Gho...

by

Saundra Crum Akers

A Mysterious Ohio

WWW.SaundraCrumAkers.com

ISBN 978-1482319194

GHOST HUNTER

Dedication

Special thanks to Charlie Colliver, for technical assistance regarding tobacco growing and processing.

Also, thank you to my readers. You make my job as a writer so much more rewarding: Steve Greer, Betty Bradley, Crystal Castle, Mike Castle, and Danielle Wahlanmaier,

This book is dedicated to those people who have gone above and beyond in supporting my writing career:

Steve Greer
Mike and Crystal Castle
Roger Akers
Noel Akers
Laing Akers
Pride Akers
Betty Mullenbrock
Dwight and Betty Crum
Victor and Sandy Crum
Betty Skidmore
Charlene Hull

Chapter 1

It had been an exceptionally happy day, a day made of the gossamer fabric of dreams, misty and unreal, until her dreams crashed smack dab into a nightmare of trouble. Carmel thought about it later wondering why she hadn't seen the problem coming; she hadn't though. Nothing could have shocked her more.

She wondered what Ash, her husband, was thinking by now; she should have been home hours ago. Studious, serious, hard working Ash Simpson might not miss her right away, but when he did, her absence would hit him like a ton of coal and he'd be worried out of his mind. He loved her; she knew that, even though his love hadn't been enough to prevent her from being tempted into a steamy affair with another man.

When Carson Wetzel had showed up one day to fix the computers in the office where she worked, she'd been captivated by his shy smile and flashing eyes. There had been something secret and enticing about him, something that she didn't seem to be able to resist. That was six months ago and their affair had been passionate and exciting although it had set up a lot of conflict in Carmel's mind because she knew that Ash didn't deserve to be cheated and lied to. He was a good man.

Lately she'd been telling Carson how she felt, hoping that he would understand her dilemma and help her to resist temptation. He hadn't been helpful though. In fact he'd pulled out all his charms in an apparent effort to hypnotize her more completely, and to keep her with him.

Angry with herself, Carmel had become almost suicidal as she struggled with the guilt she was feeling. It wasn't that she'd actually take actions to hurt herself, she thought, but if she was in danger, she wondered if she'd do anything to save her own life. She was tired of the struggle; and she felt that she should be punished for what she'd been doing. Last week she'd told Carson that she was going to try to make her marriage work and that she wasn't going to see him again.

"Give me one more day," he'd begged. "We'll make it a perfect day; we won't talk about any problems, we'll just celebrate us and our time together. It will be something to remember. Maybe we can take a ride down the river or something."

Carmel lived and worked on the East side of Cincinnati, Ohio. Carson had told her that he lived in Ripley which was farther East, but also on the Ohio River. His mother Edna Wetzel had been living with him in the family home, but about a month ago he'd told Carmel that he'd put his mother in a nearby assisted living facility because he wasn't always home to take care of her. He said she was becoming senile and needed to have someone look after her. Since Carmel had never met the lady, she had no particular thoughts about that.

She'd finally agreed to spend this one special day with Carson, in spite of having decided that they had to end the affair. Knowing the affair must be put behind her so she could try to restore her marriage to its proper place in her life, she had hesitated. But finally she decided that maybe they could end things on a good note. Carson hadn't agreed, but he was quiet about his disagreement and she wasn't sure what he was thinking. She'd taken a day off work so they'd have adequate time together. She had not told her husband Ash she was taking a holiday.

She and Carson had breakfast in a small town along the river, around 8:00am and spent the next three hours exploring as they made their way up river, sometimes crossing into Kentucky, sometimes driving a little way north of the water to see what was there. They ate lunch at a small diner along the highway and proceeded farther East afterward.

"Where do you live," Carmel asked as they came into Ripley.

"I'll show you later," Carson said as he drove on through the town. "We'll stop at my house on the way back."

In Manchester they held hands as they walked along the water and talked, spending almost an hour there; then they proceeded further East stopping to enjoy things they found of interest. Carmel felt the contagion of Carson's excitement as he showed her places he was familiar with. His eyes were fevered and fired with something new and special that she couldn't identify. His words were sweet and so were his kisses when he stopped and held her while they watched a barge push its load through the water.

"How can I give this up," she wondered while knowing that she had to.

She'd fallen in with Carson's desire for one more day, just one more chance to enjoy the fruits of the relationship that lay between them before they had to separate; now she wondered if this day together was going to make the breaking up all the harder to do.

~ 3 ~

How could she go from a perfect day with an attentive lover to the loneliness of her life with Ash, the workaholic? How could she give up the attachment she had to Carson and act as if she'd never known him? She wondered if she'd be able to maintain her resolve.

Knowing that this was the end, she felt the bitter sweetness of everything they did more poignantly. It made her happy and sad all at the same time. She laughed into Carson's eyes one minute and then the next she was doused with the ice waters of reality. As a result her emotions kept going from one extreme to another, bouncing like a ping pong ball back and forth.

It was six o'clock by the time they drove back to Ripley and Carson took her to his house for the first time. The house sat on a hill on the edge of town, overlooking the river. It looked like it had been built in the eighteen hundreds, Carmel thought. It was big and you could feel the history dwarfing its frame.

"How old is the house?" she asked.

"I think it was built in 1830 or so."

"How long has your family owned it?"

"For eighty some years I guess. I think my Great Grandparents bought it in about 1928 or 1930."

"Do you know the history of the place?"

"Not much but I'm starting to research it. Maybe I haven't told you, but I'm an amateur ghost hunter."

"And you think your house has a ghost," she asked, staring at him.

"Well, my mother thinks so, but she's senile."

"Have you seen anything unusual yourself?"

"No, he said, "But I'd still like to know the history of the house in case I do. Then maybe I'll know what to say to him."

"How do you know it will be a man?"

"Well, he or she, I'll have some idea who I'm talking to maybe."

They went into the house and he showed her through the various rooms upstairs. He ended the first floor tour at his bedroom where they spent a bit more time than the tour demanded. Later he took her downstairs to see the suite of rooms where the slaves who were fleeing on the Underground Railroad had waited for a safe passage north. There, three rooms, one of which had been modernized with a kitchen and another with a little bathroom in one end, had been equipped like a small apartment.

"I'll bet the slaves didn't have all this luxury," Carmel said as she looked around the rooms. She pulled open the refrigerator and found it stocked with food and drink. "Why do you have all this food down here? Are there still slaves hiding out in these rooms from time to time?"

"No," Carson said, "I don't think they'd know what to do with all this fancy stuff. I did all this just to impress you."

Carmel laughed. She sat down on the couch and patted the seat near her, wondering how he could have known for sure that she'd ever come here to see it. Most likely he was putting her on.

"This is comfy. Have a seat."

"I've already tried it out and I know it's comfortable. That's why I bought it," Carson said walking over to a spot by the door. He stood looking at her as she smiled back at him.

"You don't want to rethink this idea of leaving me, do you," he asked.

"No, I have to do the right thing," Carmel said. "Ash doesn't deserve this."

Turning the knob, Carson looked at her as she remained sitting on the couch, staring at the floor.

"I can't let you go," he said. "You need to stay here with me until you realize that we belong together for all time. I'm sorry!"

The sound of the closing door and the click of the lock underlined his words.

Chapter 2

Carson stood outside the door, listening to Carmel, who was yelling at him to stop playing games and to take her home right now. His heart was leaping around in his chest like a Mexican jumping bean, his breath was short and raspy, and he couldn't seem to get enough air into his lungs. He could feel layers of sweat breaking out all over him. It crept and crawled and itched at his skin.

Now you've done it! You've actually kidnapped her. You didn't change your mind at the last minute. You're in big trouble now.

The thump, thump of his heart was shaking his slightly heavy frame as he tried to get his bodily functions under control. Leaning against the wall in the hallway, he considered aborting the action he'd taken. He could pretend it was just a joke and he was only teasing her. After all Halloween would be coming up in a couple of months. She'd believe it was a joke even if she didn't think it was funny.

That would be the smart thing to do. She'll believe you if you tell her you were just playing...but then she'll be gone and you'll probably never see her again.

He wanted to go back into the room and sit with her, try to make her see how her decision to stay with Ash was going to destroy them both, but that hadn't worked before and probably wouldn't now. It was getting late and she'd want to get back home to Ash before he got worried and called the police or something.

Thinking about the police getting involved gave Carson another chill. Surely Ash would do just that when she failed to return home. He'd have all the police in Cincinnati looking for her. It would probably be on the news statewide, especially ONN, and everyone would be looking into who she'd been associating with. He wondered if she'd confided in anyone about their affair. If she had, they might come looking for him. At least he hadn't told anyone about her; that was a good thing.

He was glad that he'd arranged to have his mother live in an assisted living facility. It was close by, so he could keep an eye on her, but she wasn't right here in the house where she'd surely figure out that something was going on. Carson loved his mother, sure he did, but once he'd started to think that he couldn't live without Carmel, once the obsession was upon him, he'd known he had to get his mother out of the house. Now if she'd just stay put, that would be one problem he wouldn't have to worry about.

He'd thought it would never happen to him again after Amanda, but the minute he met Carmel, it had. He'd fallen head over heals for her, had wanted her to leave her husband and marry him. Maybe that was the problem, he'd pushed her into a decision and she'd decided against him.

But men aren't like women. You hear about women living for years as the other woman, having children by a man who won't marry her, or staying with a man who is cheating on her every day. A man can't stand that. I couldn't stand that. I didn't want to be the other man. I wanted her to choose me, divorce him and marry me. When she decided to stay with him instead, I had to do something. I had to!

He hated to think about the thing with Amanda. He'd loved her too, but now she was dead and although the grief would never leave him, he'd found a new love with Carmel. She was exciting to be around, they had a number of mutual interests and all he wanted was to give her a good life. What was so bad about that?

Thinking about the day they'd just shared together, he started to calm down a little. She'd enjoyed it; he knew she had. She loved him and they had a good relationship. With a little time to think it over, Carmel would see that she'd made a bad decision; if she didn't, Ash would take it out of her hands and divorce her for going off with another man and abandoning him. It was a win -win situation, and all Carson had done was act as a catalyst to bring things to a head. After all if Carmel really loved Ash, she wouldn't have had an affair with him, now would she?

Feeling a little better, determined not to panic and do something else stupid; Carson made a stop in the bathroom where he washed his face with cold water while staring at his image in the mirror to see if he looked normal after what he'd done. He looked at his dark hair which had started to recede in the last couple of years. His cheeks were full, his face oval, and normally his eyes were flashing bright with excitement, especially when he was around Carmel, but now guilt made him unable to look himself directly in the eye. His blue ribbed shirt was pulled a little tight over a belly that had started to round out a bit more than he wanted it to. His rubbed the stomach that had started to feel a little queasy, but rubbing it didn't help anything.

He knew he wasn't the most handsome man in the world, but Carmel had been enchanted with him, and he was sure she would continue to be, once she got over being mad at him. She was the one for him and he was the one for her. They were tailor made for each other.

The suite of rooms, where Carmel was to live for the time being, had been used for a hiding place for slaves, as he'd told Carmel. When the Rankin house was full to the rafters or there was unusual danger around, the overflow was sent to this house, where they lived in those rooms which had been carefully hidden away from casual observers. There weren't any real windows in the hide a way but in a couple of places there were slits in the walls that served as windows so the fugitives could look out. She would be able to see the light of day and she could gaze out at the river if she wanted.

He hated to have to restrict her actions this way, but for the moment there wasn't any other choice. If things went as they should, he wouldn't have to keep her in there for very long. He headed to the kitchen where he planned to put together a snack for his lady love, something to eat before going to bed for the night. Would Carmel let him sleep with her; she probably wouldn't tonight, he decided. She'd be indignant and angry with him for a day or two.

He wouldn't even broach the subject. He'd let her come to him, if she didn't take too long, that is.

Chapter 3

Carson took a snack to Carmel at 9:30 but when she refused to speak to him, he left her alone and went to his own room. His breath was still coming in short gasps as he hyperventilated. He'd taken a bold, dangerous, and illegal step by forcing her to stay with him; however, he hoped it would work out in the long run. Left alone to stew in her own juices for a while, he believed that Carmel would realize that he'd been fighting for their relationship, not scheming against her.

He pictured her as he liked her best, remembering how she looked in an old shirt and rolled up jeans sitting on a riverbank baiting a hook and laughing because she caught the first fish. She'd have her white wide brimmed hat pulled down to her eyes, her feet stuck in flip flops and she'd be happy as a butterfly and about as hard to pin down. He remembered picnics with a big basket full of foodstuff, her long blondish brown hair hanging down in two ponytails and her delight in sharing the food she'd brought for them.

Surely, she'd forgive him and become her delightful self again in a few days. Right now he knew that she'd be going crazy because she had no way to tell Ash what had happened. She wouldn't want her husband to worry about her. She was sensitive that way and didn't like to cause trouble. Ash wouldn't know what had happened; he might be scared when she didn't return home. Carson wondered how long it would be before Ash would file a missing person's report and how serious the police would take it when he did. The police would probably think that his wife had left him, run away from home, maybe with another man. In a way that is what she'd done. The only difference was that she'd planned to return home. Now she couldn't do that.

He didn't like the idea of the police looking for Carmel but as far as he knew, no one was aware of the affair between them. They had met outside city limits in places where acquaintances were not likely to see them. They'd spent hours fishing, swimming, hiking, and picnicking along the river where they didn't encounter many people, and as a precaution, he'd always gone alone to the office to check into the motel when they were ready for some intimate time together. It seemed unlikely that anyone would have guessed they were having an affair, unless Carmel had confided in someone.

Carmel had never been at his home until now, and he didn't believe anyone had noticed them arriving today, since there wasn't another house close. He thought he was safe on that score. Still his thoughts circled like a bird of prey looking for an opening. What hadn't he thought of? It would be his word against hers if it ever came to a showdown.

Although he hoped no one else knew of the affair, he had proof of it. He'd kept that proof just in case. Should Carmel say she'd been held against her will, trying to get him arrested, he could show that they'd been having an affair. He thought he could convince the police that she'd been with him willingly given the history of their time together. It would look as if she was concocting a story for her husband's benefit. He thought it provided reasonable doubt at least. It wouldn't be nice to lie about her like that, but it might be necessary.

He looked into the mirror over his dresser but just one glance and he found he still couldn't look himself in the eye. Gazing downward, he stripped off his shirt and then sat on the bed to undo his shoes and pants. In the bathroom hot water had been running for a few minutes now and he headed into the steamy room and climbed into the tub. Usually he took a shower but today he felt extra dirty.

That night Carson dreamed of a woman all night long, but it wasn't Carmel.

"Doesn't she look nice," the Undertaker said as the two men stood gazing down at the woman in the casket who was locked in her eternal sleep.

"Beautiful as always," Carson said. "Could I have a few minutes alone with her?"

"Sure, sure," the rotund man responded as he patted his shirt pocket where the bribe lay. In order to get in to see Amanda, Carson had needed to bribe the undertaker to let him in after hours. Her husband, Martin, had left orders that Carson was not allowed at the Funeral Home.

He pulled out the card and letter he had so painstakingly written for Amanda and tucked them down under her dress along with a ring which he had hoped one day to give to her. Tears slipped down cheeks that were hollow with grief. He knew that Amanda lay here mostly because of him.

He thought about their affair, a hot, torrid, and senseless thing in which they had drank and partied and made love with a hot heat. Amanda hadn't been too much for drinking alcohol until he'd entered her life but over the past few months she'd been drunk more than sober. Perhaps that had helped her to forget what she was doing to her family.

They'd been together just before her death, drinking, laughing, and loving at the river. How could he have known that she wasn't safe to drive home? How could he have guessed that she would go the wrong way down a Cincinnati freeway and be killed instantly by an oncoming truck?

Sobs were shaking his body now as he let some of the grief wash out of him and onto her still face. She would take some of his DNA with her to the grave, from his loving, and from his tears. She'd also take his battered heart. He wished they could lie together for eternity.

"I've gotta ask you to leave now," the Undertaker said from behind him.

After a long farewell glance at the beauty, which was destined to sleep eternally, Carson stumbled out of the room, heading for a lifetime of regret.

In his sleep Carson underwent the loss of Amanda again with a pain that he thought would always be raw inside him. He relived his subsequent dreams after her death, dreams in which she was always alive at the beginning of the dream but always died before the end of it. Sometimes she died in different ways but she always died.

He'd thought he'd never be able to love anyone again until finally he'd met Carmel five years later. When she'd started to talk of leaving him, he'd known he couldn't let her do that. He wouldn't have lived through a second loss.

"But you've chosen to fall in love with married women almost every time; what's up with that," an unseen voice asked him.

Carson couldn't answer that question.

Chapter 4

It was the first day of the Tobacco Festival in Ripley and Carson had a hard time driving through town on his way to Manchester where he had a job to do. The streets were congested and some were blocked off. It annoyed him, getting on nerves that were already uncovered and irritated.

He'd said 'Good Morning' to Carmel but she wasn't talking to him apparently. Knowing that she had plenty of food and water in the little apartment he'd made out of the slave's hideaway; it seemed best to ignore her moods for now. As he wended his way through the celebration, he wondered if his mother was going to be in the thick of it today; she loved to walk through the festival, listen to the music and have genuine New Orleans food cooked on an open grill by a group of black vendors. She liked the area along the river where the festival and car show spread out for blocks. She'd be here if she could manage it.

His memories went back to other years; to times when he'd gone with his mother and they'd walked the streets of the festival, sat on benches looking out across the river, and had been on happy terms with each other. Now his mother was angry with him and would probably stay that way the rest of her life.

Needing to get his mother out of the house so he could bring Carmel to it, he'd set her up in an assisted living facility against her will. It was about two miles from the family home. He figured that he could visit and would keep an eye on her while making sure she wouldn't know everything that was going on in the house. She hadn't liked the idea at all, claiming that she could take care of herself; the truth be told she probably could, but it didn't suit Carson's purposes to have her around. He'd insisted that she was slipping mentally and that she needed someone to look after her when he was away.

I'd better check on Mother on the way back. I haven't heard from her for a few days and she's probably getting restless. It's best to head her off at the pass before she shows up at the house again.

Carson shook his head nervously as he drove along the river, remembering how he and Carmel had gone that way just a few hours before. Now everything had changed.

You'd better clear your mind and put it on the work you need to do. You've a long day ahead, he advised himself.

Meanwhile, Carmel had turned the TV on to see if anyone had reported her missing. She watched the morning news, but heard nothing of interest; then she turned to court TV which was one of her favorite channels.

Today's trial was quite fitting, she thought, when she heard that the accused was a man named Fitzpatrick who supposedly killed his ex-lover's husband. Reportedly he had decided he couldn't live as the other man and had demanded that his lover leave her husband. She told him she would never leave her husband, that she'd taken a vow until death do us part. A few days later, her husband was shot to death, his passing effectively parting him from his wife. Fitzpatrick claimed he was out of town at the time and had nothing to do with the murder, of course!

Things could be worse. Carson could have done something to Ash...or to me!

Carmel thought some more about the differences between men and women when they get caught in these love affairs with married partners. Men have been known to kill the lover, kill the husband, or to commit suicide, but for the most part, men don't seem to agree to live as the other man while his lover continues to stay with her husband.

Women behave differently, and some live a back street life for years, have children by the man, standing by him no matter what. She wondered if that was because society encouraged women to "stand by their man".

There was one case that she knew about where a man had been seeing a married woman and had lived in a barn near her house so he could have access to her, for over a year, but that was an unusual situation. The man in question had been a victim of a serious head injury and perhaps that had changed his perception of things. She considered his case an aberration.

Watching the trial didn't help her state of mind any, although having the TV on was a slight diversion. Depression was sitting on her head and shoulders like a low lying cloud. It seemed too thick and deep for her to breathe normally. She could imagine the room filled with fog and that she was isolated in the mist, lost. Carmel snapped the TV off.

It's my fault; I knew better. I let my emotions and my hormones think for me; I deserve this.

Shame and humiliation swamped her in its net of sludge. How could she ever get clean again? Waves of suicidal thought drifted over her and she wondered what she should do now; wouldn't it be better if she just found a way to end her useless life? Since it didn't look like she was going home for some time, she knew Ash would no longer be there for her, even if she worked this out, and Carson let her go. Anyway, he wouldn't want her after he learned how she'd betrayed him. As for Carson…she'd never want him again.

That thought set up an ache in her stomach. She loved Ash in her own way. True, she'd done him wrong because she'd been thinking only about herself and how to get what she wanted. It was pure selfishness that had propelled her into Carson Wetzel's arms. She'd been seeking love and comfort and he'd provided it. At least she'd thought so at the time.

She'd convinced herself that having an affair with Carson was something entirely different from her marriage. It was something she did for herself, like getting a facial or a massage; it had nothing to do with Ash. Ash chose to spend his time away from her, working, not meeting her needs so she'd told herself that it was ok to fill that gap with another man. She wasn't taking anything away from Ash that he actually wanted. He didn't want to spend that time with her, Carson did, so if she went with Carson it was win, win, and win…right! Everyone had what they wanted.

Carmel went to the queen sized bed and lay down on it, her face to the wall. She'd made her bed and here she was lying in it. It was a bed in a cell, a bed Carson Wetzel wanted to share with her, and a bed that would seal the fate of her marriage. Tears mixed with snot ran down her face but she was too distressed to notice. After sobbing for a long time, Carmel went to sleep, cold and lonely, feeling condemned.

Chapter 5

Ash Simpson was worried. It wasn't like Carmel not to come home. He'd been late getting home, himself, and even later going to the bedroom, where he found the bed made and no wife in it. Usually Carmel went to bed by 11:00pm. All night long he'd waited and worried. He'd checked with her friends, called one of her co-workers and found that she hadn't been at work, and fought with himself to give her a little time before he called the police. If she was just behaving irresponsibly he didn't want to air their dirty linen in front of the police, but if she was in trouble, the police were needed. The battle raged inside him until 8:00 am and then he gave up and called the police station. They put a detective Smith on the phone and the detective asked Ash to come down to the station in person to do a report.

"Bring a picture of your wife, her social security number, a list of any credit cards that she might have, and a list of friends and family members," he said. "We won't do much until she's been gone at least 24 hours but we can maybe make a few calls and check some things out."

Ash sat at his home office desk trying to make the lists as comprehensive as he could. He was an accountant and used to a lot of paper work, so that part didn't bother him, the reason he was doing this did. His mind had been going wild all night darting this way and that into dark and implausible corners, thinking things he'd never have believed he'd ever think about his wife. Then he'd revert to a feeling of certainty that Carmel would never leave him here to worry on purpose; if she hadn't called him, it was because she couldn't. Those feelings sunk him even deeper in despair. If she couldn't call then she was hurt or in deep trouble.

Finally he had everything ready for the detective and drove to the Police Station filled with such a mixture of emotions that he couldn't have unraveled them if he had to. He was a studious, serious, and hard working man. He wasn't used to this fear tinged upheaval that was trembling through his body. He loved Carmel and his fear for her was growing stronger with every minute.

Detective Smith met him in the lobby and directed him into a small cramped space that was his office. The detective himself was a slender man dressed in casual clothes, a pair of jeans and a white pullover shirt with buttons at the top. He looked to be around, 50 his hair was black with patches of gray sliding out, and he was balding at the top. His face was set in serious lines as he motioned Ash to a chair.

Ash looked down at his own clothes which were wrinkled now from his worried all nighter and absently rubbed his fingers through his short curly brown hair. His grey eyes were red with emotion and lack of sleep and he realized that he must look a sight to the astute policeman.

"Coffee," officer Smith asked, pouring himself some from a carafe at his side.

"No thanks."

"Ok, tell me about your wife. When did you see her last?"

"Yesterday morning before work."

"Did you both go to work yesterday?"

"I thought we did, but apparently Carmel didn't go in."

"How'd you know that?"

"I called her friend Kathy, who works with her, and she told me."

"Was everything like normal when you got home?"

"I didn't see anything different," Ash said

"When did you realize that your wife wasn't there?"

"It was about 1:30. I got home at 11:30 but usually Carmel is asleep then and I don't wake her. I sat in the den watching TV for a while and then went to bed about 1:30. That's when I saw she wasn't there."

"Did you see anything in the house that would suggest foul play?"

"I don't know what I'd be looking for, but no, I didn't."

"Has Carmel ever stayed out all night before?"

"Never."

"Have the two of you been getting along?"

"We have our little disputes like everyone else but I'd say our marriage is ok. She doesn't like the amount of time I spend at work."

"Were any of her belongings gone?"

"You mean did she pack her clothes to leave me?"

"Yes."

"No, her stuff seems to all be there except for her car, her purse, and things which she'd have taken with her normally."

"I think I'd like to go back to your house with you and take a look around," Detective Smith said suddenly.

"Why? What are you thinking?" Ash asked him wretchedly. The other man's sudden decision had scared him.

"I'm not thinking anything. It's really my day off and I just dropped by the station for a while to finish up a couple of things. I'll go by your house on my way home."

The Detective followed in his own car, as Ash drove slowly back to his house.

Everything felt wrong to the hurting husband. Why was this happening? He drove slowly, his mind on his wife and his heart in his shoes. What would he do if something bad had happened to Carmel? If she was Ok why hadn't she called him? The questions came thick and fast with no answers. At his house, he invited the Detective in and put some coffee on to perk while Detective Smith walked around looking things over.

"You might want to check for messages since you've been gone a while," the Detective called out to him from the bedroom.

Ash checked his voice mail from the kitchen and found no new messages. Then he went into the bedroom to see what the other man was doing. He was astounded to see the Detective sitting on his bed looking out the window.

"Is this room the way you found it last night?"

"Yes, I never went to bed. I kept hoping she'd call but she didn't."

"So your wife made the bed yesterday morning before she left."

"I guess so, she always does."

"It sounds like whatever happened to her occurred sometime after she left home since she was following her normal routine up until then. Wouldn't you say so?"

Ash shook his head, bewildered, "I don't know," he said.

"Are you sure that the two of you have been getting along ok?"

"What are you getting at," Ash asked. "You aren't trying to say that I did something to my wife, are you?"

"It happens," the Detective said.

"Not me," Ash replied. "I'd never hurt Carmel. I love her."

"That's what everyone says at a time like this," Detective Smith said, as he checked the bedroom carpet, presumably for blood.

Chapter 6

"I want to show you some of the equipment I just bought," Carson told Carmel.

Carmel ignored him as she had all week, but he didn't acknowledge that he noticed it; instead he chattered on.

"I told you that I am an amateur ghost hunter, didn't I? Well, I bought some equipment today and I brought it in to show you." He took some items out of his bag and laid them out on the table.

"See, I have EMF testers and meters. That's to test the electromagnetic field and to detect the presence of a ghost. This tool records temperature," he said, picking up another device. "When ghosts are around it's supposed to be colder. This thing here is called an EVP, I don't know what that stands for but it's like a voice recorder that can pick up things the human ear can't hear."

He looked at Carmel hoping for a sign of interest but she sat on the couch staring straight through him. If he didn't know better, he'd think he was a ghost himself. Walking to the TV which was on, although turned down, he switched it off. He didn't want Carmel to be watching TV instead of interacting with him.

"You can help me with some of my research," he said. "I brought some books on the history of the Ohio River and some of the houses in Ripley. We had a very active stop on the Underground Railroad right here in Ripley, you know, with a lot of slaves coming through and staying here in this house, in this apartment. Maybe you'll see the ghost of one of them if you look hard enough. Let me know if anything unusual happens, okay?"

Carmel didn't say anything; she just sat on the couch looking as if she was in an entirely different world from the one he was in. Carson walked over and sat down beside her. She neither moved away nor reacted to his presence.

"We can't go on like this," Carson said. "You know I love you and that I did this for us."

He put his arm around her carefully hoping she wouldn't slap his face for his effort.

Carmel didn't react at all. It was like trying to make love to a rag doll. Carson sat quietly with his arm around her for ten minutes and when nothing happened, he turned her face toward him and kissed her. She was as pliable as a rubber doll and just as responsive. Carson kissed her again and then again with the same results.

"I see you aren't ready to start our honeymoon yet," he said, getting up from the chair, "But I know you'll realize that this is for the best when you've had time to think about it."

Carefully, Carson gathered his ghost hunting equipment and left the room, locking it tight. The history books were left lying alone on the otherwise empty table.

I wonder if she's eating anything. Next time I go in I'll check the refrigerator and see if she needs more food. I hope she's not going to make herself sick over this.

When he left, Carmel curled herself into a ball and lay down with her face to the back of the couch. Carson left her so confused. Habit, and the infatuation she still had for him, made her want to respond to him, but she couldn't do that ever again. Knowing him, she wasn't afraid of him, but she hated Carson for ruining her life. By now her marriage was over. If the police found her, her affair with Carson would be exposed and she knew Ash would leave her. If the police didn't find her, then poor Ash would be left alone to wonder and worry about what had happened. He was probably going crazy because of it right now. Her thoughts run obsessively around the problem.

I'm so sorry Ash. You don't deserve this.

I wish I had been able to reach you and talk to you instead of trying to comfort myself with someone else. Carson is attractive and I was lured by his charms but in spite of his charms, I'd have never given him a second glance if I'd really had you... but I didn't. You were more committed to work than to me. Of course I didn't really try to share my life with you either, because I felt rejected.

It's my fault and I know you hate me now.

Tears stood in her eyes like stagnant pools that had no outlet. She knew that sooner or later Carson was going to get tired of her ignoring him. He'd either force her to react by doing something so awful that she had to react or he'd open the door and let her go, having decided that although he wanted her, he didn't want her this way. She wondered what he'd do when he lost his patience.

The next time Carson came, he took a different tack. He'd searched out a poem that Carmel had written and given to him early in their relationship.

"I want you to read this," he said. "Read it and remember how you felt at the time."

Carmel didn't say anything and he went away again, leaving the poem lying on the table beside the History books he'd left before. After a while, Carmel went to look at the poem. It said:

Wake me up to love
I, who've never truly felt loved,
Show me by example, make me feel
That intimacy that melts two into one
The push and pull of partnership,
 Which will pump us higher,
 as a child's legs pump a swing.
Awaken my trust so I can appreciate
And dare to share that,
which I've never shared before.
Let me feel you melting into me
We act as one together.
In ways I've only heard of, never known
Wake me up to the potential of love.

Carmel stared at this foreign piece of writing. It seemed so long ago that she'd written those words. What had she been thinking of at the time? Carson had been a sweet diversion from her loneliness. Had she really loved him? She'd shared a lot with him, she had to admit that.

Yes, and you're paying for it now.

Sitting at the table she picked up a pen and started writing on a tablet that Carson had left for her to take notes on. He'd told her it would be there if she decided to research the Histories he'd given her.

"Keep me from a controlling man, who spouts words of love as he murders your soul," she wrote in bold letters before lying down the pen and going back to curl on the couch blocking out the memories.

Chapter 7

"Daddy's home," the four year old Carmel screamed as she ran to meet her Father who was arriving home from work.

"Don't run in the house," her mother said crossly

"Daddy, Daddy," Carmel said jumping into her father's arms. He lifted her up high and placed her on his shoulders.

"Have you been good today," he asked her.

She nodded her head vigorously and he pulled a lollipop out of his shirt pocket and gave it to her. Suddenly she was sitting all alone, crying. She knew her Daddy was gone and he wasn't coming back again. She felt abandoned, bereft, as if she couldn't endure the sadness. Getting up from the step where she'd been sitting, she started running down the street. She ran and ran for such a long time that her lungs were bursting, and then she sat on a rock by the side of the street and started crying again and wailing for her Daddy to come back.

Carmel awoke from the dream with her face wet with tears and a sadness in her heart. It only took a moment to remember where she was and why, which only made her agony greater. She got off the couch and went to the bathroom. After using the commode she washed her face and hands with cold water. Coming back into the living room she went to the slotted places in the wall which served as windows that looked out on the Ohio River.

At least I can see daylight. I guess I should be grateful for that. There isn't any chance I could call for help though. Everything's too far away and no one would ever hear me.

A barge was going down the river and she watched it push the heavy load in front of it, wondering where it was going. If she ever got out of here maybe she'd head down the Ohio River to the Mississippi. Who knows, maybe she'd even go to New Orleans before it was over. She wouldn't have a marriage any more and she didn't want an association with Carson Wetzel in her future so what was there to hold her? Her only hope would be to start over. She left the poor excuse for a window and went to the table where she looked at the books Carson had left for her. One was a History of Brown County and she elected to look at that one first.

Reading about the early churches of Ripley bored her and she turned to other pages where the book discussed the first newspapers of the town. The first was called The Benefactor, the second, The Political Censor, and the third was called the Castigator. Only the first name seemed friendly to her. She wondered just how radical the early population of Ripley might have been. Who were they castigating? Was it the slave holders? She knew that Ripley was a very important part of the Underground Railroad.

Later they had other papers called The Examiner, The Ripley Telegraph, Freedom's Casket, and Hickory Sprout. Also printed were the Farmer's Chronicle, The Ohio Whig, and The Political Examiner.

It sounds like they had a lot of hotheads in the early days, politically savvy people who were determined to effect change in the country. Even the names of the papers reflect that.

Reverend J. Rankin, who was best known for conducting the Underground Railroad in Ripley, was said to have founded a college in 1840 but it only lasted until around 1849. Ulysses S. Grant attended school in Ripley according to the book. Carmel rubbed her forehead. She liked History but she didn't like to be told what she should read or study. Carson hadn't given her any other reading material.

Well, I'll be darned if I'll take any notes for him. I might read the books but I'm not helping him do research so he can figure out which ghost he's talking to. I think he's bonkers to be looking for ghosts anyway.

Looking at the papers again, she saw that although Ripley was noted for helping blacks escape slavery, they had a separate school for the black population; the schools weren't integrated. However, papers in 1882 reported that some former black students had been hired to teach in the schools and were doing well. It didn't say if they were teaching in the colored school or in the white school.

They were probably hired to teach the black children, she decided.

She read about a big flood in 1832, and another one that hit in1847. Both floods covered a great portion of Ripley but the one in1832 was reportedly worse. She went back to the window slit and looked down toward the river again. Would a flood reach up to this house? She didn't think it would since the house was fairly high up.

At the table again she turned the pages and found a series of biographies of the early inhabitants of the town of Ripley. Not being into personalities at the moment she scanned those pages hurriedly, and then started reading about a mammoth tusk that was found in Red Oak creek in 1869. A Mr. W.H. Dunn found this tusk about 15 feet down imbedded in the sandy bank of the creek near its mouth. The removal efforts caused it to be broken in three pieces, but it was conjectured that it was about seven inches at the thickest point and maybe fourteen feet long. It got soft and crumbly when exposed to the air. He made a deal to ship it to P.T. Barnum, who supposedly paid him $50.00. Others reported finding teeth, a scapula bone and other bones that may have been from the same animal, which they supposed to have been a Mastodon.

She thought she remembered seeing Red Oak Creek where it ran down to the main street of town. She couldn't remember if it had run under the street and down to the river but most likely it did. Carson had pointed out houseboats that were anchored in its waters. Something about house boats drew her to them. She didn't know what it was because she tended to get sick with motion but she thought it would be cool to stay on a houseboat for a few days. She'd heard that people sometimes rent them by the week.

"Ripley is said to be the mouth or entrance to the Underground Railroad. It is Ripley, Ohio where Harriet Beecher Stowe's fictional character Eliza crossed on the ice of the river," she read. Carmel was fascinated in spite of herself. At least Carson had given her something interesting to read, even if he did have ulterior motives. She put the book aside for the moment though. If she read it all today, what would she do tomorrow?

Chapter 8

Ash Simpson sat hunched over his laptop trying to do his work. He was working from home today hoping that he'd hear from his wife. He wanted to be available to get the call. His vision wavered over the numbers in front of him and he struggled to focus on the page. His eyes were red and irritated and he could hardly keep them open. He hadn't had much sleep for the past few days. His short curly brown hair was matted to his head, a product of the sweat that had overcome him from time to time today. His open necked white shirt seemed to be confining him and he pulled at the collar every few minutes although it wasn't tight.

Detective Smith had grilled him for hours yesterday and then had called an hour ago to say that he was planning to stop by again this morning. Ash was feeling like a suspect in his wife's disappearance and that set his nerves on edge. He knew he hadn't done anything wrong but he also knew that if there had been foul play, the spouse is usually the first one the police suspect.

Another wave of cold sweat broke out across his forehead and Ash left his desk to go wash his face. He looked at the pale face reflected in the mirror and wondered why this was happening. Carmel would have told him if she was leaving him, therefore something must have happened that left her unable to tell him. A chilled sickness entered him.

You should go out and take a walk. You might as well since you've only managed to do a handful of work in the past few days. Maybe a walk will clear your head.

Instead of going to the computer on his desk, Ash threw on a thin jacket and headed out the door into the drizzle of the day. It was early September when it was usually cool and dry in Ohio but one of the hurricanes must be sending its spray northward because it had been wet and cold all morning.

Briskly Ash walked down his street and headed toward the river. He liked the waterfront for some reason. In the early days of their marriage, he and Carmel had walked down to the water frequently to fish off the pier or at their favorite spot on the river bank. He felt more in touch with his wife going to a place where they'd been happy.

At the river bank he walked down to the water and then headed west along the edge until finally he took off his washable jacket and put it on the ground, then sat on it staring at the moving water.

Meditating on his situation, Ash remained in a state of inner isolation for nearly an hour as the hum of cars hit the splash of puddles not far away. The jacket he sat on was wet through and his pants had become soaked but still he sat as if the cold and wet could leach the pain out of him. Finally he got up and stumbled back to the street; he took the long way home, wondering if Carmel was somewhere thinking of him as he was thinking of her. How could she vanish into a cloudless day? Tired and wet he returned to his house and started up his steps. He didn't see the other man until a voice jerked him out of his reverie.

"Hello, Mr. Simpson," the Detective said. "Been out for a stroll?"

"Yeah, I hoped the fresh air would clear my head," Ash said.

"Have you heard from your wife," Detective Smith asked him.

"Not a word unless she called while I was gone," Ash said hopelessly.

"Aren't you usually at work at this time of day?"

"Yes, but I wanted to be here if Carmel called."

"You wanted to be here, but then you left; you took a stroll to get out of the house?"

"Whatever you're trying to say, you're wrong. I couldn't take it any more and I went out for a little bit trying to walk off my anxiety. It's not like I don't care about my wife as you're trying to imply."

"Let's go inside and see if she's called then."

Inside, Ash checked the answering machine but there had been no calls.

"We have some new information," Detective Smith said. "My partner will be here in a few minutes and we'll update you."

"Tell me now," Ash said. "Is it good news?"

"We'll wait for my partner."

When the other Detective arrived, Detective Smith identified him as Detective Davis. They all sat down at the dining room table.

"Why didn't you tell us your wife was having an affair with another man," Detective Smith asked.

"She's not!"

"Yes she is. One of her co-workers says that Carmel all but admitted it to her but wouldn't tell her his name. Other co-workers had suspected something like that was going on too."

"That's just gossip."

"No, we checked her work records and she's been leaving early regularly and she takes a full day off about once a month. We think she's been meeting the other man at these times."

Ash's face was as pale as skim milk, his eyes burned and were tearing up; he couldn't look at the two men in front of him. This was more than a blow to his manhood; it was a blow to his heart. He coughed weakly.

"Who is it," he managed to ask.

"We don't know; we thought you might be able to tell us," Detective Davis said.

"I'll believe it when Carmel tells me it's true," Ash said defensively.

"That will be hard for her to do if she's dead," Detective Smith said.

Ash flinched at the suggestion made. Carmel couldn't be dead; he'd be able to feel it if she was, wouldn't he?

"Here," Detective Davis said, "We have a warrant to search this house."

Ash didn't say anything; he just buried his face in his circled arms and left them to go about their business of destroying his life.

Chapter 9

Carson Wetzel was awakened by a sound in his hallway.

"What the hell was that?"

Quietly he crept from his bed and sidled over to his doorway where he stood silently listening. Through the early morning gloom he could see the clock across the room which said it was seven am; it was a Sunday morning. Another sound from the hallway had Carson questioning what he was going to do if he had an intruder. He didn't have a weapon of any kind. He looked around for something to use to defend himself if needed.

On his wall he'd hung a decorative letter opener that looked like a small saber and he tiptoed to it and took it off the wall. Pulling the semi-sharp saber out of its sheath, he decided it would be sharp enough to at least puncture a burglar. At any rate it was better than nothing.

As he stood there listening he wondered why Carmel hadn't tried to defend herself. Why had she passively allowed him to lock her up in those rooms without attempting to fight him, to force her way out the door, or anything like that.

I'll think about that later.

Right now I might have a murderer standing outside the door.

Holding the letter opener like a knife, he jerked open the door to the hallway but saw no one. Cautiously he headed down the hall toward the kitchen area. He could hear someone in there rattling and clanging something.

Is someone trying to steal the family silver?

He smiled grimly at the thought because he had nothing but department store silver-wear; it was hardly worth the stealing. At the door to the kitchen he paused unable to see the source of the noise but still hearing it. He opened the door to the old pantry and jumped in surprise when he saw his mother, Edna Wetzel, standing there fiddling with something.

"Mo-ther! What are you doing here," he yelled; his fear and anger mixed to form indignation.

"It's still my house no matter what you say and I'll come here if I want to."

"Where'd you get a key? I took your key."

"Well I had a copy made before you took it. I've a right to come to my own house and I'm not going to let you stop me. You've done enough by making me live in that soulless place with old people who I have nothing in common with."

"What are you doing here so early?"

"I've things to do today and I'm looking for my favorite scissors. I'm doing some scrap-booking at the Senior Center."

Carson sat down in a kitchen chair and looked at his prodigal mother. She was a handful all right. However, Carson admired her for not plopping down somewhere and giving up on life.

"What's all that stuff you have setting there in the living room? Is that your ghost hunting stuff," Edna asked.

"Yeah, I'm about ready to get started. I still don't know how to use some of it though."

"Well, you'll find some ghosts here alright if you know what you're doing. I heard one this morning already."

"What'd you hear?"

"There was a wailing coming from the slave hide out, and as you know, I've heard and seen things in that room that looks down over the river, the one with the fireplace. Something was rustling around in there the last time I was here. It's the one just above the slave quarters."

"Tell me exactly what you've heard and seen and I'll focus in those areas, although it was probably just a mouse," Carson said, glad to be on neutral territory.

"That window in the room with the fireplace was always coming open. I'd leave it closed and go back a few minutes later and the curtains would be blowing because the window was up. I also heard sounds in there that weren't normal and I can feel the hair on the back of my neck stand up when I'm in there sometimes, it's like someone's watching me."

"That's all the more reason for you not to be coming around here when I don't know you're coming. It will confuse my ghost catching equipment. It will pick up sounds you make and I'll think I've a real ghost and all it will be is you sneaking around the house," Carson said.

"That's a good test to see if you can tell the difference," Edna said.

Carson gave up. His mother had a head harder than the asphalt on route fifty two.

"Are you going to church this morning," he asked her.

"No. I've something else to do today."

He waited but she didn't offer any more information. Thinking the best way to get her out of the house would be to stop interacting with her, Carson set about making coffee and some toast. He didn't offer any to his mother but she didn't seem to care. Her mind appeared to be on other things. When she found the scissors she'd been looking for she held them up triumphantly.

"See, I knew they were here," she said. "Well, now that I've found these, I've got to run. Behave yourself."

With a flounce and a flurry, Edna headed down the hallway and out the front door before Carson could decide if he wanted to say anything like,

"Goodbye".

He followed her to the door and watched her walk down the pathway. *What a character,* he thought with both pride and annoyance. As he drank his coffee and ate his toast he listened to see if he could hear any sounds coming from Carmel's part of the house. He couldn't. That area had extra insulation and he didn't think sounds from inside would penetrate the walls, but what had his mother heard?

He walked through the house to the room his mother had designated as possibly haunted. It was an ordinary room with a fireplace at one end and a large picture window looking toward the river. He liked the room which had been used as an extra bedroom when his parents were younger and entertained a lot. He couldn't remember any guests running in terror or saying it was haunted.

Carson was one skeptical ghost hunter. In a way he was setting out to prove there weren't such things as ghosts. He liked to have his information first hand so he didn't rely on what others said. He knew they had a lot of reality shows like Paranormal State and similar shows on TV. He watched them sometimes just for information as to how to go about ghost hunting. He didn't believe what they said necessarily. He'd believe it when he saw it happen himself.

Maybe I should set up some of my equipment in here and see what I find, he decided as he looked around.

The room still had a double bed in it and an armchair by the window. He liked this room but never had any occasion to use it. It was one of the nicest rooms in the house.

His mother had argued that the house was haunted since he was a child and his father had agreed with her. Funny, Carson had never seen or heard anything that couldn't be explained. He'd have to quiz his mother further about the reasons she believed the house had a ghost the next time he saw her. Meanwhile, he was going to put bolts on the door so she couldn't just turn the key and surprise him whenever she liked. This morning's surprise had taken a decade off his life.

Chapter 10

Carmel stood at the window slits looking down toward the river. She had paced back and forth from the window to the wall to the window again all afternoon. The dejection that had been immobilizing her had somehow changed to agitation today. It was the seventh day of her captivity. She'd been marking each day on a little calendar Carson had left in the drawer of the table. It wouldn't do to lose track of time; suddenly it had hit her that time was passing and she was stuck here in limbo.

Carson hadn't physically harmed her. He'd given her adequate food and water supplies and he hadn't raped her or anything like that. Mostly he'd been leaving her alone.

What does he want with me? I know he doesn't want me like this.

I'm no good to him for conversation, lovemaking, or any other purpose.

Does he think that I'll magically decide to go on with my life staying with him willingly after what he's done to me?

She plopped herself on the seat of the kitchen chair, her anger licking flames of liquid frustration inside her stomach, but her mind seeking to rebel. She'd gone through most of the books Carson had left for her and she had a notebook to write in, but she didn't feel like writing. Boredom, anger, and anxiety caged her in misery. There was nothing to do here and no one she wanted to talk to, even if talking to someone was a possibility. She didn't want to have to explain what had happened. After all this time she didn't even want to talk to Ash. After all what could she say to fix things now?

Deciding to check out the TV she put that on and searched for a news channel as she did every day. So far she hadn't found anything about her on the news. Didn't anyone know she was missing? Surely Ash would have reported her missing within twenty four hours. Now it had been a week. Something should be on the news about her! Why wasn't it? Not finding anything she wanted to watch she turned the set off again within half an hour.

Poor Ash, he's probably thinking that I'm lying dead in a ditch somewhere.

He knows I'd have called him even if I was leaving him; I'd never just let him wait and worry.

She sniffed as the tears threatened to flow again; no need to give Carson the satisfaction of seeing her cry. Anyway she didn't deserve pity. She'd gotten herself into this and it served her right! A part of her was glad she was being punished. It was what she deserved.

Picking up a book of Folklore that had been among the other things that Carson had left in the room, Carmel struggled to focus on it. She knew there was a legend about someone known as Mike Fink. He was supposed to be a riverboat man from the 1800's she thought. Maybe she could find a story about him in the book. She looked in the index and found one story about Mike Fink and the Brindle Bull. Reading it, she decided that the story wasn't all that interesting. Most likely the character of Mike Fink never existed. If he had, the legends had made him into something superhuman and thus unreal.

At another point in the book she found a section on superstitions and ghosts. That made her think of Carson and his assertion that he was a Ghost Hunter. He'd admitted that he was an amateur so he wasn't trying to brag but still it had annoyed her. Everything he said and did annoyed her now that she knew he was capable of confining her in this little prison of his.

"When two people of the same name live in a house, ghosts stay away," the book said. "Ghosts hate new things so hang something new over your door to get them to leave. A ghost will knock on a wall before someone dies; and you should never get mad at a ghost because it will resent you for it."

Well that last one makes some sense anyway.

According to the book, ghosts like singing and will listen if you sing for them. Carmel thought about that. Of course she didn't believe in ghosts and was too depressed to sing anyway. Maybe she could sing the blues, but no, she didn't even have enough energy for that! She closed the book. At least it had some stories in it. Maybe that would give her something to think about.

Back at the window she watched as a woman she'd never seen before walked toward where she suspected the front door was. The woman was slender with shoulder length brown hair. She was wearing a black knit sweater and a straight skirt with heels.

I guess we have a saleswoman at the door.

It's too bad I can't yell down and get her attention, but she'd never hear me all the way out there. I wonder if she'd go get help or just get out of here and go home if she heard someone screaming from inside the house.

Carmel strained to see where the woman had gone but she couldn't see her. She stood there bouncing back and forth on legs that seemed to have gone to sleep. Everything about her seemed to be in a state of hibernation. She felt numb.   Just as Carmel was about to walk away from the window, she saw the woman come around the house and head down toward the spot where Carson parked his car. She knew where it was although she couldn't see it. That's where they'd parked when he brought her here. The woman must have left her own car in the same place.

Carmel went and sat on the couch again; she flipped on the TV. That's all her life had become, a repetition of movement back and forth to the window, couch, TV and table. How boring! She wondered when Carson would tire of his little game. When would he decide that he'd made a mistake and let her go?

By then I'll have nothing to go back to.

Ash will be gone.

All that will be left to do is get a divorce and start over again.

Tears hovered in her eyes but did not fall. Sadness wrapped her tight in a cocoon of isolation. She pulled a blanket around her but its warmth couldn't annihilate the chill that was eating at her bones.

Chapter 11

Carson arrived home and noticed a car parked in his driveway. He wasn't familiar with the car, and wondered who it could be. The last thing he wanted was company. He climbed the steps to his house and walked around the deck to see if his visitor was sitting on the other side. She was.

April Mayes sat in one of his lawn chairs, her long legs crossed tidily and her arms folded across her chest. Her shoulder length hair was parted in the middle and she was dressed in a skirt and sweater which was her trademark. Her brown eyes looked serious as she got up and came to him giving him a long hard hug, and before he could intercept it, a kiss on his lips.

"I've missed you," she said.

"How have you been," Carson mumbled, too surprised to say much.

"I'm fine. Aren't you going to invite me in for a drink?"

"It's nice out here tonight," Carson said. "After that wind storm we had, well, at least the weather got cool behind it. Did you have any problem with electricity or phone?"

He was referring to the remnants of a hurricane which had swept through Ohio with heavy winds and a lot of destruction two days before. Actually he hadn't been affected and hadn't thought much about it but now it represented a subject for small talk while his mind churned wildly looking for ways to get rid of his unexpected visitor.

"I didn't have any problem, my electricity stayed on," she said as she sat looking at him speculatively. "Well, can I at least have a drink out here?"

"Sure," Carson said, getting up and unlocking his door. "I'll be right back."

April shifted her body and looked around the deck. He had a grill and table at one end, a planter with some marigolds in it on the other. They had been sitting in chairs which were arranged around an umbrella table. At the back of the deck you could see all the way to the river. April liked the view. Carson returned with two strawberry martinis which he knew to be her favorite. He hadn't made them from scratch but had poured the drink from a bottle over ice from his fridge.

"Here you go," he said handing her one and sitting down opposite her with the other glass.

"You didn't answer me," April said. "Did you miss me?"

"I didn't hear a question. You said you missed me. That's a statement, not a question. Anyway, we didn't part on good terms if you recall."

"It was just a silly argument. It wasn't anything to break us up over. It's been almost a year now. You should be over it," she said.

"I don't think I'm going to get over you seeing another man," Carson said.

April set her drink on the table, got up and walked over to where he sat. "You know you're special. I only went out with Tony because you were neglecting me. I'm sure you wouldn't do that this time; how about we try again." She twined her arms around his neck, tightening them like a slip knot.

~ 50 ~

"You're too late, April," he said, pulling her arms loose. "There's someone else now."

"If that's so, where is she?"

"She's around. I need you to leave before she comes and asks questions about you."

"So… she's the jealous type," April said, smiling her wickedest smile. "Good. I can work with that."

"I'm not kidding April. We're history. Don't try to cause me trouble now or I'll get a restraining order against you."

Scowling at him, April said, "That's a little mean don't you think. So what if I care about you and want to get back together; I don't think we did our best last time and I want to try again. What's wrong with that? It's not very nice for you to threaten me."

"What happened to Tony?"

"He's not around any more. What about this woman you claim to be seeing? What's she like? What kind of job does she have?"

"That's none of your business."

"There isn't really a woman is there? You're just making that up so I'll be jealous because of Tony," April accused, stepping back to look him over for telltale signs that he was lying.

"There is another woman. I love her and it's over with you and me," Carson said. "I think you should leave before this gets ugly. We should just agree to disagree and go our own ways."

"I'll go, but I'll be back. I know you still care about me. Your ego is just bruised, that's all. See ya soon," April said, as she walked casually over to the table, picked up her drink and took a sip, set it down and walked jauntily down the hill toward her car. She didn't look back or acknowledge Carson any further, but he watched her until all he could see was the taillights of her Infinity as it drove away.

Restless and upset, Carson tried to calm himself down with the rest of his martini and then he finished off the one that April had been drinking. Still agitated he decided to go get pizza and have a pizza party with Carmel. It was time they got back to normal before both of them forgot what that felt like. An hour later, armed with a CD player, tapes, and a large pizza, he went to visit his captive lover. He wasn't prepared for the flurry of arms, legs, and fury that greeted him at the door.

Carmel came barreling at him the minute the door opened, trying to push her way out past him. The pizza landed on the floor as he dropped it to grab her and pull her back. She fought like a wild woman, kicking and biting at him but he maintained a secure hold on her.

"Calm down," he yelled as he panted and struggled to get the door closed and locked again. "What are you doing?"

"Let me out of here," Carmel demanded, her face flushed a bright red, her hair standing up with sweat and exertion. "I refuse to stay here with you any longer. You've already ruined my life."

"I haven't ruined your life. Sit down and we'll discuss it but you can't attack me every time I come in the door. Next time I'll backhand you into the next room," he said, finally getting the door closed.

The pizza box hadn't come open but the pizza was scrambled together looking like a butcher had been at work with all the red tomato sauce sloshed around.

"Now," he said. "Here's your pizza, don't blame me for the shape it's in."

Chapter 12

Carmel hadn't even known she was going to take action. Suddenly as she heard Carson at the door, she decided she'd had enough of this charade. Enough was enough.

In the flurry of battle her adrenaline had been running high, and she felt better fighting back against her fate; however, once Carson managed to lock the door and the battle was over, she fell back into despondency. Having slammed the pizza box down on the table, Carson strode angrily around the room glaring at her. She sat on the couch and ignored him as she'd been doing for a week. After a while Carson stopped and sat at the table. He opened the pizza box.

"Come on and have some scrambled pizza. It doesn't look good but I'll bet it tastes just as good as when it was made," Carson said, trying to smile at her.

Carmel didn't move. Carson picked up a piece of the pizza and started eating it. He'd carefully restored most of the sausage and mushrooms onto his piece in such a way that it didn't look bad at all.

"Tastes good," he said, mouth full.

Without speaking, Carmel got up and went to the table. She picked up a piece of pizza, restoring it as Carson had done, then sat on a chair to eat it. After they'd eaten in silence for a few minutes, Carson got up and went to get the dropped tapes and CD player.

"I hope these didn't get broken," he said. "I thought we could use some dinner music."

He selected an easy listening CD and started the player. Soft music enveloped the room. It could have been one of their earlier dates when things were good between them, although they wouldn't have had scrambled pizza. They both liked the gentle sounds of the music as a romantic background. Carmel was aware that he was trying to seduce her.

It would be easy to fall back into the old relationship and forget what has happened, but I won't.

She turned sideways on the chair and looked toward the darkened window, wishing she could see outside. Probably if she stood at the window she could see the lights of town and maybe light from a boat on the river. However, she instinctively knew that if she walked to the window, Carson would be right behind her. He'd put his arms around her and stroke her hair and she'd be lost in the past, forgetting the predicament she was in now. Choosing to stay where she was, she made her posture unfriendly and cold, while trying to relax and let go of her anxiety. She ignored the soft music and focused on what her lover had done to her. He'd had no right to imprison her.

Tomorrow I'll write down that verse about "If you love something, set it free, if it's yours it will return to you, if it doesn't, it never was", And leave it where he can't miss seeing it!

"It wouldn't hurt you to be friendly to me," Carson was saying. "You might be mad at me right now, but we both know that you love me. We can disagree about me keeping you here when you want to leave but I think you'll see the benefit of it sooner or later."

Carmel didn't answer; instead she reached for another piece of the pizza and spent time spooning sauce back onto it. It was so hard to know what to feel in a situation like this one. If Carson had been a stranger who had abducted her, there wouldn't be this confusion. She'd hate him, fear him, and be one minded about her desire to escape him.

If Carson had raped her or abused her in some way like that, there would be no question in her mind. As it was, he'd been kind. He hadn't raped her, he'd provided food, drink and for other needs for her as he understood them, and he hadn't hit her when she attacked him at the door, although he'd threatened to next time. All he'd actually done to her was to prevent her from leaving him to go home. He had imprisoned her.

She smoothed down her hair which was a mess from the scuffle. Would Carson lose his patience if she didn't come around to his way of thinking and rape her, or would he let her go when he saw that his tactics weren't going to work? And what about Ash; he must be going through an awful time wondering and worrying. Tears started sliding down her cheeks as she realized what a mess she'd made, not just of her own life but the lives of everyone around her.

"I'm leaving now," Carson said, getting up abruptly. "Do you need me to bring you anything the next time I come?"

"The key to the door," Carmel said.

"Other than that?"

"No."

"Alright then, good night," he said.

She noticed that before Carson unlocked the door he stopped and looked to make sure she wasn't close by waiting to make a break. Glad that she'd remained in her chair, Carmel, watched as he unlocked and went out the door, closing it behind him. The sound of the key told her that she was locked in again.

Looking at the table she saw that the box still had a few pieces of pizza in it. She cleaned that up, putting the extra pizza into the refrigerator. She liked cold pizza but if she wanted it hot, at least there was a microwave. Her eyes scanned the room she was in again. There was no exit big enough to leave by. The door was the only way out. Just to be sure she checked in the other rooms, but saw no way out of them either. She feared it was a game of chess now, waiting to see who'd give in first. Although she was determined not to be lured into continuing her affair with Carson, would he accept that decision? Would he try to force her, or would he let her go?

Checking the kitchen drawers, she saw plastic knives and very blunt flat-wear made of metal. Her mother had called those knives butter knives, probably because the only thing they'd cut was butter! Not much of a weapon. She flipped the tine of a fork against her palm. It had a point but wouldn't do much damage. Still, just in case, she took one and hid it under the cushion of the couch and another went under the bed. If Carson tried to rape her, she'd give him what for, stabbing him with the fork in as sensitive a spot as she could manage! He'd imprisoned her so he could continue to have sex with her. It was definitely against her best interests to let him get his way about that!

Chapter 13

The nightmare started with Amanda. Carson was sitting with her in his car at the lake, laughing and drinking, watching the drizzle of rain pinging the water with tiny circles. He felt happy and at peace, as if this idyllic moment would never end.

"My husband knows about us," Amanda said. "I told him."

"What did he say?"

"He told me to stay away from you. He threatened to take the kids away from me if there's a divorce."

Carson felt his hopes plummeting. He didn't think that Amanda would give up her kids although he wasn't sure he wanted them. He wanted Amanda but wasn't looking for a package deal.

"Would it be so bad if they lived with him at least for a while," he asked her.

Amanda frowned at him as she tipped the bottle and drank deeply from it. "Of course that would be bad. I want my kids with me!"

He could see her struggling with her thoughts and he reached out to hold her but she pushed him away. When he persisted she slapped at his face with her open hand. She turned to the door and struggled to get it open but for some reason she couldn't seem to do it. She was pushing and shoving at the door as if desperate to get away from him. Carson tried to talk to her but she was saying that he never really loved her, and then she had the door open and was running across the parking lot to her own car.

Carson ran after her but she roared out of the lot and then everything started to swim and sway as he heard a loud crash. As the light around him seemed to shift, first to black and then to red; Carson tried to get to Amanda, but instead he found April Mayes standing over him.

"We're meant to be together," she said. "Don't let a little thing like infidelities throw you. You don't want commitment. That's why you choose unavailable women."

The aching in his heart was suffocating him and he reached out to April to shut her up but she evaporated from his grasp and he saw her at the other side of the lake with another man. He felt himself crying in frustration and agony over the loss of Amanda, along with humiliation over the betrayal of April.

"Why me, why me," he groaned.

And then the dream shifted again and he was smiling at Carmel. She was sitting on the bank of the river with her rolled up jeans and bare feet perched on a rock. She was reaching for something in a picnic basket. Carson sat drinking a bottle of water and watching the way the sunlight fell on her hair. He was feeling loving and warm toward her. Suddenly the wind shifted and the dirt was kicked up by it hitting him in the face. He could see Carmel through the haze, her smile replaced by a frown as she gathered the picnic basket and started to walk away from him.

"Don't go," he said to her, but she kept walking away.

He got up to follow her but trees seemed to be growing in his path blocking him and he called out to her to stop.

"I have to go home to Ash," she said; she kept walking away from him. All at once he had a chain saw and was cutting down a large tree, making it fall across her path to block her from leaving. She climbed through its branches and kept moving away without a backward glance.

After that the dream backpedaled and he was back at the lake with Amanda.

"I'm sorry," he was telling her. "Stay here with me; don't drive until the alcohol wears off."

Amanda looked at him and then got into her car and drove away. He woke up screaming at her to come back to him.

After the nightmare, all chance of sleep was blocked for a while and Carson wandered around his house thinking about his life and his many mistakes. Was this new ghost hunting venture actually a grasp at the possibility of communing with loved ones who had gone on before him? Was he really hoping to talk to Amanda again? Amanda had never been to this house so her spirit wouldn't be likely to make an appearance unless it had attached itself to him somehow. It would be nice to tell her how sorry he was. He'd never had the chance to really say "Goodbye". That late night visit to the funeral home was all he'd had and it was not enough.

Of course that's not it? I'm in love with Carmel now. Amanda is gone. I loved her but she's gone.

Thinking about the ghost his mother said inhabited the house, Carson took his equipment to the room directly above the slave hideaway. He wondered what Carmel was doing right now. She should be sleeping, just as he should be sleeping. What would she say if he went in to see her in the middle of the night? Thinking about her temper, Carson decided not to find out.

He'd read the directions and now he hoped it would be as easy as setting up the equipment and leaving it in the room to measure the presence or absence of any spirits which were around. Once he had everything set, Carson turned the lights out and made his way to his bedroom again. He flipped on a late night show and watched it until his eyes finally started drooping. Gratefully he flipped off the light and slipped into an uneasy rest.

Chapter 14

Edna Wetzel and her friend Ted Zimmerman slipped into the Opry House and took their seats. On the stage in front of them a group of men called the Ragtime River Rats had their fiddles primed. They were dressed in the style popular in America during the 1920's and 30's, with top hats, canes and a certain flair not seen since. The room was full of older people with a scattering of younger folk mixed among them. Edna couldn't wait for the show to start.

She looked at her date for the evening. Ted Zimmerman was seventy nine years old but he still had a zest for life. He'd taken her all around the area to shows at the tiny Opera Houses that many small towns still have. She liked the man a lot, enjoyed his company, and liked the musical events he took her to. Tonight was promising to be one of the best shows they'd seen. Ted was wearing a blue baseball cap, a blue and yellow print shirt and his smiles were showing off his extensive dental work to good effect. She admired him quietly.

"Would you like something to drink," he asked her.

She turned to look and saw a small snack bar at the back of the room.

"Maybe at intermission," she said.

The show started with the band's version of Alexander's Ragtime Band followed by Somebody Stole my Gal. These songs were a little before her time but Edna had heard them all her life and she found herself singing along. Looking over at Ted, she saw him smiling indulgently at her and smiled back. He liked to see her enjoy herself. Carson's father would have been mortified if she'd sung out loud along with the band in his presence. She felt a rush of affection for Ted.

On stage they were encouraging audience participation and the lead singer was dancing down the aisle shaking a hand here and giving a high five there. Everyone was in a rollicking good mood it seemed. Edna kept smiling all through the first half of the show and when they walked outside at intermission, Ted said,

"I see you're having a good time tonight."

"I sure am," she agreed.

He'd purchased drinks while she waited in line for the bathroom and now they stood with others in the late September air, enjoying the evening to the fullest.

"How'd it go with Carson this morning," Ted asked her.

"He was being difficult as usual," Edna said. "He doesn't like me coming home. I think he's up to something but I can't imagine what it would be."

"I still think you should get an attorney and make him let you move back into your house. Your son has no right to come along and dispossess you this way. You're no more senile than I am. If anyone has to move it should be him. It's your house, right?"

"I've been thinking about what you said," Edna acknowledged, as the crowd started moving back inside for the rest of the show. "I might see that attorney you told me about."

The second half was as good as the first and the band ended the show with an animated version of "Those Were the Days". Singers were going down each aisle whipping the audience into excited song and Edna's heart expanded with the shared camaraderie. It felt so good to be a part of something. She felt vibrant and full of life in spite of her age.

On the way home, Ted stopped at a restaurant for pie and coffee and they sat talking for a half hour or so. Finally, Edna was back at her own place, alone. She looked around the little apartment style area where she'd been living this short time and thought about her house sitting there with only Carson to make it a home. Maybe Ted was on target. Carson didn't have the right to dispossess her this way. It's true that someday the house would be his, but she wasn't dead yet. It was still hers and maybe she'd fight to take back what belonged to her.

"I'll see that attorney Ted told me about tomorrow," she thought as she drifted to sleep, glad she'd finally made a decision.

While all this was happening, Carmel was drifting deeper into her own problems. Carson had gone back to leaving her alone most of the time. She supposed he thought he could wear her down with isolation. She had to admit that sometimes she'd have been happy to see him just so she'd have a human being to talk to. As it was, there wasn't anyone, not even one of Carson's ghosts to ease her loneliness. Today she'd finally heard her name on TV and it had only made matters worse. According to the newscast, police were investigating Ash, suspecting him of murder in her disappearance.

"No one has seen Carmel Simpson for two weeks now and foul play is suspected," the commentator said.

Poor Ash! He is truly the victim here, not you!

That made her feel even worse; all this had happened to him because of actions that she'd taken. He was innocent. Guilt is never an easy guest and her guilt rode her night and day until she wanted to end it all. Even when she tried to see light at the end of the tunnel, she could only see dreary unending clouds. Today she'd even looked around the apartment for something she could use to hang herself. Later she'd been scared by her own thoughts, but the idea had never fully left her mind.

Now at the end of the day she stood staring out the slit in the wall that passed for a window, watching a lighted barge on the river. The free world was so close, but it might have been a thousand miles away as inaccessible as it was to her. She wondered if Carson was home. It was impossible to hear what was going on in the rest of the house down in this place.

You need a plan and you have to get out of here to put it into effect.

Somehow she needed to let the police know that she wasn't dead so they'd leave Ash alone. That was the least she could do to put right what she'd done wrong. She wondered if Carson would let her send a postcard or something. Surely if Ash got a card from her saying that she'd left of her own free will, the police would leave him alone, wouldn't they?

I'll ask Carson about it the next time he comes.

Chapter 15

"The police are giving Ash a hard time because they think he's responsible for my disappearance. I want to send a postcard or letter to him, so he won't worry, and so the police will stop hassling him," Carmel said.

"How'd you know?"

"I saw it on TV."

"I'll think about it," Carson said, glad that Carmel had finally asked him for something, that she was actually speaking to him.

"It won't hurt anything," Carmel insisted. "It's not fair for him to be blamed. He's guiltless."

Carson considered that. It was true. Ash was blameless in this matter, but Carmel might be trying to trick him. Maybe she was going to write something in a code that only she and Ash would know; she might have an idea how to tell Ash a way to find her. He had to think this through before agreeing to it.

"I don't have any postcards," he said, stalling. "I'll buy one tomorrow and we'll send it."

Carson had just had a brilliant idea. He'd write the note himself on a separate piece of paper. She could copy it word for word so it would be in her handwriting, but using his words instead of hers would prevent her from putting any hidden messages into the text.

Carson hadn't been watching much TV himself but later that night he put the set on and watched the news from Cincinnati. Carmel had been right. Ash was suspected of murder in her disappearance. It reminded him of the Lacy Peterson case and of a case out of

Northern Ohio where a pregnant woman had gone missing and then was found dead. Her boyfriend, the father of one child, and suspected father of the unborn baby, admitted to that murder.

If they knew about me, they'd be on my case just as hard as they are on Ash.

Carson felt sorry for Ash. He didn't deserve what he was going through. He didn't wish any harm to Ash...he just wanted his wife. Sitting down at his desk, Carson attempted to write a note that could be mailed to Ash and would satisfy the police. If he could get the right note written, just a paragraph or so, and have Carmel copy and send it; that should get Ash off the hook.

She needs to tell him that she left him, she's ok, but she never wants to see him again.

"Dear Ash," he wrote...

"I'm sorry to have left so abruptly but I don't want to be married to you any longer. I didn't want to talk to you; you'd have tried to change my mind. I'm fine but I intend to live my life without you from now on, and I advise you to move on as well. We aren't meant for each other. I'm sorry if this hurts your feelings. You're a good man, but not the man for me. I've found the perfect man for me and I want to stay with him always.

Best Wishes, Carmel"

Carson sat back and looked at the words on the paper. If Carmel wouldn't burn her bridges with Ash, he'd burn them for her. He doubted that Ash would ever give her another chance after this note. Carson knew that he wouldn't, if the roles were reversed. The note would clearly tell Ash that there was someone else in the picture, and that she'd left him for the other man.

Once she realized there was no going back, Carmel would see things his way. She'd realize that they were soul-mates and that everything he'd done was for the best.

As much as he liked the note, Carson knew Carmel would hate it. She'd give in and write it though, in order to save Ash from the police. She had a soft heart that way. That's why he'd added the part about Ash being a good man. He knew that if Carmel was writing a letter like that, she'd probably try to be gentle with Ash. She wouldn't want to hurt his feelings any more than necessary.

He pulled out some old postcards and took them and the writing he'd done to Carmel. Laying them on her table, he explained that she was to write only what was on the paper. If she really wanted to help Ash, she'd do it his way. If not, then Ash could just get out of the hot water he was in the best way he could manage. Carmel looked at the paragraph he'd written and snorted but she didn't say anything. Instead she walked to the TV, tuned it on and tuned him out. He could see she wasn't happy.

You knew she wouldn't be happy but she'll write the card anyway.

"I'll be down in the morning," he said. "If you have the card ready, I'll put it in tomorrow's mail."

He didn't tell her that he'd decided to drive all the way to Cincinnati to mail it so the postmark would be from there, not from Ripley. He had no intention of leading trouble to his door. If Carmel had any idea that she could signal Ash or the authorities as to where she was, she was naïve. He'd wipe all prints off the card to be sure his weren't there, in case they checked. He'd go over every word to be sure she'd copied his message exactly. Nothing about the card would point to him or to Ripley as a location.

As he'd predicted, the card was written by the next morning. As he picked it up he asked Carmel if there was anything she wanted him to bring home for her, but she declined to ask for anything. Unhappy that she was still dissin him, Carson left the house and headed toward Cincinnati.

He had a job to do in Hamilton and thought that he might as well mail the card from there. He'd brought a damp cloth to wipe down the missive, which he carefully did using rubber gloves to prevent leaving new prints. Then he put the stamp on the card and tossed it into the nearest mailbox. He'd checked the words on the card earlier; Carmel had written exactly what he'd told her to. Perhaps that was a good sign.

He hoped the card would do the work intended, that Ash would be believed, the police would stop searching for Carmel and chalk the disappearance up to her being a run away wife, and that Carmel would thaw in her attitude toward him.

All in due time, he decided.

Chapter 16

Carmel wasn't very happy with the words that Carson had made her write but it was essential that a message be sent as soon as possible. Even though the message wasn't exactly true and would cast her in a bad light, Carmel believed that it would satisfy the police that she was ok, and had left of her own accord. She'd hated to give in to Carson's demands that she write the letter his way but she knew that if she objected it would cause a delay and Ash couldn't afford a delay. It was the least she could do for the man she'd married.

She'd thought a lot about where she and Ash had gone wrong during her days of captivity. They'd been close and happy during the first year but as Ash had taken on more and more work, and she'd seen him less and less, that had changed. Now she was wondering if the loss of her father during her childhood had affected her perception of Ash's inaccessibility. When her father left her mother, Carmel had been eight. She'd been a Daddy's girl. The hurt he'd inflicted by moving away and starting another family had never left her. Although Ash hadn't gone anywhere, it felt the same. Emotionally he wasn't there when she needed him.

It doesn't matter why. I ruined my life because of the way I handled things.

It was right that she stop the torture for both of them, make a clean break; just end it. She wouldn't have chosen to do it this cruel way, but in the circumstances she had no choice. She loved Ash. She hoped he'd forgive her some day and they could be buddies again, friends at least. No one wants to be the bad guy, but she needed to stop dragging out the pain.

If I can't give the marriage what is required, then I need to end it. That should make us both happier.

Ash might forgive her, go to counseling with her and try to work it out. It wouldn't be fair to him to put him through that though. She should have been happy with a man like him, but it wasn't enough and now she felt paralyzed and hopeless. She had tried not to be a drag on the marriage, but she had helped to pull it down further and further by turning away from him and finding someone else. Now all she could do was to keep Ash from being suspected of murder and to give him his freedom to find someone to love him. She watched the news every day for a sign that the police had accepted the postcard as legitimate and stopped investigating Ash. However, the few mentions made of the case seemed to indicate that he was still a suspect.

Why? Didn't he get the card?

She'd questioned Carson about when he'd mailed the card and he'd sworn that it had been mailed on Tuesday. It was Friday now and the card should have arrived at its destination but nothing had changed in the media. At least she didn't think so. There weren't any mentions of the case either way. She couldn't think of any reason that Ash wouldn't give the card to the police if he'd received it.

Meanwhile she'd sunk even lower into despair and self loathing. She hadn't paced today; that took too much effort. Mostly she'd lain on the couch with a blanket over her staring at the wall. It was time to put herself out of her misery, and the only question was how she should do it. Various ideas went through her head but she was too frazzled to make a plan at the moment.

It will come to me what I should do. I caused this problem and the world would be better off without me in it. The only concern I have is that I need to know that Ash is safe and won't be blamed for what happens to me.

Meanwhile, Ash had received the postcard from her and it had confused his emotions even more. Had Carmel really taken off and left him for another man? The handwriting looked like hers. If she'd left him in this predicament on purpose he was furious at her. He'd not believed that she would leave him to worry and fret this way, let alone let him be suspected of murder. She could have told him if she was unhappy. Maybe they could have resolved it.

Of course he had to take the card to Detective Smith because the Detective was on his case daily asking if he'd heard anything from her. Maybe this would solve that problem anyway. When he gave the card to the Detective, the man looked at him suspiciously, but accepted the card and read the message.

"Does this look like her handwriting to you," he asked Ash.

"It looks like it to me. I don't like to believe what the card says but maybe she did leave me for the other man. You said she'd been having an affair and I guess this confirms that."

"Maybe," Detective Smith said.

"What do you mean, maybe? It's right there in black and white. She's gone off with another man and wants a divorce I guess."

"Well, let me know if her lawyer contacts you for a divorce. I'm betting that's not going to happen."

"Why not?"

"I'm not at all convinced that she wrote this card. Do you have examples of her handwriting? I want an expert to authenticate it before I accept that she wrote the card."

"Surely you don't think I sent the card to myself to get off the hook, do you?"

"Why not, it's happened before?"

Ash shook his head in disgust and got up to leave the Detective's office. Things just got worse and worse.

"Don't forget to get those samples to me," the Detective called as he left.

As Ash drove home he wished that he'd asked if they'd identified the other man. Was it someone Carmel worked with? How had she met this pirate who'd stolen her away? When he got home he searched through papers they'd filed jointly looking for samples of her handwriting. The sooner Detective Smith verified that this was her writing, the sooner the police were off his back.

When he flipped on the news later, the first thing he saw was that the mother in Florida who had failed to report her three year old missing for over a month, and who had then reportedly told the police a number of false stories about it, had been arrested.

I hope she isn't an innocent person caught in a web of circumstantial evidence like I am, he thought.

He hadn't lied to the police, but even so they'd failed to believe him. He didn't know what more he could say or do. If Carmel was having an affair, he hadn't known it. He hadn't confronted and killed her as they seemed to think he had. He took his shower and prepared for bed automatically, his mind on other things. Hurt and puzzlement were uppermost. He just couldn't believe that Carmel would do things this way. She had a sensitive nature and would have tried to let him down easily. It just didn't sound like her, but what was he to believe? She'd told him so in black and white.

Ash knew he spent a lot of time at work, of course, but it was for both of them he'd rationalized. After all they wanted children some day and he wanted a nice house in the suburbs for the kids to grow up in.

I've been putting myself up on a pedestal patting myself on the back for what I've been doing for my family. Now I've been rudely shoved off that pedestal and I'm drinking a bitter dose of reality.

He climbed into his empty bed and lay looking at the ceiling for the next few hours, unable to put his problems out of his mind. The loneliness ate at him like a cancer, the whys echoed hollowly through his head. Finally he slept.

Chapter 17

Carson looked at the letter in his hand in disbelief. How dare she do this? He stared at the words going over them again and again, but the meaning was plain. His mother had hired an attorney and was planning to force her way back into her home if need be. They were questioning Carson's decision to put her in an assisted living facility and ready to go to court to rectify the matter according to her attorney.

"Why, that old biddy!"

In spite of his anger and dread of the things to come, Carson admired his mother for her spunk, but he'd have never told her that. He'd been heavy handed with her and had taken the house which was hers lawfully, and justified his action by saying that she'd be better off somewhere else; the house would belong to him anyway, sooner or later.

I put her in a better place where she'd be taken care of.

She doesn't even have to fix her own meals unless she wants to.

Of course she does love to cook!

He looked at the letter again; the attorney, one Charles La Kemp, said in the letter that unless Carson contacted his mother and arranged for her to move back into her home within a week, they were launching a lawsuit against him. Carson swallowed down the bile in his throat gagging at its bitter taste. Nothing had been going right lately. Carmel was still mad at him; he was beginning to think they could never go back to the way they'd been before, and his mother was angry enough to sue him. Nothing was working according to his plans.

He was even getting repeated calls from April Mayes, calls that annoyed and dismayed him.

He wondered if it would do any good to talk to his mother about the matter. Probably not, since she'd made her position clear. Maybe the attorney would be easier to talk to. Should he call Mr. La Kemp and try to discuss the matter? He wondered if they would come to inspect the house if a lawsuit was launched. If he claimed she couldn't be left alone due to some hazard, then they'd surely check the house, wouldn't they? He couldn't risk that right now. Deciding to put off a decision about that, he headed toward Aberdeen and a small job he had there today. Best to let the problem marinate for a while before making a decision as to what to do.

Meanwhile, Carmel was sizing up the bed clothes to see if she could rip them into strips with which to hang herself. She'd thought about ingesting detergent or something poison, but that didn't seem feasible. Carson hadn't left anything but mild cleansers in the apartment. The only knives were dull and useless although she might use the knife to sort of saw part of the way through the material and rip it the rest of the way, she thought.

Believing that she could manage to rip the sheets into strips that would make a rope, her eyes searched the ceiling for something strong enough to hold her weight. She found a beam that seemed sufficient to that task, and so her mind moved on to thinking about when she'd do it. When should she take this final action? Should she do it at all? Even though her life looked bleak right now, there could always be something good down the road to look forward to. She wondered if she would be punished eternally if she took her own life as some religions believe.

Well, at least I'll be ready and have a plan if I decide to do it.

So far she hadn't heard anything to say that Ash was beyond suspicion in her disappearance. There hadn't been anything on the news about the matter at all lately. If she was missing and later found dead, would they blame Ash, or maybe if her body was found here, Carson? Should she even worry about whether Carson was blamed? After all he had precipitated this entire fiasco. What would Carson do when he found her dead? Would he take her body off his property and leave it somewhere, call the police, or bury her under the garden?

He deserves something bad but he doesn't deserve to be charged with murder.

Now that she'd almost decided what she was going to do, she felt better. It had been the indecision that was paralyzing her before.

"Even if it's a bad decision, at least it's a decision. I don't see any future."

She went to the TV and turned it on, then settled down to wait for news. If Ash had taken her card to the police wouldn't they announce that the missing wife had been heard from and appeared to be all right? Maybe the police would just let it drop and not tell the media anything. That could be why she hadn't heard anything about it. Still she wanted to be sure that Ash was in the clear before she took any action. There were no updates on her disappearance on any channel.

A few days later she started to work ripping sheets as soon as she thought Carson had left for the day. Managing to get three long strips of linen ripped from the sheet and tying them together, she climbed up and looped the linen rope over the beam on the ceiling, loosely for now because she planned to take it back down and hide it until she was ready to use it.

Satisfied that she now had means to end her misery, she hid the rope and went on as if nothing was amiss. Carson continued to be aloof, apparently in an effort to wear her down. He was silent and preoccupied. It was working on her nerves but she had no intention of letting him know it. He visited her every evening and sometimes sat and watched TV with her for a while in the evenings, but he seemed to be waiting for a sign from her before doing more. She had no intention of giving him that sign.

"I need to know what has happened to Ash," she told Carson the next time she saw him. "I want to know if the police have stopped looking for me or if they're still accusing my husband of having done something to me."

"How are you going to find out? You aren't in the news anymore."

"They do that sometimes, stop reporting on a case and then the next thing you hear is that the husband has been arrested. I'm not that important to be in the news every day, but that doesn't mean they aren't doing things, investigating and such."

"What do you want me to do about it," Carson asked, staring at her. "We sent that card. That should be enough."

"I want to be sure. Maybe I could call the police and tell them I'm ok. You could stand right there and listen," Carmel said.

"Maybe I can call and ask if they're still investigating the husband or maybe I could call Ash and ask him," Carson said.

"Don't do that?"

"Why not, asking Ash would be the best way. He'd know what's going on."

"Then let me be the one to call him. I swear I'll only tell him that I'm ok and ask if the card I sent got him off the hook with the police, and then I'll hang up."

"I'd have to think long and hard about that," Carson said; but he hadn't ruled it out.

Chapter 18

"I talked to Ash," Carson said.

Carmel stared at him. "Why? You were supposed to let me call him."

"I thought I'd better do it."

Carmel was angry. She'd wanted to be the one. At least that way Ash would know that she cared what happened to him. She wanted him to know that. Also, she didn't trust Carson to tell him the truth. She sat down in her chair and tried to tune Carson out but her curiosity wouldn't let her and so she asked him,

"What did he say? Is he off the hook with the police?"

"He said that they were checking to see if the handwriting is yours or not, of course it is, so that's not a problem. He said they hadn't been around for a few days."

"So he thinks everything is ok?"

"It seems to be."

"Who did you tell him you were?"

"I told him I'm the other man, of course, the one you left him for," Carson said, watching for a reaction.

Carmel tried not to give a reaction to that. Carson was just rubbing in the hurt, being cruel and he shouldn't get what he wanted. He shouldn't see her cringe or squirm because of what he'd told her husband. She looked at the TV set instead of at him. The set was on but muted.

"He didn't seem surprised," Carson said.

Carmel said nothing. Carson got up and came over to the couch where Carmel was sitting and sat beside her. He reached over and took her hand and held it. She didn't move away nor did she acknowledge that he'd touched her. She just stared straight ahead.

"It's time to put this behind us and to go on with our lives," Carson said, trying to maneuver her to where he could give her a kiss. She ignored him. He took her face and pulled it toward him and kissed her on the lips. Carmel turned her head away.

"We're wasting a lot of time here," Carson said. "You know there's no turning back now. Ash knows about us and he's moving on. We need to move on too."

"Did he say that," Carmel asked, stricken.

"Not in so many words but that's what it is. He knows you're in love with someone else, so it's time for him to find someone else too."

"I'm not in love with someone else. Not any more."

"I don't believe that," Carson said. "You're just mad at me because I took the decision away from you, but you'll see that it happened for the best."

"No, I won't," Carmel said, jerking away from him and running into the bedroom where she turned her face to the wall and sobbed.

Carson started to lie down at her side, aiming to hold her and try to soothe her, but then he decided against it. She was going to have to come to terms with things on her own. As for him, he had other problems to worry about. The week was nearly up and he hadn't talked to either his mother or the attorney yet. He needed to do that because he couldn't afford to have a lawsuit filed against him.

"What do you mean, she has a right to live here; I told you, she's not able to take care of herself and I'm gone a lot. She needs an assisted living arrangement," Carson said to the lawyer.

"She's perfectly capable of taking care of herself and you know it, Mr. Wetzel," The attorney said. "If we don't get your permission for her to move back into her home by tomorrow, we file the lawsuit. Is that understood?"

"I'll let you know," Carson said.

He hung up and called his mother but Edna had stiffened her backbone now that she was backed up by a legal opinion and she was adamant about moving back into her own home. He couldn't sway her in the least.

"I'll call you tomorrow afternoon," Carson said and hung up.

After staring at the wall for a few minutes, he got up and headed for the state liquor store. He needed a stiff drink of whiskey to help him think this problem out.

Carmel lay on her bed crying for a long while after Carson left. Now she was tired and washed out, the tears having leeched out all her desire to go on. She thought about the rope of sheets she had hidden under the bed. That rope was a means to nirvana, the way to escape all the pain of being earthbound. It looked more and more tempting to her today.

"I'll rest here for a while and then maybe I'll get that rope out later when I'm sure that Carson has gone to bed for the night and won't be popping in here. Maybe when he sees how far I went to escape, he'll finally get the point that I no longer want anything to do with him," she thought.

Carson returned to the house with a bottle of whiskey and a desire to drown his sorrows. He poured two jiggers of the stuff and drank those down before making a drink with whiskey and coke together. He sat staring out a window at the night sky, all lights in the upstairs off. After a while the warmth of the liquor started to ease his anxiety a little and he drifted into another world.

Thinking about his mother's insistence on the presence of a ghost in this house and of his equipment, which had been set up for a week, but never checked, Carson got up and carried his drink with him to the room where he'd set up the monitoring devices. He turned on the light in that room and went over to see if any strange sounds or pictures had materialized on his monitors.

First he listened to the sound equipment but hadn't heard anything unusual on the tape after half an hour. He checked the video tape, fast forwarding it, but didn't find anything of interest there either.

"Well, if you're here, you're awfully quiet," he said to the empty room.

Immediately he heard a loud scraping sound coming from the fireplace. Spooked by the sound, the meaning of which was amplified by the alcohol he'd consumed, Carson hi-tailed it out of the room. Uneasily he settled back down into his chair in the living room, all lights on now and his peace disturbed.

It just figures that on top of everything else that's wrong I really do have a ghost, he thought.

Chapter 19

Carmel woke up cold and stiff, still wearing her daytime clothing, at 1:15 AM. She got up, used the bathroom, made herself some tea and sat thinking in the gloom of the night. The only light she had on in the room was a small night light near the door to the bathroom. She liked the darkness though. It was her friend. She could hide in its shadows and avoid having to look at her actions in the light of day. Putting down the empty cup, she went to her bed and pulled the sheet rope out and tested it for strength. It seemed strong enough to hold her.

I don't want the rope to break or take forever to kill me. I want to do this right and get it over with.

Picking up a footstool that had been sitting in front of her chair, Carmel set in an appropriate place and climbed on it. She looped the rope over the beam and tied it. Pulling down on the material she saw that it had a little give to it, but not that much.

Good it won't let me slide on down to the floor because it stretched.

She tied the loose end around her neck and prepared to kick the footstool away. The footstool wouldn't budge. Taking the rope loose from her neck again, she got off the stool and moved it easily. Back on the stool again, she got the rope in place but the stool again refused to budge.

"Ok, then I'll just jump off it and let my neck catch my weight. That will probably be all it takes."

She tried that, but when she jumped the rope undid itself and she landed on her knees on the carpet.

What's going on here?

She didn't realize she'd been talking aloud until a voice answered her.

"You can't do this stupid thing," the voice rumbled, its vibrations striking the walls and bouncing at her from all sides.

Unnerved, she looked around the room. She couldn't see anything. Trembling inside, she asked the voice,

"Why not?"

"Because of the baby," the voice said.

"What baby," she asked but already an awful suspicion was gripping her. She'd been so upset lately that she hadn't paid attention to signs that might have alerted her before now. Could she be pregnant? How awful if she was! She settled down onto the footstool, the air leaving her lungs, an awful tightness gripping her chest. She was taken by a violent trembling that was beyond her ability to control. The shaking chilled her.

A baby?

"Who are you," she asked the empty air.

At first there was only silence and then the voice said,

"Tut Jackson here, pleased to meet ya."

"Who are you? What are you? Are you a ghost?"

An outline formed above her, the shape was that of a man dressed in vintage clothes which Carmel thought were from the 1800's. She saw long black hair and eyes like brown sugar. The image wore a scowl and looked mean. She trembled but asked him where he came from anyway.

"I'm a river-boat-man," he said proudly.

"Why are you here?"

"Looking for Virginia," the voice said, but the voice was fading away as was the image in front of her. A minute later, Carmel had all the lights on and was searching the rooms for the apparition but it had vanished as fast as it had come. She huddled in the armchair, legs tucked up in front of her. How could things get any worse? To top it all off, she might be pregnant and if she was, who was her baby's father? Most likely it was Carson since she had been with him more than with Ash during the past few months.

I can have DNA tests done to see who the father is but this means I can't escape. It's one thing to take my own life but another thing entirely to take this baby's life. What will happen to it if I die? Of course if I die before it's born, it dies too, but if I wait and then take my life, who will raise the baby?

Carmel got up and started to pace around the room. Was she really pregnant and if she was, how did that man, that ghost know it? He said he was a river-boatman not a doctor. If she was pregnant what should she do? Carson would figure it out soon, she wouldn't be able to hide it very long. Calculating, she decided that she couldn't be more than a month and a half pregnant, if she was pregnant at all. She could hide the pregnancy for another two months or maybe more if she was careful.

Sighing, she realized that everything was different now. She didn't want either Ash or Carson to know if she was pregnant; she needed time to think. Suicide was no longer an option. There didn't seem to be many options available to her.

Maybe this is all in my imagination.

I dreamed up that spirit and I dreamed up what he said.

None of it is true.

But she knew it could be true. She should have thought about that possibility before. What would Carson say if he found out she was pregnant? Would he claim the baby as his and use that as further reason to convince her to divorce Ash and marry him? What would Ash say if she told him? He'd want the baby if it was his, she thought but he'd probably want a DNA test to determine who the father was. That would be humiliating and she wasn't going to submit herself to that.

Crazy thoughts circulated through her mind. Abortion wasn't an option even if she was free and could make that decision. It would be one thing to take her own life, another thing to take the life of her baby. She'd never murder the poor little thing. Nothing about the situation she was in was its fault. She sat in the chair thinking and crying until Five AM, and then finally she lay down in her bed. She hadn't seen any more of the ghostly river-boat-man, for which she was thankful. He scared her but other things scared her more.

What am I going to do?

Chapter 20

Carson had gone through a heart wrenching, soul searching night and now he was spent with the anxiety of it. He felt he'd been backed into an impossible position and that he had no choice. He had to let his mother move back into the house and if he did that, he had to let Carmel go.

If you love something set it free, if it's yours it will return to you and if its not, it never was.

He thought about this old line and wondered if Carmel had ever been his or had he just borrowed her without her husband's permission. Through out the night he'd squirmed and schemed as to how to have things the way he wanted but had found no solution. If he refused to let his mother move back into her house, she'd file a lawsuit to force the issue. Since he claimed she couldn't handle being alone in the house, they'd send someone to inspect the house to see why not. They'd check to see if there were hazards or anything of real concern. They'd find Carmel. If he let his mother move back, Edna would have the run of the house and she'd find Carmel. Carmel would tell whoever found her that she was being held against her will. The only solution was to let Carmel go and let his mother move back into her house. He hated it!

Carson decided to call his mother and her attorney during the day and to tell them that she could move back into her house next week. He'd say that he was using areas that had previously been hers and that he needed to clean that up in order to get ready for her, as a way to explain the delay. He was sure that she'd wait just as long as she was assured that she was getting what she wanted. That way he could let Carmel go and he could clean up any trace of her having been in the house so that his mother would not suspect his reasons for having made her leave home.

Edna Wetzel seemed happy when he told her that she could move back home the next week but there was something reserved about her response. He guessed it upset her that she'd had to go to extreme measures, threatening him with a lawsuit, in order to get back what was rightfully hers.

Carson dreaded the talk with Carmel which he must have tonight. He planned to discuss things with her, first over wine, cheese and pizza, and then open the door and tell her she was free to leave whenever she wanted to. At least she could leave on a more positive note that way.

I wonder if she's ever going to forgive me.

Through the long whiskey soaked night he'd tried to put himself in his mother's place and he hadn't liked how that felt. He'd also looked at things from Carmel's side of the situation. He'd taken away her freedom of choice. She'd chosen to do what she thought was the right thing; in spite of her obvious attraction to Carson, she had been planning to try to make her marriage work. He'd taken away her free choice and he had ruined her chances for happiness with Ash. It appeared that he'd also ruined any chance that he and Carmel had for a future together. At least if he let her go now, she could start a new life without either of them. Maybe, if she was really his, she'd forgive him and come back to him.

He wondered how she'd take being set free after a month and a half. Would she run to Ash and try to explain what had happened? Would she just go off on her own away from both of them? What would she do? Would she gloat because he'd had to release her? Would she go to the police? Carson cringed at the thought of police. However, he still thought he could convince them that she'd stayed with him willingly; and that the story about abduction was to make her husband believe that she'd been coerced.

I won't tell her about my mother.

I'll let her think I'm doing it to please her, just because I love her.

He did love her. The fear of losing her was niggling at his decision to release her. He tried to consciously let her go, to accept the inevitably of that. Perhaps once he was no longer restraining her or limiting her life, her anger toward him would go away. He wondered about that. Either way, he wasn't looking forward to tonight.

He brought a supreme pizza, minus the anchovies, along with a bottle of wine and a cheese plate when he went to the slave quarters to see Carmel that night. He'd put it all into a cardboard box so he could carry it.

She was sitting on the couch her legs pulled up under her; she barely looked at him when he entered the room. Finally she looked up as he set out the cheese tray and pizza and poured the wine into their glasses.

"Sorry," he said, "I'm not much of a cook."

Carmel joined him at the table her mind in turmoil; her indecision and worry overwhelming her. After the experiences of the previous night, her suspicions were paramount. Once the possible presence of a baby growing inside her had come up, she immediately felt that it was true. She was pregnant. She had wanted a baby ever since she and Ash had married but it never seemed to happen. Of course this baby was probably not Ash's. Maybe something in Ash's makeup had prevented her becoming pregnant, something that Ash lacked but which Carson did not. Another reason to believe the baby belonged to Carson.

She'd struggled with what it would mean if she found out that she was carrying Carson's baby. He'd find out eventually and then demand visiting privileges. Would he step up his campaign for her to divorce Ash and marry him? What would her pregnancy mean to Carson? Maybe he wants me, but not a baby. Maybe that information would make him let me go so I could get medical treatment and deliver a healthy baby. A doctor isn't likely to make house calls to this place. The possibility of a pregnancy had altered the situation in a lot of ways and she needed to think it all out before making any decisions.

She couldn't think straight but she noticed that Carson had bought her favorite pizza and that he seemed to be trying to make the meal festive. Deciding to go along with that mood for now, she ate pizza and discussed mundane things with him. She had declined the wine and chosen milk with her pizza, just in case there was a little life inside her that shouldn't be exposed to alcohol.

"You know I love you," Carson was saying. "I might not have expressed my love in the proper way but everything I've done is because of that love. Other than not letting you leave, I've been nice to you, haven't I?"

"I suppose so," Carmel said grudgingly, wondering where this conversation was going.

"Maybe I'll do something that will tell you how much I love you, and how much I believe in us. It might be the biggest risk I've ever taken but I'm about to give you something very special," Carson said.

Carmel stared at him; finally, she had actually listened to his words.

What is he saying?

Chapter 21

Carmel shook her head a little trying to make sense of what Carson was saying. He'd said something about giving her an important gift; a gift which he thought would make a difference. She hoped he hadn't bought her a ring or something like that. He'd already declared his intentions as pertained to marriage. She didn't want to have to discuss this with him again.

But your baby would have a name, a father to help support and take care of it.

Don't burn any bridges just yet.

"I can't imagine what that would be," she said.

She was shaken up a little, hearing the voice of the spirit in the night all over again. The man, or ghost, had sounded gruff and illiterate on the one hand, but on the other hand, he'd made sense. She wondered who the Virginia was that he claimed to be looking for, an old girlfriend probably, or maybe his sister? Carson was saying something but she couldn't seem to grasp it. She tried to focus on his face but instead she was seeing the image of the spirit whom she'd glimpsed for a moment in the night, superimposed over his features. It was eerie!

What's happening to me? Am I going crazy?

"I'm going to finish my wine, give you a brotherly hug and a kiss on the cheek, and when I walk out the door, I'll leave it unlocked. You're free to leave whenever you want. .I won't try to stop you," Carson said. "That's my gift."

Carmel strained to process that statement. Did he mean it? If so, what had changed his mind? Surely he hadn't been talked to by the ghost, had he? That vapor-misty river-boat-man from last night could have made a visit to Carson, she supposed, although it wasn't likely since he was only a figment of her own imagination. She wondered what Carson's response would have been if he'd been told that she might be carrying his baby. Would he decide to set her free?

"Why are you doing this now," she asked him.

"I've been thinking about things and I decided that if you're really mine, if we belong together, you'll see that and come back to me. If not I just have to get used to the fact that you never loved me at all."

Carmel decided that she'd believe it when she saw the open door and not until. What was she going to do if it was true? She could leave but where would she go? Ash wouldn't want her back and she didn't have any money for a place to live. In fact, by now she didn't have a job either.

Smiling at Carson to encourage him to do what he'd said he'd do, she said,

"Why don't you give me the keys then?"

"No, because you'd probably leave as soon as you had the keys and I'd like to talk a while before that happens," Carson said.

"Just as I thought..."

"I mean what I said," Carson told her. "Let's finish this food, drink a toast to our futures, either together or apart, and then I'll leave. When I do, the door will be left open so you can walk out anytime you want."

They sat eating the pizza, tension hot in the air, watching each other guardedly. Carson was trying to assess how Carmel was taking her prospective freedom and she was trying to figure out if he meant it, and if he did, what did that mean for her.

Eventually they were finished eating and Carson proposed a toast, as he'd suggested he'd do earlier; the toast was to them both whether they happened to be together or separated. He'd poured more wine for himself and a glass for Carmel as well. Not wanting to make a fuss about the alcohol, or to alert him to any change in her habits, Carmel took a sip of wine with the toast, and then set the glass down on the table.

Carson walked over to her and gently pulled her up out of her chair. He put his arms around her and held her, then gave her a kiss on her forehead and then one on her right cheek. Letting her go, he went to the door, unlocked it and walked out leaving it standing open, the key still in the door.

"Have a wonderful life," he said as he left her there, riveted to the same spot, looking at him in amazement.

Carson had expected another terrible night but was pleasantly surprised the next morning to realize that he'd slept through without waking once. Somehow he'd come to terms with his losses and although losing Carmel made him terribly sad, he thought he could move on with his life, following whatever opportunities came his way.

He was scheduled to do work in Cincinnati this morning and in West Union in the afternoon. Although it was early November, Ohio was having its Indian summer, and the weather was perfect. It was supposed to get up to 72 degrees today. Somehow it was hard to stay down in the dumps when the sun was shining so brightly.

He hadn't gone to the apartment where Carmel had been living this morning. He figured that would make him too sad, which was one of the reasons he had asked for his mother to wait a week before moving in. He knew he'd have to clean to remove signs that someone had been living in the apartment before his mother got home, but he wanted to wait a few days, in order to get used to the idea of Carmel being gone. Even then he'd probably have to fortify himself with strong liquor to deal with it.

As he finished his last job of the day and headed back toward Ripley, Carson wondered what he could do to entertain and distract him tonight. Maybe a movie and dinner out, he thought. He wasn't in a hurry to go home. If he got home late enough he'd be just in time to go to sleep and forget his worries for the night.

"Yeah, that's the thing to do," he decided and took a street heading away from his house, hoping to distract himself from his pain.

Chapter 22

A couple of days later Carson came home, fixed himself some dinner, and consumed a couple jiggers of whiskey, hoping to fortify himself enough to go and clean out the apartment where Carmel had lived. He expected to feel a lot of grief and maudlin sentiments and thought the alcohol might help him to cope. When he'd left her there with the room unlocked, the key in the door, he'd known that she would leave as soon as she realized that he really meant it. He'd gone to his bedroom and closed the door where he'd watched TV until bedtime, feeling that he couldn't bear to see her leave. He hadn't returned to those rooms since, not wanting to face his loss.

As he ate, Carson thought about his ghost hunting equipment and wondered if there was anything new recorded. Checking it out first would be a way to put off doing what he needed to do in the rooms downstairs. Once he'd finished his dinner and put the dishes in the dishwasher, Carson headed to the room where his ghost hunting paraphernalia was. Again he didn't find much of interest but he took the audio tape to listen to it further at a later time. To be sure he didn't miss anything he needed to listen to hours of recordings. He replaced the tape he took with a new one.

Finally he headed down stairs to the hidden rooms. He saw that the door was shut now and that the key he'd left in the lock was missing. Had Carmel taken it with her or maybe she'd left it on the table inside. He turned the door knob and found that the room was unlocked. Hesitating, afraid of the emotions that he

~ 101 ~

expected to assail him when he faced the empty apartment, Carson took a deep breath and then turned the knob.

"I wondered if you were coming back," Carmel said.

She was sitting on the couch where she usually sat; Carson was so shocked to see her that he dropped the bucket and cleaning supplies that he'd brought with him. A bottle of detergent rolled back out the door; confused he automatically stooped to pick it up trying to figure out what had happened, what did it mean that Carmel was still here?

"I thought you'd be long gone," he finally said.

"I don't have a car. Remember, mine's parked in that grocery store lot in Cincinnati."

"Oh, I guess you want me to take you there," he said, the words stumbling from his mouth as if he was drunk. He was sure he wasn't though.

"Yes, I'd like to get my car back, if it's still there after all this time."

"What have you been eating?"

"There was enough food in the refrigerator."

Carson slumped down in the chair not knowing what to say or what to hope for. Since she was still here, could that mean that she wanted to be with him after all and might stay willingly?

"Why are you really here," he asked. "Did you decide that I was right and we should be together?"

"No. I'm really mad at you for making me a prisoner. You had no right to do that, and I'll never forgive you! I 'm still here because I haven't decided where to go yet and since its your fault that I'm in this predicament, I think you're obligated to let me stay here until I can get on my feet again."

Carson looked at her not knowing what to say. He thought it was a good thing that she'd stayed in his house after he'd set her free to go wherever she wanted to. The more time they were together the better the chance that they'd reestablish their old relationship, but what about his mother?

"My mother is going to move in here next week," he said.

"What does that mean?"

"How will I explain you, if you're still here?"

"It's simple; tell her I'm a friend who needed a place to stay for a little while."

"Okay, maybe that'll work. Are you planning to stay down here?"

"Sure, why not, as long as you don't lock me in."

"I promise I won't do that again. I'd like for you to be with me because you want to."

"That's not going to happen so don't misunderstand me. You took away my life, as it was, and it will take time for me to rebuild it. Until I figure out what to do, I plan to stay here because I think you owe that to me for the problems you caused. That doesn't mean that you and I will be an item again," Carmel said.

Carson didn't think it would be good to argue with her. He didn't want to scare her away. For whatever reason she had stayed and for now that would have to be enough. He had to be patient and let her come to him now. He was sure that if he gave her enough time that could happen.

Ok," he said. "Friends first and then maybe later we can go back to the way things were."

"Why's your mother coming back? Doesn't she like the place where she's been living?"No, she's homesick.

I'll tell her that you're down here in the apartment so she won't be surprised. I'll say you're a friend who needed a temporary place to stay, as you suggested."

"Will you take me to get my car?"

"What are you going to do if it's been towed?"

"Then you're going to pay to get it out of the impound lot since it's not my fault the car was abandoned."

"I guess that's fair. I have a job in Cincinnati tomorrow so if you want you can go with me; we'll see what's happened to it."

"Okay."

Not wanting to risk causing more ill will with Carmel, elated at the chance, however slight, of winning her back, Carson decided to leave her alone for now. He put the bucket and cleaning supplies on the table, said good night and told her that he'd be ready to leave at 8:00 in the morning. He thought about his mother. Why hadn't he thought of that? If Carmel wasn't a prisoner there was nothing to hide from Edna. He had a right to let a friend stay here if he wanted to.

Carson whistled as he walked up the steps and headed toward his room. As he went by the ghost room, as he'd started to think of it, he could have sworn he heard a man's booming laugh, although it sounded muffled as if its owner didn't want to be heard.

Imagination is a wonderful thing!

Although sure he'd imagined the sound, Carson noticed that he was almost tiptoeing as he went down the hall. Perhaps he was afraid that if he made too much noise it would wake the dead.

Chapter 23

After that horrendous night with her suicide attempt, the appearance of a ghost, being faced with the possibility of pregnancy, and then all the emotion that followed when Carson had set her free, Carmel had been drained. After Carson had left her there, the key in the door, her options open, she'd wilted into exhaustion. All she'd managed to do was to go to the door and retrieve the key, just in case he decided to change his mind and lock her in again; then she'd just sat there staring into space.

Where do I go? What do I do? I don't have a car, a job, or a husband any longer .I can't go home. I don't think I can face Ash after all of this, knowing that he knows about the affair.

This was Carson's fault. Yes, she'd committed adultery but it wouldn't have led to such a disastrous situation as this, wherein she'd lost everything, if Carson hadn't abducted her. He still had a job and a home but he'd taken that away from her. Thinking that, she'd made up her mind to stay and use his house as hers until she could figure things out. He owed her!

For the next two days she'd wondered what Carson was doing, what he was thinking. She supposed that he believed she'd left, but why didn't he come down and check? There had been a decent supply of food so she hadn't gone hungry. Mostly she'd sat and meditated on her situation and how she could get out of it. More and more she was convinced that she was pregnant. All the signs were there. Should she reconcile with Carson if that was the case so the baby would have a father? What about Ash?

Her thoughts had chased each other like a pack of dogs after a rabbit. She had trouble calming them down so she could think straight. First of all she didn't want to burn any bridges. Her inclination was to try to get on her feet and to leave both Ash and Carson behind, making a new life for herself. However, if she was pregnant, and either or both men knew, she could be faced with demands for child visitation and the like. She didn't want that kind of complication. Right now she needed to play her cards close to her chest as she tried to get her life back in order.

First things first, find out what happened to the car.

Once you have transportation, you can figure the rest out.

You should have a paycheck coming.

Pick that up and use it until you can find another job.

Work long enough to pay for an apartment and you'll be on your own again.

Better hurry though before the baby starts to show.

In spite of her mind urging her to hurry, Carmel was enmeshed in a drowsy state of unreality. It worried her that she'd imagined a ghost had spoken to her. Clearly, she'd known about the pregnancy in the deeper recesses of her own mind and had somehow conjured up a ghost to tell her about it. Since then she'd seen and heard nothing.

Why did I conjure up a river-boat-man? It must be because of the material Carson gave me to read. I'm sure all these old houses have a rich history with the river and the men that have sailed up and down it these many years.

Now that she'd talked to Carson she felt better. He knew she was here and wasn't going to throw her out, spoiling all her plans. He was going to take her to see about the car and had tentatively agreed that he'd get it out of impound if it had been towed away. She'd parked it in a Kroger parking lot. The store was open twenty four hours a day and so she'd hoped no one would pay any attention to it with all the cars coming and going constantly, however, after a month and a half, it had probably been impounded.

Turning on the TV she decided to listen to the news to see if they were still mentioning her disappearance. She hadn't seen anything in two weeks. By now the police should have a handwriting analysis to confirm that she'd written the card. Her bridges were burned but at least Ash wouldn't be in trouble with them any more.

All the news was about the president elect, Barrack Obama. She hadn't paid any attention to this year's political zoo, having had too many problems of her own to concern her self. She thought about what the country was going through. There were massive problems with the economy and she wondered if she'd be able to find another job.

"The worse thing you can possibly do when you're depressed is to watch the news," she thought and snapped the set off. It was time for bed anyway if she wanted to be up and ready for the next phase of her life tomorrow morning.

She dreamed of a baby boy who pranced around on top of her bed in a little sailor suit. He had her eyes but she couldn't tell who else he might resemble. It didn't matter because her heart was hurting with love for him. She woke up with tears wet on her face. If she was pregnant the baby was the most important thing. Every thing she did, every choice she made had to be made for him or her. The baby was the future.

Chapter 24

Carmel was ready when Carson had told her to be; she left the secluded apartment and found her way to the upstairs kitchen where she joined him for a cup of coffee. She watched Carson as she drank his swirling black brew. He seemed ill at ease with the new arrangement between them which made her feel more confident. She no longer felt like a victim.

"I forgot where you said you had to go today," she commented.

"It's in Cincinnati, not all that far from where we left your car. I should have remembered about that car. I could have gone and moved it to a safer location."

"I wish you had," Carmel said.

"Well, we'll do whatever we need to, starting today," Carson promised.

They drove in near silence all the way to Cincinnati. To their great relief and surprise, the car was still where they had left it. There would be no need to deal with an impound lot or anything like that.

"What are you going to do," Carson asked.

"I'm going to start my car and drive it away."

"What if it won't start after all this time?"

"You have jumper cables don't you?"

"Yeah, I threw some in, just in case we needed them."

Carmel got into the car and although the motor dragged and hesitated, the car started without need for the cables.

"Goodbye," Carmel said, preparing to drive away.

"You'll be at the house later, won't you?"

"I told you I'm staying there for now. When will you be home? I can't get into the house you know."

"Here," Carson said, taking an extra key off his key ring. "This will open the front door."

Not saying anything, Carmel took the key and attached it to her key ring. Driving out of the lot she thought about what to do now that she had a measure of freedom. First I want to stop and have another cup of coffee while I think this out, she decided, pulling into a fast food place. After she had the coffee in front of her she sat staring out the window at the November sky. The day was grey and rainy, dampening her spirits which had just started to dry out a bit.

I've made progress at least. I have my car back. I can go to see about my last check and make sure I really am fired. I can look for a job. I could even go to see Ash if I want to.

Seeing Ash would be too traumatizing, she believed, so she decided to go to her old job and talk to accounting about her check. With a little money in her pocket she could then start looking for a job.

That sounds like the most reasonable step for me to take right now.

At her old company the staff registered surprise at seeing her.

"The police were here and everything," the payroll officer whispered to her. "They think you're dead or something. I told them I didn't know nothing!"

"Thanks, it was just a big misunderstanding," Carmel said.

Although the woman tried her best to get the real story from her, Carmel blocked her attempts and got out of there, check in hand. As she left she saw numerous heads turning her way but her attitude was adequate to block anyone from speaking to her. Gratefully she got into her car and left the place forever. She'd seen several people reach for the phone as she passed. Most likely some of them were notifying the police that she'd been spotted.

That chapter is closed. It's time to write a new chapter to my life, she thought.

Unfortunately she didn't know what to write or to do with the rest of the day. She went to the bank and cashed her check, tucked that money away and then sat in her car wondering what to do next. Today wasn't the day for looking for a job. She hadn't taken any clothes with her the day she and Carson had gone for their fateful drive and she'd lived in the clothes she'd worn and a couple of Carson's T-shirts and shorts ever since. Now she looked at the black slacks and cream colored blouse she was wearing and realized that she'd have to have something to interview in before trying to find a job.

Okay, today I buy a pair of shoes, some hose and a very cheap suit. After that I'll be ready to start a job search.

She looked at the money in her purse. It wasn't much, especially if she had to buy clothes with it. It was too bad she couldn't go home and get a few of her own clothes and take them with her. That would save money for gas and whatever else might come up before she had an income again. Sitting in her car she pondered the option of trying to go there while Ash was at work, sneak in, she still had her key, and get a few things…just enough to get by. After all they were her clothes. Why shouldn't she go get them?

Something whispered that to do this would be taking a risk she didn't need to take. She was 100% sure she didn't want to see Ash right now. However, economy won out. It was the economic thing to do. Why buy clothes and shoes when she had them already? What was the risk in going to the house anyway? She felt like a burglar breaking into her own house, but she shouldn't feel that way. Maybe she'd lost some of her rights but she still had a right to her possessions.

Starting the car she headed toward what used to be home. Everything looked different today. The familiar streets seemed changed somehow, her own house foreign. That increased her anxiety and worry. She drove by first making sure that Ash's car wasn't in the drive, and then she came back and parked. Fumbling for her house key, she suddenly wondered if Ash would have changed the locks. After all he had no reason to think she'd ever return and he wouldn't like having his house key out there in some unknown place.

The key worked, so he hadn't changed the lock; hesitantly she opened the door. Hurriedly like the thief she felt she was Carmel ran up the stairs to the bedroom. Inside the room she saw several boxes. When she went to her closet, she found it bare.

Where are my things!

She felt panic and pain as if she'd been slapped hard. Ash had given away her clothes! Running around the room, she checked his closet and found everything of his there as usual. Now she stopped a minute to look at the boxes. The first one she opened had some of her clothes in it neatly packed away.

He really hates me. He's giving away my things because he can't bear to see them! He can't bear to be reminded of me!

Carmel sat down and cried, her heart broken.

Chapter 25

It was half an hour before Carmel could stop the sobbing long enough to take action. There were five boxes in the room. She decided to take all of them so Ash wouldn't be able to give them away. Anyway, she never wanted to come back here. It took another forty five minutes to get the boxes into her trunk and back seat. After that she went back inside, looked around the house for the last time and then laid her key on the hall table.

That's that!

She drove back to Ripley getting there at 3:00pm. She didn't expect Carson until 5:00 or 6:00 so she hauled the five boxes into the house herself and lugged them down the steps to the apartment. It felt good to have her possessions again but horrible to know that Ash had been systematically disposing of her starting with these boxes. She'd known he'd be upset and angry but she hadn't expected this. What was she going to tell Carson about the boxes? She didn't suppose she had to tell him anything except that she needed her things and had gone to get them. If she kept on it would take a moving truck to get her from his house to the next place.

I wonder what Ash will think when he comes home and finds my key on the table and the boxes gone.

It was five thirty by now and Carmel debated whether she should go to the kitchen and fix dinner or what her new role in this house should be. She wanted to pull her own weight. Essentially she was now a house guest who was not paying rent or doing anything to earn her keep. She decided to wait and see what

Carson's thoughts on the matter were. He should be home soon.

Carson had told her that his mother would move things in tomorrow. Carmel didn't want to be here when that happened. She'd have to ask Carson if he'd told his mother that he had a house guest yet. It could be ugly if Edna came and found a stranger in the house and wasn't expecting it. She busied herself putting things away and going through boxes, even if she didn't plan to actually unpack them, she did it just to see what they contained. It looked like her life up until now was the sum of five boxes of possessions.

When she heard Carson come into the house, she went upstairs to meet him.

"Do you want me to fix dinner," she asked.

"I'd rather go out to eat if that's ok with you," he said.

"I want to start earning my keep around here. I need to find things to do to make myself useful."

"My mother loves to cook so that job's taken. You can do cleaning and things like that if you want to and maybe I can find some other things needing done if you want. For tonight let's just go out and grab something. I don't care if it's pizza."

They ended up at Slugger's pizzeria on Second Street. Carson had declared pizza to be his favorite food and Carmel didn't care what she ate, so that worked out ok. Back at the house, Carmel told him that she didn't want Edna to come home to a disaster so she cleaned up the kitchen which Carson had left in a mess while he went into the living room and sat with a glass of wine watching TV.

She was glad that he was respecting her boundaries and hopeful that with this new relationship she'd be able to earn her way while preparing to go on her own. The next step would be to find a job. She stopped to say 'Good Night' to Carson before heading down to the apartment.

"I don't suppose you'd like to share my room with me tonight, would you?" he asked.

"No," she said and headed downstairs.

Carson didn't try to stop her, nor did he follow her, which was a relief. It was going to be hard to re-define their relationship once again. They'd gone from lovers to prisoner/jailer and now to host/house guest. How confusing this was!

Carson sat in his chair staring at a TV he didn't really see. What was he going to do to get Carmel back? He'd been trying to stay his distance and let her make the decisions she needed to make hoping that she'd eventually forgive him and renew their previous relationship. His patience and faith was wearing thin now. He wondered how long he'd be able to cope with this.

Well, starting tomorrow, Mother will be back in the house and I have to adjust to that too. I wonder what she'll think about Carmel being here. It's best not to rock any boats right now.

He thought about his ghost tapes, the tapes he'd extracted from his equipment a few days previously, and decided to listen to them as he went about getting ready for bed. He put the tape in the recorder and let it run; minute after minute of silence ensued and he almost forgot the tape was playing. Picking up his night clothes and heading for the shower, Carson jumped when a husky voice said

"Who are you?"

He stopped and went back to stare at the tape recorder. Backing the tape up, he played the message again. It repeated the question. Letting it go on, he wondered if there were other anomalies recorded. He felt an internal chill of apprehension, but he'd decided on this course and he planned to stick with it. Forgetting his shower, Carson sat down and listened until the end of that tape and then started another. Although he listened to the very end of the recordings, he didn't hear anything else, no chains thumping, whispered words, or other questions.

Playing the question over again and again, he decided the voice was that of a man who might be British or maybe have a touch of Irish. It was hard to tell much with so few words to go on.

So my Mother was right. This house does have a ghost. It's apparently a man. Why would he ask that question? Does he want to know who I am as much as I want to find out about him? I guess a ghost could be curious too.

Finally Carson went off to bed but not to sleep easy. There was too much going on in his life for that.

Chapter 26

A couple of days later Carson was thinking about the upheavals in his life as he drove home from work. His mother had moved back into the house and he'd adjusted to that better than he'd expected to. She hadn't seemed upset meeting Carmel and being introduced to her as a friend. In fact his mother seemed to see her presence as a good thing for some reason. It could be because Carmel had been helpful around the house. It could also be that Carson's mother wanted him to meet a nice girl, marry, and settle down to produce Grandchildren for her.

Last night at dinner he'd told his Mother and Carmel about the recorded voice on his ghost hunting machine, in an effort to make safe conversation. At their insistence he'd gone and retrieved the tape and played it for them. Carmel had seemed particularly interested and had him play it several times.

"I told you there was something in that room," Edna said. "There's something in that apartment where you're staying too," she cautioned Carmel.

"What have you seen and heard," Carmel asked her.

"I've heard sounds of movement and seen curtains and rockers suddenly start moving back and forth as if something had brushed by ; things like that mostly."

"What about the room where your equipment is, have you checked the tapes since you took this one out," Carmel asked Carson.

"No."

"Let's go check the next one then," Carmel said and the three of them trouped into the room and extracted the voice activated tape, then they went back to the living room to listen to it.

"What about the video equipment. Have you checked that?" Carmel asked.

"No. I haven't had time to sit and watch a blank tape for hours," Carson said.

"Get it out and I'll watch it tomorrow while you're at work," his Mother suggested and so he'd gone back to the room and taken the old video tape and replaced it with a new one.

They'd sat and listened to the audio tape for an hour that night and hadn't heard the voice again. They had heard rustling and a sound of movement that they couldn't explain unless it was mice or some other small animal, but otherwise, nothing.

Carson smiled as he remembered how friendly the evening had been. Maybe it was for the best that his Mother had come home. Although he'd been sure Carmel would leave, she hadn't done so, and he liked having his Mother around, as long as she wasn't interfering with his plans. He was lucky enough now to have both his mother and Carmel under his roof. Maybe things would work out after all.

He pulled his car into the driveway and grimaced at the sight of April Mayes car in his parking space. Carmel's car was here too, so it looked like everyone was having a grand ole party in his absence. Why hadn't April stayed away? He'd been very clear with her the last time. When he entered his kitchen he found the three women seated together at the table with coffee and sweet rolls in front of them.

"What's going on," he asked.

"I'm just telling your Mother and Carmel here about all the fun we had last year," April said, grinning at him insolently.

"I told you not to bother me anymore, April. I want you to leave and I don't want you to come back."

"Be nice Carson. April is a guest and I invited her to have some coffee and rolls. Be a gentleman and sit down and join us," his Mother said.

Instead, Carson stomped his disapproval as he headed for the refrigerator where he got a beer. He opened it and headed for the living room. In the living room he could hear the three women talking and his anger festered and congealed. All April wanted to do was to cause trouble. He'd been hopeful that Carmel might rethink their relationship; that wasn't likely to happen if an old girl friend kept hanging around. He didn't want to discuss the matter in front of his mother or Carmel, although he believed he'd been clear that he didn't like for her to be here.

He put the TV on and halfheartedly watched a game show as he listened with the other ear to what was going on in the kitchen. April was animated showing off her quick wit, he guessed, building up the relationship they'd had to heights it had never attained. He'd have to talk to his mother about letting that woman into the house, but for now, he'd try to ignore her. It he did that enough, perhaps she'd go away and stay away.

What does Carmel think? I told her the truth that she was the only woman in my life, but here an old girl friend pops up. Maybe it will make her so angry she'll want to leave, or maybe she'll be jealous!

He hadn't thought about that. Maybe this visit from April Mayes was a good thing after all. If it made Carmel jealous she might be inclined to renew their relationship sooner.

I should have greeted April like an old friend with a hug and kiss.

That would spark Carmel's interest I bet. I missed a golden opportunity.

Looking up he saw April coming into the room where he sat. He'd been daydreaming and hadn't heard any indication that she was leaving. The other women had remained in the kitchen.

"I'm going home now," she said. "Will you walk me to my car?"

Carson was ready to refuse and then he decided that this wouldn't be a bad thing. It would give him a chance to speak to her privately. He got his jacket and went with her without saying anything. Once outside, he turned to her and said,

"I warned you not to stalk me. You are not welcome in this house. If you don't stay away, I will get a restraining order."

"I understand it's your Mother's house, not yours. She hasn't told me not to come back."

"She will."

April shrugged and opened her car door. "Your new girlfriend isn't much," she said.

"Carmel's twice the woman you'll ever be."

"She doesn't even claim you. She told me you're fancy free, that you're just friends," April said.

That hurt but Carson tried not to show it.

Stay away," he said, and turned back toward his house as April roared down the driveway in her car. He wondered if Carmel had really said that to April, but knew she probably had because that was the story they'd given his Mother. If Edna suspected that her son was having an affair with Carmel, she hadn't alluded to it. Anyway, they weren't having an affair now. He remembered the past though and was sickened by how everything had changed.

Chapter 27

Carmel had been putting in applications all day. She'd decided to try places in Ripley, Aberdeen and Manchester first since money was limited and she hoped for a job nearby to start with. That would save gas and stretch the money she had until she could get a paycheck. At three o'clock she decided that she'd done enough for the day and so she headed for the library to do some research on who Carson's ghost might be. She thought that the river boat man she'd encountered must have had some kind of tie to the house. Otherwise, why would he be there? Maybe he'd lived in the house or had family who did.

She searched for history on the house but couldn't find anything specific. With an eye out for anyone named Virginia, since the phantom she'd seen was looking for Virginia, she looked at death records from the 1800's. Records were sparse until the later 1800's after it had become law that deaths and births be reported. Before that some were and some weren't recorded.

There was a Virginia Wiseman who had died from Scarlet Fever in 1850, a Virginia Bradford who died with pneumonia in 1866, and a sixteen year old Virginia Rankin who had died from unknown causes in 1865. She couldn't find any residences listed for these women.

As a matter of fact, I don't even know the exact address where I live, she realized.

Ripley was settled in 1812 and named Staunton by its founder Col. James Poage. In 1816 the name was changed to Ripley to honor Gen. Eleazor Wheelcock

Ripley. It was settled mostly by Irish/ Scot peoples with a later influx of Germans who helped to make it a vital port. It was known for shipping pork and tobacco. Many buildings are still standing that date to the Underground Railroad era, one book proclaimed. These include the Rankin house, Parker house, and the Campbell and Beasley homes. She wondered why Carson's house wasn't mentioned.

Carmel found this all to be fascinating but it didn't help her identify a spirit who called himself Tut Jackson, nor was she finding a woman named Virginia that looked promising. Surely he hadn't meant he was looking for the state of Virginia, she thought suddenly doubting her strategy. If he was looking for the state of Virginia he really was lost!

She hadn't told Carson or his Mother about her encounter with the ghost. She didn't want to explain what she'd been doing at the time she'd seen him, nor did she want to tell them what he had said to her. The baby; she'd been thinking about the baby a lot, wondering if she should go to a doctor. Most likely she was pregnant and should be under a doctor's prenatal care. Right now she didn't have that much money and now that she had no job, she had no insurance either. She would have to wait to see a Doctor

It's mandatory that I get a job right away. I have to get hired before the baby shows.

When she thought about her predicament her fears escalated. There wasn't much time and it might take a while to find a job. The economy wasn't stable. Tut Yeager, as the ghost called himself, had been good at telling her what she couldn't do but he hadn't given her any answers as to what to do. Most likely the spirit had been a figment of a crazed mental state. After all she wouldn't have been trying to kill herself if she'd been in a normal state of mind, would she?

The past few months had been all ups and downs for her. She'd ridden the crest of joy with the new love she'd found with Carson for a while but guilt had yanked her down to the pits eventually. It was due to that guilt that she'd decided to break with Carson and try to make her marriage work. It had been just too much for her when that good intention had been blocked by Carson's actions; he kidnapped her preventing her from returning to her marriage. She'd been teetering on the edge already. Now she owed her life to a ghost in the night, a spirit who claimed to know things he couldn't possibly know.

If I'm pregnant, how would a ghost know?

What am I thinking about? How can there possibly be a ghost?

I was distraught and imagining things.

She decided to ask Tut Jackson, if she ever saw the spirit again, how he could know intimate details about her life and her health. Yikes! If he had a way to know she was pregnant, could he tell her who the baby's father was also?

Now that she had some distance between her and the dark night when she'd met the river boat ghost man; Carmel was more and more certain that the ghost had been a figment of her imagination. She knew the signs of pregnancy and that they were present in her. She had been aware on some level that she was pregnant and had invented a spirit to tell her what she already knew. That's the explanation she fixed on.

I'd better see a doctor soon. Maybe I should see a head doctor as well as a gynecologist. It's not normal to try to commit suicide, nor to be talking to spirits.

Later she found herself sitting at the dining room table eating Edna Wetzel's meatloaf and mashed potatoes and listening to Edna and Carson talking about his father and the Ripley tobacco industry. She had tried to avoid Edna, not knowing what to tell the woman as to why she was here. Most nights she joined the conversation at the table in a limited way, then cleaned up and headed for her private area in the apartment. Carson had been giving her space and Edna had seemed to pick up on her reluctance to talk and so had left her alone.

"I remember Dad saying there were five grades of tobacco and they had to be sorted. I think he called one flyings and trash. At least that's what it sounded like to me," Carson was saying. "He said the best tobacco leaves are at the bottom of the plant where the sun doesn't hit them."

"Flyings and trash is a weird name," Carmel said, "What were the other grades called?" She wasn't interested in the subject but at least it was a safe one.

"I think he called them Lugs, Bright, Red and tips," Carson speculated.

"He used to sell the tobacco here in Ripley or in Maysville, whichever one was paying the most," Edna added.

"All I know is I had to sow the seeds in the tobacco bed. Dad mixed those tiny little seeds with a half bag of manure before sewing them. After the plants got bigger I had to set them in rows in the tobacco base."

"It didn't hurt you none," Edna said.

Carmel stood and started clearing the dishes from the table. "You two sit here and reminisce as long as you want. I have to go out and find a job tomorrow so I'm going to bed early," she said.

Chapter 28

Ash knew something was different the minute he walked into his house. There was a different smell in the air as if it had been disturbed by another's presence. Hastily he went from room to room finally arriving upstairs where he immediately saw that the boxes that contained Carmel's things were gone.

Was she here?

His breath started coming in gasps as he hyperventilated. Why would she come like this and take her things without staying to talk to him. Was it true that she was in love with someone else and wasn't even willing to give him the courtesy of an explanation? A fast flutter in his chest told him he needed to slow his breathing down, to calm down before he passed out. He sank into a chair and sat there forcing himself to slow everything down.

Maybe she left me a note.

He leaped to his feet and ran into the kitchen where she'd always left notes for him in the past. No note. Finally he saw the key lying on the dining room table, alone and forlorn, just as he felt himself to be.

It really is over. She doesn't love me anymore.

He wondered if he should tell the detectives about this. They'd been leaving him alone for a while but occasionally he noticed them in the neighborhood and wondered if they were discretely doing surveillance on him. He didn't think they'd gone away, just undercover. They'd never told him if the handwriting analysis had proven the card was in Carmel's handwriting, but he was sure it was. He knew his wife's handwriting.

The call he'd received from the man who said he was Carmel's lover had been the pits for Ash. The man had refused to identify himself. He'd only said that he and Carmel wanted to make sure the police didn't arrest Ash on suspicion of murder. When he'd told him that the police were doing a handwriting analysis on the card, the man had seemed satisfied and hung up.

Ash had wanted to punch the other man who'd pretended to be such a cool customer, so smug in his assurances that Carmel was happy with him, and didn't want to see her husband again. If only he'd been able to defend his interests as a husband should; Ash sighed. He fingered the worn key. It was like Carmel was returning the key to her heart and saying that she was no longer open to him. That hurt.

Knowing that his grief was consuming him, Ash had packed up her things, planning to store them in the basement until such time as Carmel indicated that she wanted them. It hadn't occurred to him that she'd come into the house while he was away and take them without a word. None of this seemed like the Carmel he knew. His Carmel was sensitive and thoughtful and would not have done these things in such a hurtful way.

Maybe I really didn't know her.

Wordless tears were dripping onto his cheeks as Carson turned toward his kitchen, automatically resuming his routine of fixing dinner and then going to work in his home office. He supposed that Carmel would contact him through her attorney sometime soon to ask for a divorce. She was gone and he didn't even know what had happened or why.

Why wait like a whipped puppy for her to sue you for divorce. She left you, abandoned her marriage, you

~ 132 ~

have perfect grounds for a divorce. Sue her before she sues you.

He thought about that. How could he sue for a divorce from a wife whose whereabouts were unknown? A good attorney would be able to advise him about that but he wasn't sure it could be done if there wasn't a place to serve the papers.

The next afternoon he sat in the law office of Charles Jackson, someone he'd picked out of the phone book. He explained the circumstances and then waited for the attorney to comment. Charles was a plump man with a scraggly black beard. He wore a white shirt and blue dress pants; his suit jacket was draped haphazardly over his swivel chair. Leaning back in his chair a little, he tapped his index fingers together in thought.

"How do you know that Carmel took the boxes?" he asked.

"Of course she did, who else would?"

"I guess you're right, so that means she's probably alive and well and the card she mailed you must be a true representation of her feelings. If someone had abducted her he could have made her write the card so it would be in her handwriting, but he wouldn't have known to go get the boxes of her things and leave the key."

Ash was thinking from a different angle now. Could Carmel have been forced to write the note she'd sent to him? If so why had that man called him to see if the police were still questioning him about her disappearance?

"What if he thought she had something of his in her possession? He could have come with her to the house for all I know, and made her retrieve it. I wasn't there."

"I know that's what you'd like to believe, so let's assume for a minute that's the case. He abducted her and wouldn't let her come home. He made her write to you telling you that she was leaving you. He wanted something that she had in her possession and made her come with him to your house while he expected you to be gone. Why did he leave the key? What if the thing he wanted wasn't in the box and he'd have to go back to get it?"

"I don't know."

"Why did he care if the police arrested you for foul play in her disappearance?"

"Maybe he didn't care about me at all. If the police keep investigating they might find him, find out what really happened, so he wanted them to drop the case for his own benefit," Ash said hopefully.

"It would be good if we could actually talk to Carmel and make sure of the facts. It also makes it easier to serve her with papers. Why don't I put a guy I have a contract with on the case to locate her first and then we can proceed from there," The attorney said.

"I'd rather do it that way," Ash decided. He'd been dreading the finality of the divorce and this allowed him to put off that decision for a little longer.

Chapter 29

Carson brought home the items his mother had asked for so she could make a nice Thanksgiving dinner. This included a 12 lb. turkey, whole cranberry sauce, potatoes for mashing and canned turkey gravy, as well as things to make pumpkin pie and other desserts. He was a pie eater but Carmel had told him that she preferred applesauce and other fruit cakes. Carson grimaced when she said that but bought a fruit cake anyway.

He'd also bought some cans of soup which he liked to take with him when he worked out of town during the winter. He had a heating device that he could plug into the cigarette lighter in his car and make hot soup to warm him up. Carmel had offered over and over to help in the kitchen but Edna had refused every time saying she worked best when no one got in her way and she liked to cook.

"I'll tell you what," she'd said last night, "I'll stay in the kitchen before the dinner is served and you can be in there afterward, cleaning up."

Carson knew that wasn't what Carmel wanted, but she agreed to it. He knew his mother liked the cooking but hated the putting away and cleaning up afterward. Watching the way Carmel had tried to be useful around the house in an unobtrusive way, Carson had been impressed. Even though she'd told him that he owed her for having messed up her life and leaving her homeless, she was never-the-less trying to earn her own way.

Yesterday she'd told him that she had a good chance of getting a job in a small business in Manchester. She had an interview tomorrow. It would just be something small to start with, she'd told him and she planned to keep looking for a better job.

"At least I'll be able to contribute to the food bill and it will make it sooner that I can stand on my own two feet again."

Carson wasn't anxious for her to be able to stand on her own two feet just yet. At this point she'd surely leave but maybe down the road, if he didn't press her, she'd realize how much she cared for him and they could go ahead with their lives as it should have been all along. He wasn't sorry for having imprisoned her but he had to admit that his strategy had backfired. She'd hated him for it and now they had to find a way to move past that, for her to forgive him and come around to his point of view. At least it had kept her from going back to Ash. Surely Ash would have nothing to do with her after all of this. Carmel hadn't said anything about Ash but he'd noticed that she had boxes of her possessions with her now. The marriage must have ended.

Carson pulled up to his house and started pulling the groceries out of the car. Hearing a sound he looked down the hill and saw April Mayes car chugging upward toward him.

"Well that just makes my day," he thought.

April pulled in, parked, got out, and said brightly.

"Hi there lover; need a hand?"

Without waiting for him to answer, she grabbed a couple of bags and started toward the house with them. Carson grabbed some more and started after her.

"Just what do you think you're doing," he huffed, out of breath with anger and exercise.

"I'm helping out my friend; can't you see that?"

"I don't need any help. I told you to stay away from here," Carson said, irritated that his voice came out high pitched like a wail. "I don't want to be around you anymore. Can't you get that through your head?"

He saw the anger pop into April's eyes in a flash and hoped she'd be mad enough to go away. Instead she set the bags down, grabbed canned goods from one of the bags and started pelting him with it. Carson held the bags he was carrying in front of him as he dodged flying soup cans and choked on the expletives on his tongue. He lunged past her, dialing 911 on his cell phone and dropping one of his own bags on the ground. A can hit the facing of the door and dropped on the toe of his shoe.

Carson rushed inside the house and locked the door as he tried to explain to the operator that a mad woman had attacked him in his driveway using soup cans for weapons. The woman seemed skeptical but said she'd have someone there momentarily.

Peeking out the window, Carson saw that April must have realized that he was calling the police because she had headed back to her car and was out of the driveway before the police had driven in. Once the police arrived, he went back outside and tried to explain what had happened.

"I've threatened to call you before because of April's stalking behavior," he said but I always kept putting it off, thinking she'd lose interest. "Today she escalated it just too far."

He was questioned about his previous relationship with April Mayes, about who was currently living in his house, and concerning what had set off the conflict today.

"I guess it was because I rejected her. She just pulled up and grabbed some of my grocery bags and headed for the house as if she'd been invited. I asked what she was doing and told her once again that I didn't want her here. I saw fire flashing in her eyes and then she started her attack."

"Was anyone else home when this happened?"

"No."

"Who's this woman Carmel? Is she a new girlfriend?"

"She's just a friend who's down on her luck and needs a place to stay. April's probably jealous of her though."

"So you aren't co-habiting? She has a separate place to sleep and everything?"

"That's right."

"You might want to get a restraining order for April Mayes. These things tend to escalate. She might hurt you or if she's jealous, even Carmel."

"I'll consider that," he said.

After the police left, Carson started wondering where his mother and Carmel were. As he picked up cans and torn bags from his driveway and carried everything inside, he thought how lucky he was that April's visit had occurred when neither was at home. It embarrassed him for his mother to see a former girlfriend in this light, and he didn't know how Carmel would react. Why was April doing these things anyway? The breakup had been her fault. She was the one who'd gone out with a third party. Her only excuse had been that he was ignoring her and she was lonely, and it had all happened a year ago.

Why now?

Reflecting on his previous relationships, Carson agreed with himself that he just didn't seem to get things right with the ladies. One lover was dead because of him, another had turned into a maniac stalker, and Carmel despised him because he'd essentially kidnapped her. Apparently he'd made deadly mistakes in his dealings with all three, although he wasn't ready to give up on Carmel yet. She was still here in his house and now she was here willingly, not because he was holding her prisoner. He liked that situation a lot better.

Chapter 30

Carmel was sitting in a business office waiting for the results of her interview. She'd spent an hour answering questions as well as she could and the woman who'd interviewed her had sent her back to the front office to wait. She felt optimistic about this job. Any job for now was a plus, but she wouldn't rest with this piddling little job. No, she'd keep looking until she found something that would support her and the little one coming.

She suspected that she was about two months pregnant right now and wondered how long until the pregnancy started to show. She'd heard that since it was the first child and her muscles were tight, acting as a girdle, she might be almost five months before anyone could tell. That seemed overly optimistic to her though. She figured that everyone would be able to tell by four months or sooner, so she'd better get a job and leave the area way before then.

"Come on back, Carmel," the interviewer was saying and she got up gladly and went into the office with her.

"We're going to hire you. Can you take time to get all the paperwork done before you leave so you can start work on Friday the day after Thanksgiving?"

"Yes, thank you. I can."

"Well, see the receptionist and she'll tell you what we need. I'll see you back here on Friday," the woman said.

With a sense of expectancy, Carmel went through the employment hoops the company demanded and was out of there by 2:00pm. She sat in a McDonalds, a half hour later, making a list of things she needed to do now that she had a job. This job wasn't going to pay much, and it was Monday through Friday which made it harder to search for a better job, but it should allow her to start putting money aside for the future. She planned to buy a certain amount of food for Carson's household as long as she was there, and to earn her keep any other way possible, but everything else would be set aside and saved.

She'd come from a thrifty family and before her marriage to Ash she'd been very thrifty herself. After marrying Ash and adding his income to her own, she'd been less careful although she'd never been a spend-thrift. Now it was back to penny pinching but it would be good to have some pennies to pinch for a change!

On her list she put as a number one concern, seeing a doctor. She didn't have a doctor any longer so she'd have to find one. It would probably be best to find one not too far from Carson's home, although later she'd have to transfer to a different one.

Should I tell the doctor my real name?

Maybe it would be better if I give a false name so I can't be traced.

Later when I disappear for real, someone like Carson might come looking for me and find out about the baby.

Deciding that was the best plan, she put the words See Doctor and Name on her list so she'd be reminded to think of a name before the appointment. Now that she knew that Ash was through with her, and now that she was feeling she could never trust Carson again, Carmel had decided not to tell either man about the baby. There was no use in complicating her life any further. She'd probably be embarrassed by both men requiring a paternity test and by the father demanding visitation. She didn't need any of that. The easy way would be to go off and make a new life for her and the little one, one free of such aggravations. It would be better for the baby too.

As she got up to leave the restaurant she saw April Mayes entering. She stopped a minute to say a friendly hello to her but was surprised at the venom in April's attitude.

"You don't really have him, you know," April almost spat, moisture flying from her mouth. "He's mine. You'd better watch out."

"I don't know what you're talking about," Carmel said pushing by her.

"You know! Leave Carson alone," the other woman yelled.

Carmel fled to her car, angry and afraid. "That woman acted as if she's insane," she thought.

Well this is one more reason to save some money and get away from Carson.

He has a crazy ex-girlfriend, he locked me in a room for over a month before releasing me, and this certainly isn't the life I want for my baby!

She thought about this all the way to Carson's house. It really wasn't fair to blame Carson for what April Mayes did. There was plenty he deserved to be blamed for however. He was certainly responsible for what he'd done to her. It was odd though because otherwise Carson didn't seem to be a controlling man. Once he'd decided to release her he'd gone back to the way he'd been before all this had started.

It's a mystery!

At dinner she told both Carson and Edna about her new job. They congratulated her and asked her questions about it then they went off to watch TV while she cleaned the kitchen. That was the pattern they'd fallen into and it suited her fine. She didn't feel like talking to them anyway. Really, she had nothing against Edna but the bitterness that Carson had generated in her when he'd treated her like a possession, when he'd locked her up to keep her from leaving him, still stung. If he could do something like that to her just because she was leaving him, what else might he do if the situation was stressful enough to push him into panicked behavior?

When Carson had released her she'd considered filing charges against him but there were so many negatives associated with that that she abandoned that idea. First of all they wouldn't believe her. She'd had an affair with Carson and no one would believe that she'd been held against her will. Even Edna had only seen her as a free and voluntary house guest. There was also the card she'd written to Ash; the story would leak out and be tied into the older story of her disappearance and the fact that her husband had been suspected of foul play. It would be a major scandal and maybe in the process they'd find out about the baby. No, it had been better to leave well enough alone. Ash had gone through the worst of the pain by now and it would just reopen the wounds if she tried to tell him the truth.

That didn't mean she forgave Carson though!

Chapter 31

Edna Wetzel was puzzling over a few things as she sat with a second cup of coffee waiting for Ted Zimmerman to show up. One of the things that had her confused was the relationship between Carmel Simpson and her son Carson. She hadn't wanted to ask Carson about it because he already seemed to think that she was a nibby, nosy, old woman, which hurt her feelings considerably and which she believed was unfair.

If Carmel's such a good friend of his that he's giving her a place to live; why isn't Carmel more appreciative? She acts like he owes her something. The thing is; Carmel isn't like that in other ways. She's always polite and works hard to pull her own weight. Something's going on between those two that they don't want me to know about.

She thought of the possibility that they were having an affair while telling her they were just friends. However, there had been no clandestine visits between bedrooms between the two. She'd paid attention to that. In fact they seemed uneasy with each other.

Carson seems to be trying to stay out of her way and Carmel avoids spending time with him too.

If they aren't really friends, why's he letting her stay here?

He certainly sent that April Mayes packing.

Edna's impression of Carmel was good so far. She was quiet, respectful and helpful. She was always polite and Edna thought maybe Carson should be looking toward Carmel as a romantic interest. What was wrong with the boy? Hearing a knock at the door she muttered to herself about Ted's refusal to use the doorbell even though it worked just fine. He hated using technology for something so simple, he'd told her.

"Come on in," she told him. "You're as slow as a herd of turtles."

"It's some cold out there," Ted said, "Would you build me a cup of tea?"

Edna busied herself with the teapot, tea bag, and a cup to put it in as she chattered to Ted about the Christmas shopping she wanted to do today. Yesterday had been Thanksgiving Day and it had gone well. Ted had come to dinner with Edna, Carson and Carmel. She'd wanted Ted to see the two younger people together so she could get his impression of what was going on, but she hadn't had a chance to ask for his opinion yet.

"I think yesterday's dinner went well, don't you," she asked.

"Yep, lots a good food."

"What did you think about Carmel?"

"She's like the girl next door, you know, she's cute and nice. At least it seemed so to me."

"Didn't you think there was a strain of some kind between her and Carson?"

"Yeah, they seemed a little distant."

"Well, what do you think that's all about?"

"Maybe he made a pass at her and she didn't like it; how would I know," Ted asked as he sipped the hot tea and looked at the ads Edna had left strewn about the table.

"I guess that might be it," Edna mused. "Maybe she feels bad having to take his hospitality knowing that he's got ulterior motives. That would put a stress on things."

"Why's the girl homeless anyway? You said she didn't have anyplace else to go and she's here trying to get a job so she can get on her feet again," Ted asked.

"That's what Carson told me," Edna said. "He didn't say what had happened but I got the feeling that there was a nasty divorce or something and maybe she got the short end of the stick. Anyway, she's got a receptionist job now. She started today."

"That's good," Ted said absently looking at a JC Penny add. They were going down to Cincinnati so Edna could get a start on her Christmas shopping. Maybe Ted would buy a couple of things for his kids today too; maybe he'd even buy something for Edna.

Later, Ted stayed for dinner after they returned from the trip to Cincinnati. Edna was happy because she'd found some good deals and Ted was just happy it was all over. He and Carson sat watching TV as Edna and Carmel fixed dinner. Edna had decided to let Carmel help her tonight, thinking it might be a good idea to get to know the girl better.

"How'd the job go today," she asked Carmel as she chopped vegetables for a salad.

Carmel shrugged. "It was ok."

"Well, at least it's a job. With this economy you're lucky to find one at all," Edna told her.

"I know that's right."

Once the men came in to eat, the conversation was a bit livelier. Carson told them about his job at a business in Cincinnati where the office was having a "dog day"

"They had more mutts in that office than I see in six months otherwise, and it was a zoo. Not very easy to work in that atmosphere, I'll tell you."

"I just can't imagine the company would let the workers do that," Edna said.

"One woman told me that the owner is the biggest dog lover of all," Carson said.

After that Edna, Ted, and Carson started talking about the old days again when almost everyone in the county had a tobacco bed and a yearly crop of tobacco for sale.

"I knew a family that charged their groceries from year to year and then paid the bill off when they got paid for the tobacco crop," Edna said.

"A lot of people did that in those days," Ted agreed.

"I remember Dad and the other men gathering wood to put around the seed bed for months before the tobacco was ready to plant," Carson said. "I helped. Then when it was time to plant they'd set the wood on fire and burn it so the old seeds in the ground would be destroyed and there wouldn't be any weeds. Of course there were some anyway."

"Yeah, do you remember mixing the tiny seeds of tobacco with fertilizer or manure and planting it in the bed," Ted asked.

"I remember it; especially the smell of the manure. I remember the white canvas that looked like cheesecloth to me. They put it over the bed, I guess to help warm it up. It let the sun come through. They'd let it stay like that with the tobacco growing underneath. I still had to help weed it though Dad put a board across the bed and I'd sit on it and pull the weeds. You had a little area at the end where you grew leaf lettuce and radishes, didn't you," he asked his mother.

"Yeah, it was a family tradition to use a little area at the end for food."

"It sounds like you enjoyed your childhood," Carmel said suddenly.

Everyone looked at her since she'd been so quiet though out the meal. She looked down at her plate as if embarrassed.

"I did have an awesome childhood," Carson said. He looked at his mother with a new eye, one that was a little more appreciative.

"Those were the good old days," he said.

Chapter 32

Carmel sat thinking as the conversation stirred around her. She was half listening to the discussion; Carson was telling how he'd been sent to pull the plants from the tobacco beds and put them on a burlap bag to be conveyed to the field.

"You have to make a hole in the ground to put the plant in, so you use something called a tobacco peg. Dad had one that was like a curved metal pipe made sharp on one end. You jab that into the ground, make a hole, and put the plant in, then cover it and go to the next one," Carson said. "Sometimes it's just a wooden peg they use."

"Did you work in tobacco," Edna asked Ted, who was ladling up some more mashed potatoes and gravy.

"Yep, that's what most of us did in those days."

"You forgot about taking the suckers off," Edna told Carson. "You did a lot of that when you were a kid."

"You have to pinch the blossoms off to make the plant put out better leaves, otherwise it will be tall and spindly instead of leafy like you want it," Carson said turning to Carmel as if she'd asked about this. "And then the plant will try another way and will put out suckers. You have to take those off too."

Seeing that she was being included in the conversation whether interested or not, Carmel said,

"Well, it sounds like a lot of work."

"A lot of work but a way of life, a way that nobody seems to remember any more," Ted told her.

"I remember how yellow the plant would turn when it was ready for harvest. You'd drive along and see all those yellow fields," Edna said.

"That just started a whole new round of work," Ted agreed.

"You had to have a tobacco stake and you'd put about five plants on it," Carson went on explaining, continuing to talk as if for Carmel's benefit. "You'd hang these stakes on tier rails in the barn starting at the top and going down. You did that in August or September and then the tobacco would get dry. A little later on the weather would change and get moist; the tobacco would come in "case". That meant it was damp and could be worked with."

Carmel was restless wanting to get up and start clearing the table, but the others ignored her lack of interest and continued on with their reminiscences. She wanted to be polite but she was nervous as she settled down again; it wouldn't hurt to listen to them a bit more, she guessed.

"That's when they'd drop the tobacco off the tiers and take it off the sticks (or stakes, my Dad called them). Then we'd take it to the stripping room and grade it. Every stripping room had to have a source of light from the north so you could see to grade it. After that we'd make what we called a hand of tobacco and press it, then pile it together until we took it to the warehouse," Ted informed them.

"We used to run to different tobacco markets up until February. They'd stay a few days and then move on to a new location up until then, and then the market would close," Edna said.

"And I'd be put back to gathering wood to burn on the next tobacco bed," Carson said. "It was all one big cycle."

That statement by Carson seemed to wrap up the conversation because Ted decided to go outside to smoke and Edna stood up and started to clear her dishes. As Carmel worked around the now empty kitchen, she thought about this community she'd landed in and how different it was now from the one the others had been describing just a few years ago. She was not used to farming of any kind but the life they'd been talking about was a culture in itself, one full of hard work and an affinity to the land. She wondered what she'd have been like if she'd been raised that way. As important as it seemed to these people, it was no wonder Ripley had a tobacco festival every year!

After the kitchen was cleaned, Carson came and asked her to join everyone in the living room. Carmel had hoped that she could go off to her rooms and be alone but she dutifully followed him in and sat down in an armchair.

"We're talking about the history of this house and about our ghosts. Ted has been telling us about a man who used to visit a girl who lived in this house back in the 1800's. He says the man died here but no one seems to know why. The girl he was courting died before he did as the story goes," Carson told her.

"Don't tell me, the girl was named Virginia," Carmel said before she thought to curb her tongue.

She saw everyone staring at her and wished she'd kept her mouth shut.

"How'd you know that? Did you hear us talking," Carson asked again.

"I don't know; I must have. Was her name Virginia?"

Carson looked at her as if she suddenly had grown a second head. "The story is that the girl was called Virginia Caroline Walker."

"I must have heard about it somewhere," Carmel muttered,

She was aware that she couldn't explain about the ghost. It would start them asking too many questions. She thought about the night when she'd encountered Tut Jackson. He was looking for Virginia, he said. She didn't remember a Virginia Walker in the files she'd looked at, but of course they were incomplete.

"Does the story say where he was in the house when he died," she asked Ted.

"Not that I recall. I've heard everything from him being down in the slave quarters to his being in the kitchen. Don't put any stock in what I've heard on that subject."

"And people think he's haunting this house?"

"Something is," Edna said. "I can feel it."

"Was he a good man or bad," Carmel asked fearing the worst.

"He worked on a river boat they say. I don't know if it was a gambling boat or just a regular boat. Some rough characters lived on those boats but I don't know about this one," Ted answered her.

Carmel thought about going down to her apartment and then thought again. It didn't seem as appealing now. She really didn't want to run into Tut Jackson again. Maybe she'd stay here with the others a little longer tonight.

"Did you ever hear what this man's name was," she asked Ted.

"Nope," he said, "I never heard."

Chapter 33

After Ted left and Carmel had gone back to her apartment, Carson and his mother decided to check out the equipment in the room upstairs to see if anything new had been recorded on it. Instead of playing the tapes while in the room, Carson replaced them with new ones and took the used ones to the living room. He and Edna sat down to listen to whatever might be on the tapes, after making themselves fresh cups of tea. They sat quietly for an hour but didn't hear anything that sounded preternatural.

"I'm through for the night. You can go ahead and check those out if you want to," Carson said. He left Edna still sitting in the living room, head cocked toward the sound equipment that was quietly turning but which had recorded no sounds so far.

The next morning he found five balloons tied to his car, when he went to get into it. A card stuck to his windshield said

"Thinking of you,"

"April," Carson said and looked around stealthily to see if she was somewhere nearby. He'd told the officers that he'd get a Temporary Restraining Order after the last incident but since nothing more had happened he'd forgotten to do it. He took the balloons off the car and set them free into the air, and instead of heading for work, he headed for his lawyer's office. Finding him unavailable, Carson left a note about the problem and went on his way. That action made him feel somewhat better.

He'd told everyone in the house that April was stalking him and that if anyone saw her, that person should tell him right away. Carmel had mentioned running into April at a store and being confronted by her in an aggressive manner. There was no way that Carson was going to let April mess up the small chance he felt he had with Carmel.

Thinking about April, he remembered that she'd always been afraid of never having anyone who loved her and ending up an old maid. However, it seemed that all her behavior was geared toward driving people away instead of making them want to be with her. She had been possessive with him, but unfaithful when he didn't give her as much attention as she wanted. She'd always been self centered and seldom had worried about his needs, Carson thought. If the other man hadn't broken them up, other things probably would have. April wasn't stable.

I don't want her to scare Carmel away. She's only hanging on here by a thread anyway and might leave at any moment. April's shenanigans might be enough to push her into leaving.

The next morning Edna was listening to the tapes while cleaning the kitchen. Everyone had gone about their days work and she considered this to be her work for the day. A sudden shriek almost caused her to leap into the sink with the dishes. Realizing that the sound had come from the tape player she went to it and backed up the recording. Sure enough there was a shriek and then a groan recorded on the tape. After playing that sound a couple more times, she let the recording go on. Again it was a quiet hum with nothing to hear. Edna went back to her dishes.

It was forty five minutes later when she heard the voice. A deep timbered male voice spoke from the tape repeating the name Virginia three times in a questioning manner. It was as if he was calling for her. Edna listened; she was fascinated, thinking about the story Ted had told them of the riverboat man and the girl Virginia who had lived in this house. Although she listened to the tape all the way through, there was nothing else on it.

When Ted arrived, Edna told him what she'd heard and then played it back for him.

"That shriek gets to ya," Ted said when he heard it.

He agreed with her that the voice saying 'Virginia' seemed to be desperately calling out for a loved one. Edna questioned him about what he'd heard regarding the girl Virginia who'd died in the house and the riverboat man who'd been her beau. Ted couldn't remember much more than he'd already told them but said there might be records of some kind if they knew what to look for. He suggested that they might drive to the Historical Center in Columbus, go to the archives, and search the newspapers of the area for some reference to the couple, when spring came.

"I don't want to wait until spring. Isn't there some way to find out before then?"

"Well, you can go in there and ask him, I guess. Maybe he'll answer you," Ted said.

Edna looked at him and realized he was being sarcastic. That annoyed her and so she said,

"Ok, that's just what I will do. I'll figure out a question and ask it and then see if he answers me."

~ 157 ~

She sat thinking for a few minutes and then got up and headed toward the room where the recording equipment was set up. Ted followed her, smiling at her in a way which she did not like.

He thinks I'm crazy. Well, we'll see what happens. I hope the ghost scares him out of his sox!

Inside the room, Edna stood looking around and then she called out, "Mr. Riverboat man, sorry, I don't know your name. Can you tell me what I should call you?"

Silence in the room, excepting for the voice activated recorder which had captured her words, then stopped.

"Maybe I can help you," Edna said. "Are you looking for Virginia?"

"Virginia, where is she?" a voice boomed suddenly and Ted rocketed back as if a rattlesnake had bitten him.

Edna's nerves jumped to alert inside her but she was determined not to show any fear in front of Ted. She was grimly happy that Ted had obviously been scared after he'd made her feel foolish earlier.

"What is Virginia's last name," she asked the unseen presence.

"Where is Virginia?" The voice came as a wail of anguish.

"Are you looking for Virginia Walker," Edna asked, determined to hold her ground as she saw Ted edging toward the door.

"Yes," the voice thundered out, shaking her resolve.

"Virginia?"

"She's not here but maybe I can find her for you," Edna said. "What's your name?"

"Tut!"

"Your name is Tut?"

"Tut Jackson."

"Ok, Tut, I'll try to find Virginia for you."

Edna backed out of the room slowly, afraid to turn her back on the presence she'd been communicating with. She hoped all the conversation was on the tapes but for now she planned to leave them there. Carson could replace the tapes with new ones when he got home. Ted had gone on before her, silent and ashen in color. The gray dryness of his skin made him look sick and she realized that he might have a heart condition that could be worsened by a shock.

"Come on Ted," she said. "Let's go sit down and have a cup of tea and some applesauce cake." She made a comfy place for him in the living room and served the tea and cake to him.

"You were actually talking to a ghost, and the ghost answered," Ted said shakily, his tea dancing in his cup as he trembled with the realization.

"I know," Edna said.

Now that the shock was over she was inordinately pleased with herself. She'd surely have an interesting subject for dinner conversation tonight!

Chapter 34

Dinner conversation was lively that night as everyone discussed the sounds on the original tape. After dinner Carson went to get the newer tapes while everyone, excepting for Ted, trooped after him. Ted hadn't stayed to dinner saying that he'd had enough excitement for one day.

The three of them settled into the living room with the tape player and the newer tapes. About halfway through came the conversation between Edna and the spirit of Tut Jackson. Everyone looked at the others in confused delight.

Carson was happy because his amateur attempts as a ghost hunter had borne fruit. Edna was happy to have vindication. She'd told Carson all along that there was a spirit of some kind in the house. Carmel had mixed feelings. She was glad that others were able to hear the entity Tut Jackson, whom she'd encountered on that awful night when she'd wanted to end her life. It was good to know she hadn't imagined that, or if she had, she wasn't alone in her delusions; but she felt uneasy knowing that this all seeing ghost knew her secrets. If he was talking to the others in the house, he might tell them about the baby or about her suicide attempt.

She left the others early and went to her apartment. She was wondering if she could talk to the ghost and ask him not to tell her secrets. Would that be a good idea or would it give him ammunition to use against her? Was he a vindictive ghost who would try to hurt her?

"Are you here Tut," she whispered into the room.

She looked at the couch, the tables, and the rest of the area. It was so normal a setting. There was nothing ghostly about it. If the ghost was in the room above, maybe he'd moved out of her area. Maybe she'd have to talk to him upstairs if she wanted to communicate.

No, that won't work because our conversation would be recorded, she thought.

"Tut, I want to talk to you about what happened that night when I first met you," she said into the stillness. "Please don't tell anyone anything about what happened. I don't want them to know what I was doing or about what you told me. Will you promise not to tell?"

There was a stillness that was deeper than normal and Carmel waited with nervous apprehension. She felt stupid talking to thin air. It also seemed unwise to be communicating with a ghost since who knows what a ghost might be able to do.

"I won't," a voice rumbled from somewhere near the window. Carmel jumped.

"You mean you won't tell?"

"I won't tell."

Carmel felt the chills on her skin and it was as if she was hanging by a thread over a mountain cliff. This was scary. She wondered how she'd been so casual about her talk with the ghost the first time.

I guess I was so upset that I was in an altered state then. I wasn't thinking straight enough to be afraid.

"Thank you," she told the ghost, then reached over and turned on the TV as a way to dismiss the entity. The TV sputtered and turned itself off. Frightened, Carmel sat on the couch staring around the room.

"Did you do that," she asked the spirit.

"No."

"I guess we need a new TV then," she said, and turned it on again.

This time it played normally. She wondered if the ghost was lying to her or if something else had interfered. Her space was suddenly less secure with the knowledge that her every move was being watched by a male ghost. Would he be gentleman enough to turn away when she was changing clothes? Probably not, because she'd heard that the riverboat men were a rough lot.

Trying to focus on Court TV which was now playing, Carmel attempted to ease some of her fears. She realized that the channel was playing tapes of jailhouse conversations between the Florida mother, who had misplaced her three year old and was being charged with murder, and her parents. According to the police, the mother had lied over and over about what had happened to her child.

That is so depressing.

Carmel put her hand over her stomach as maternal instincts kicked in strongly; she thought of her own little one. She had an appointment with a doctor when she left work tomorrow. She was pretty sure the doctor would confirm that she was pregnant.

Once that's confirmed I need to make my plans more concrete; I need to get out of here before anyone knows.

She made herself a cup of sleepy-time tea and decided she'd drink that and go to bed early. Tomorrow would be a long day.

Sometime in the night she heard a sound at her door. Was it Carson? She'd been surprised that he was leaving her alone as she'd requested. Maybe he was tired of waiting. She lay still listening. It sounded as if someone was trying to open the door but couldn't get it to open. There shouldn't be a problem because the door wasn't locked. She continued to listen and heard Carson whisper her name. He must be afraid his mother would hear him and know what he was about, Carmel realized.

She had no intention of opening the door to him but she was confused as to why he wasn't able to do it himself. She refused to respond to his whispered requests and eventually she heard him leaving the area. After she was certain that the coast was clear, she carefully got up and went to the door. It swung open easily to her touch.

"Why couldn't Carson open it," she said aloud to herself.

"Because I was holding it," Tut Jackson answered from the blackness around her.

Chapter 35

Ash called his attorney as soon as he got home. He'd been wondering all day what progress the private investigator had made in locating Carmel. At last report he'd been told that they'd narrowed down the location of her boyfriend to one of three river towns. Those were Aberdeen, Ripley, and Manchester. Maybe by now they had a name and an exact location. If it was a divorce that Carmel wanted, if she was so cold toward him that she could leave him as she'd done without a word, then he was anxious to get the paperwork done and the divorce in process.

I won't waste my time on someone who obviously doesn't love me, who is obviously not the person I thought I knew, and who I loved.

His attorney informed him that he had a plan. There was no new information, but since they were sure that Carmel was in one of three towns, they could post a message to her in the local papers.

"I think you should put an open letter to her in the paper and ask her to contact either you or me. Then if she calls us we can get an address and serve the papers on her," the attorney said.

"I guess that is something worth trying," Ash agreed.

"It would also be good for us to have a way to prove she's alive in case the police decide to charge you with murder down the line," the attorney added.

"That sounds right," Ash said half-heartedly.

He sat for the next hour trying to write an ad that would encourage Carmel to contact him without telling the world all their business. Of course, he'd already been in the media as a suspect in her murder, so it didn't seem he had anything more to lose. Finally he came up with a short ad which said:

Ash Simpson requests Carmel Simpson to contact him regarding mutual interests.

Under that he printed his attorneys name and address as an alternate address to contact.

He called the newspapers and arranged to post the ads in the Sunday paper.

On Sunday, Carmel was approached by Edna Wetzel in the late afternoon. Carson was out of the house and the two of them were alone.

"Have you seen this," Edna asked her.

Carmel looked at the newspaper in Edna's hands and her heart thumped down into her belly. She had a premonition of bad news. She took the paper and read the ad which Ash had placed without comment.

"That's you, isn't it," Edna asked her.

"Yes, it's meant for me. I'll take care of it," Carmel said and walked away before Edna could ask her anything else.

Having noted the attorney's name and number she knew that this was probably about a divorce. Ash had washed his hands of her. That hurt her deeply. Even though she'd made a big mistake, had betrayed him, she'd never stopped caring for Ash. It was painful to see how easily he was flushing her out of his life.

Her mind drifted to the other night and the clandestine visit Carson had intended to make to her quarters. That event made her realize that she couldn't stay in his house much longer. She didn't want to fall back into their old relationship, nor did she want him to realize that she was pregnant. She knew she was pregnant for certain now, the new doctor having confirmed it this week. It was funny but Carson never mentioned his visit to her rooms. He acted as if the event had never occurred.

She was only paid twice a month and the first check had mostly gone to paying for the doctor and some food items for the house. She had managed to save 100.00 toward her emancipation though. Hopefully the next pay would allow her to set aside more money. At this rate it would take forever to get out of here.

I guess I'd better call the attorney and see what's up.

She picked up the phone and dialed the number listed in the paper. It didn't take long to get an answering machine which told her that the office was closed and she should call back tomorrow. She hung up and smacked herself in the forehead with the heel of her hand. Why had she called a law office on a Sunday? Of course they were closed!

When Carson arrived home that evening, Carmel was still in her apartment but his mother was waiting for him in the kitchen. As she bustled around finishing the evening meal, she looked him over and then decided to tell him about the ad in the paper.

"I think you should talk to Carmel," she said. "There was something in the paper. I think it was from her husband. He wanted her to call him or his attorney."

"That doesn't sound like good news," Carson said, but inside he wasn't sure. Maybe Ash was going to divorce Carmel and then she'd be a free woman, just as he'd hoped for.

"She's been in her apartment ever since I showed the paper to her. She took it with her so I can't show you, but I told you the main thing," Edna said.

"I'll go down and talk to her before dinner then," Carson said.

"Better make it fast. We eat in twenty minutes," Edna said.

Downstairs, Carson knocked on the door and when Carmel opened it, walked in before she could tell him to leave her alone.

"My Mother told me about the ad in the paper. What do you think it means," he asked her.

"It means my husband is through with me and wants a speedy divorce," Carmel said bitterly.

"I see that upsets you," Carson said, a little disappointed that she didn't see a divorce from Ash in the same way he did.

"It's your fault," Carmel said bitterly, her eyes throwing knives at him.

"It's for the best. You don't love him."

"How do you know how I feel?"

"You feel sad because your marriage is ending but that doesn't mean you love him. It will be for the best. We can make a new life together."

"I don't want a life with you," Carmel said stepping away from him.

Carson decided to back down for the moment.

"I hope you change your mind about that," he said.

He was sure that she would once it was certain that she couldn't go back to Ash. All he had to do was to be patient and things would work out the way he wanted.

"Mother said dinner is about ready," he said and headed out the door. "See you upstairs."

Chapter 36

Dinner was a quiet meal this time since nobody seemed inclined to aggravate Carmel with questions. They discussed the ghost, as a safe topic, but no one added anything new. Carmel could have added a report of new ghostly contacts, but she didn't. Her conversations with the ghost were personal and she chose not to mention them.

After dinner, Edna and Carson went into the living room to watch the news. Carmel stayed behind to clean the kitchen and dining room. That suited her fine because she felt compelled to think things out, and she didn't want to have to make conversation with anyone. When she had finished cleaning she went to her apartment and this time she locked the door. She didn't want Carson bursting in or demanding answers from her. Distracting herself from her problems with a little TV, she soon fell asleep on the couch.

She dreamed of Christmas which was coming soon although she hadn't thought about it. In the dream she and Ash were still together and they were having a baby. It was the best Christmas present they could have, something they both wanted. She saw them sitting together before a fireplace watching the fire and making their plans. Outside she could see snow falling, encircling them, closing them off from the world, but in their snug little house they were warm and happy.

Just as she was reveling in the joy of it all, Ash suddenly turned to her with condemning eyes and said,

"I want a divorce. The baby isn't mine."

Her dreams shattered, she woke to a chilled room. She was lying on the couch, uncovered. The contrast between what could have been and what was, slapped her into the reality of what she'd done with her life. Now, her baby would be condemned to a life without a father and she'd have to struggle to make its world right, the best way she could. She would be alone, a single mother condemned to loneliness for how long? Maybe it would be the rest of her life. Feeling incredibly sorry for herself she got up, stretched her aching muscles and started preparing to go to bed. As she moved around her bedroom turning back the covers and preparing her clothes for the next day, she thought about the holiday.

Christmas! I hadn't been thinking of that. Should I buy a gift for Carson and Edna?

If I get them one, I should get one for Ted Zimmerman too.

He might be around for a Christmas celebration.

I don't feel like doing anything for Carson but he is my host; I live in his house.

I can't really afford this!

Ash is the one I'd like to buy a gift for, but he wouldn't want anything from me. That's over and I might as well accept it and move on.

She realized that she was still being influenced by the dream as she thought of Ash. The dream had been of an idealized marriage to him, one she hadn't really had. They had moments such as she'd dreamed of, but work and day to day life had intervened, and soon they'd been going separate ways; that had left her lonely and vulnerable.

The next day, at work, she found herself thinking about Christmas again. It was a season she used to love.

In fact, she'd been known to celebrate in some small way every day of December, even if it was just by listening to Christmas songs or baking cookies.

This year I won't even be mailing out cards. The sooner it's over the better.

Of course the company was playing soft Christmas music in the background. That annoyed her even more being in the state of mind she was in. Christmas, the holidays, just focused her attention on her predicament and on all she'd lost. The holiday reminded her of how different things were from last year.

"Christmas music makes me want to cry," she told the woman working beside her.

With her emotions weighing her down, she thought she'd never get through the day but finally it was over. When she got home, she was ready to scream when she found Edna sitting in the kitchen listening to Christmas music on a small radio while she baked pies. After making sure that Edna didn't need any help right now, she went off to her own quarters. There she busied herself with cleaning and organizing her space and her possessions.

Lately Carmel had been keeping everything in readiness so she could leave at a moment's notice; although she had no idea where she'd go. She had asked a girl she worked with about cheap housing in the area and had been told about a sort of rooming house a few blocks away. She had kept that in mind but hadn't checked it out yet because she didn't have the money to pay for it.

She had made up her mind to leave if Carson tried to force the issue of their relationship in any way. Fortunately he hadn't been pressuring her. Maybe she'd forgive him for imprisoning her and causing the end of her marriage some day, but it wasn't this day. Right now it was a reminder of what he'd taken from her every time she saw him.

Think of the baby. The baby is all that's important now.

You can figure out the rest later. Like Scarlet O'Hara in Gone with the Wind, you can think of that tomorrow.

Outside it was dribbling down a cold rain and the day was gloomy as the wetness slid into a dark and murky night. Carmel stood at the slit of a window watching the change as it came. At this time of year in Ohio it was fully dark by 5:30. Sometimes on days like this it came earlier. She felt like going to bed and skipping supper but knew that would cause comment, so she went upstairs to eat. She definitely didn't want to call attention to her health at this point in time. Someone might figure out she was pregnant. When she walked into the dining room, she didn't see Edna, but Carson was already seated at the table. He sipped from a cup of coffee, set it down, and looked at her.

"Did you call Ash or his attorney," he asked.

"No. Not yet."

"Why not?"

"I didn't feel like it."

Carson looked like he was going to say more but Edna came back into the room at that time and he didn't. Carmel thought that Edna knew something was going on, because she seemed determined to get a conversation started.

"So," Edna said to Carson, "Has April Mayes been leaving you alone since you got that restraining order?"

Carmel saw Carson wince, before he said, "No, she left two messages on my cell phone today."

"I wondered," Edna said. "I saw her leaving the house earlier when I came home. She was just pulling out when I pulled in."

"Well, I don't know what more I can do. I need both of you to keep me informed if you see her," Carson said. "All I can do right now is to notify the police if she violates the restraining order."

Chapter 37

When Carmel decided to call Ash's attorney, she made sure that first she had rented a Post Office box in Aberdeen. She didn't want either Ash or the attorney to know exactly where she lived. When she had the lawyer on the phone, and he asked her for an address, she gave him the PO Box address. He tried to pin her down to an actual address but she refused.

"What is this about," she asked, and was told that her husband was filing for divorce.

A lonely sad woman made the drive home that afternoon. Carmel grieved for the marriage as if it had been a loved one. What a pity it was that things had come to this point. She didn't blame Ash though. What was he to think after she'd sent that postcard?

It's all my fault...well, no, its mostly Carson's fault. I would have gone back to my marriage and made it work. He prevented me from doing that. It's his fault.

Her bitterness toward Carson doubled and for a time she wondered how she could go back to his house and stay there for even one more day. After thinking it through though she knew that she had no good choices. She'd do what she had to do. So with new resolution she went back to the house and started to work cleaning. She didn't want to be indebted to Carson for anything. Not being able to pay in money she would pay in work for her room and board, at least to the degree she was able to.

No one else was home. Carmel was in the middle of dusting when she saw a movement outside the window that drew her attention as being unusual. When she went to the window, she saw April Mayes leaving the house.

What is she doing sneaking around here like that?
I'm sure she didn't knock or ring the bell.
Edna said she was here yesterday too.

Putting on her coat, Carmel went outside and looked around the perimeter of the house. Had April left something here? Was she looking through windows? What was she doing? At the base of the house under Carson's window she saw a ladder leaning against the wall. She also saw a pile of wood that looked as if someone might be planning to build a fire. Although she didn't understand exactly what April was doing, Carmel felt a thrill of fear racing through her.

Was the ladder so April could climb up and look into Carson's window or maybe go into the house through his window? Had she managed to get into the house? That woman was dangerous; Carmel wondered why she didn't just go away and leave Carson alone, since he had made it clear that he didn't want her in his life. Stalking never had made sense to her. Why get rejected over and over?

And she's jealous of you. You'd better watch out. She might try to hurt you.

Leaving the ladder and wood as she'd found it, Carmel went back inside and resumed house cleaning. She wondered where Edna was this afternoon. Usually she was fixing dinner by now. It was five o'clock and Carson would be home within the next hour. She hoped Edna would be back before he arrived. She felt uneasy being alone with him now. She dreaded his making a pass at her or pushing the issue of their past relationship. Her mind reverted to April again.

"What are you up to April," she said aloud.

"Stay away from that woman, she hates you," Tut Jackson's voice said with a sudden rumble that made her jump.

She was silent for a few minutes not sure whether to believe she'd really heard the ghost or if she was imagining it.

"How'd you know?" she asked the empty living room, realizing suddenly that Tut had now appeared in a different room of the house. Apparently he could go where ever he wanted to and wasn't limited to just that special room and the apartment downstairs, where she'd first seen him.

Be careful," Tut said not answering her question.

She wondered why she'd been able to see him the first time but had only heard him speaking since that night, his voice appearing to come from thin air.

"Tell me about you and Virginia," she said.

"I'm a riverboat man. Virginia lives here," he said "Where's Virginia?"

"I don't know, but I think she must have died here a long time ago," Carmel said.

"No she didn't!"

Carmel jumped at the loudness of the ghost's reply. He didn't like to hear that Virginia was dead. Didn't he realize that he was dead too? His angry reply had made her cautious and she reminded herself that she was dealing with a supernatural being here. For some reason she had been accepting him as if he was just another resident of the house.

"I didn't mean to upset you," she said and went back to her work, thinking she'd certainly be glad to get out of this house for many reasons. Having to deal with a ghost was one of them. It was making her nervous because she felt that her every move was being watched. Although so far the ghost had only tried to help her, she wasn't sure if that would continue to be the case. He'd just shown his potential for anger.

Later at dinner she told Edna and Carson about having seen April as she'd left the house, having gone to check the area where she'd been and finding the ladder and the pile of wood under Carson's window.

"I see why you don't want to deal with that woman," Edna told Carson. "She's unhinged!"

"What are you going to do," Carmel asked Carson; she was curious.

"I'm calling the detective I talked to before. At least I have a couple of witnesses to her having been here, which clearly violates her restraining order."

"Are you going to move the ladder and the wood? Could she be planning to start a fire or something," Edna asked him. "This makes me nervous. I don't want to wake up to the house on fire."

"I'm not going to move either one. I'm going to watch tonight to see if she comes back," Carson said darkly.

Carmel thought maybe he was channeling all his frustrations with life into this one problem. She could see a tremendous anger in him.

"What are you going to do if she creeps up and tries to climb in your window," Edna asked him.

"All I can say is she'd better not," Carson replied. "I might just shove her backwards, ladder and all."

"That could kill her," Edna said.

"So…"

Carson got up to leave the table. "I'm going to bed for a while so I can be up watching later," he said as he went out the door.

"Do you think he'd really hurt her," Carmel asked Edna.

"Well, she's a trespasser with who knows what bad intentions. If she gets hurt because of that, it's her problem," Edna said.

"Maybe she's just trying to be romantic or something, you know, knock at his window in the middle of the night, invite him to climb out to look at the moon or something," Carmel suggested.

"Carson made it clear to her that he's not interested," Edna said, getting up to take her plate to the sink.

"Why did they break up," Carmel asked.

"He said she went out with another man," Edna said. "I think she's not wrapped right and that he's well away from her. Maybe you and Carson could get together," Edna suggested.

Carmel paused, not sure how to reply to that. Carson was Edna's son and Carmel didn't want to say anything negative about him to her. After all she was availing herself of his hospitality and Edna didn't know the details of how she'd lost her own home and how Carson was responsible. However, she didn't want Edna to get any matchmaking ideas either.

"I don't think Carson and I are compatible," she said, then walked away before Edna could argue with her.

Chapter 38

Carson sat at his window looking out at the dark sky. Tonight was particularly black, he thought, although it did seem to get better after he'd stared into it for a while. He'd checked his watch a few minutes ago and saw that it was 1:00am. Even though he'd slept earlier, his body was still telling him that it was bedtime and that he should be asleep. He had to work tomorrow and he expected that would be a difficult day for him after tonight's lack of rest.

So far nothing had happened. He tried to think about where April worked and why she would be free to come to his house in the afternoons. He hadn't asked her what she was doing these days because he'd been in a hurry to get away from her.

Down on the river he could see a barge going by; its light moving slowly through the night, made him think of the ghost who'd supposedly been a riverboat man. It had certainly been eerie to hear a strange voice answering his mother on the tape he'd set up. So far he hadn't asked the spirit any questions of his own. He called himself a ghost hunter but he was an amateur and the truth was that he was somewhat spooked by the idea of another world that he couldn't see. He couldn't even think why he'd bought the equipment and set it up in the first place. It was curiosity he supposed.

He hadn't checked the tapes for a few days and it was time to do that. He'd been worrying himself over the intentions of April Mayes and his fear that she might spook Carmel into leaving. He wanted that problem solved as soon as possible. Now he sat there wondering what April was up to. Apparently she had placed the ladder and the wood under his window. Did she intend to climb up and try to get into his bedroom or did she plan to start a fire? Maybe she had meant for them to find the wood and the ladder and had put it there as an attention getter.

I sure know how to pick em! For some reason none of my relationships ever work out. I think I've blown it with Carmel now, although I won't give up on that yet.

What was that?

He had heard a rustle somewhere under the window. Straining his eyes, he tried to see the area below but it was dark. Suddenly he saw a spark of light that flicked on and off again so fast that he wasn't sure he'd really seen anything at all.

"What am I going to do if she starts a fire down there?"

He suddenly thought of a couple of buckets that he'd left in the closet of his bathroom. He ran in and started filling both of them with water, running back to the window to peer out every few seconds. When both buckets were filled he carried them to the window and sat looking down at the blackness. If April was down there and she intended to start a fire, she hadn't done so yet. He'd be able to see the flame if there was a fire and he couldn't see anything.

What's she doing? I know I heard something and I think she's down there, but no fire, and April is not *climbing up the ladder either. Maybe she's just trying to mess with my mind.*

Listening, so hard it hurt, Carson couldn't hear anything now. Perhaps it had only been his imagination after all. When a few minutes had passed he saw a spark of light again somewhere near the ladder and he could hear sounds as if someone was climbing up the wall.

Why would she come up to my bedroom?

She probably thinks that Carmel is sharing it with me since I told her I had a girlfriend and she's met Carmel.

The only reason she'd do such a thing has to be something to cause trouble.

There's no telling what a rejected lover might do.

He peered out again but it didn't look like April was on the ladder. Maybe she'd changed her mind. He eased the window up a little feeling the icy air from outside. It was a particularly cold night for someone to be prowling around outside his house. It was then that he caught a faint smell of smoke. He leaned into the window and saw a small flame up against the house. A figure stood there feeding wood into it.

Acting on instinct, Carson pushed the window up, grabbed a bucket of water and poured it, not on the tiny flame but on the figure near it. He heard a woman scream out in surprise just as he snatched up the second bucket and emptied it partly on the fire and partly on the figure which had collapsed into a ball below him.

"That'll teach ya to prowl around my house at night," he yelled out the window.

He headed for his bedroom door and started down the stairs hoping to catch April in the act before she could get away. He grabbed a coat from a hook by the door on his way out, having remembered how cold the air had been. He carried a flashlight for use as a weapon if needed.

She really got a ducking this time!

Deciding to be cautious, Carson eased himself out the door and around the edge of the house. There wasn't anyone there when he got to the soggy pile of wood. The flashlight showed charring from a small fire but no embers remained. He turned out the flashlight and stood near the wall listening. Abruptly he heard the sound of a car engine starting; he ran to the edge of his lot to look down the hill. He could see a car moving away from his house but couldn't tell the make or model.

After all the excitement he went inside and to bed. He didn't expect April would be back tonight. The water must have felt like an ice bath to her standing in the cold air as she had been. It should be enough to cool her off for the night. Amazingly he slept like a baby, having a feeling of accomplishment. At least he'd taken steps to solve one of his problems.

Chapter 39

At breakfast, Carson related the night's events to Edna and Carmel. He was a bit proud of himself it seemed to Carmel, as he described throwing ice water down on April as she attempted to set a fire beside the house.

"What if that girl catches pneumonia and dies from having ice water poured on her in 20 degree weather," Edna asked. "Her family might bring a wrongful death suit against you."

"That would be absurd. Anyway, I was just trying to put out a fire that was threatening my house. Can I help it if she was standing over the fire?"

Carmel listened fascinated at how Carson's mind worked. To tell the truth, she'd have probably done the same thing if someone was trying to set fire to her house, though. She had no sympathy for April who had turned into a stalker, trying to get the man she wanted, but Carson should have understood her better. After all he'd turned to kidnapping to get the woman he wanted. How was that different from stalking? It could even be a form of stalking. It had certainly ruined her life, hadn't it?

"I doubt that will be the end of it," she found herself saying.

"Why do you say that," Carson asked her.

"Now you've declared war on her, in her mind you probably attacked her, and I don't think she's the type to let that go."

A few minutes later, Carson left the house to go to work; however, he was back in a few minutes.

"My tires are slashed," he said. "Will you drop me off on the way downtown," he asked Carmel. "I'm doing a job here today."

"Sure," Carmel agreed.

"I'll call that roving mechanic I used last time. He comes to your house, changes oil, fixes tires, and things like that," Carson told her. "I might be able to get him to pick me up and take me home."

"I'll call your cell phone to see if you need a ride," Carmel promised.

When she called at the end of the day, Carson told her that the mechanic was giving him a ride home. That way they could settle their bill while they were at it. Since she wasn't needed anywhere, Carmel decided to go to the library and do some research before going home. She was still looking for Tut Jackson and his Virginia, or any history of the house that she could find. To her joy she hit pay-dirt after only an hour of searching. At least she thought she had. It was going to be a sad story, she thought.

A newspaper article said:

Girl imprisoned after she refuses to name the father of her child.

It has come to the attention of this county that Ms. Virginia Walker is currently with child. The county has required her presence for the posting of a Bastardy Bond. Most of my readers will know that in a situation like this, the court of the county where-in the woman resides, demands such a bond so the county will not be required to support the child in later years. Ms. Walker appeared in this court and was questioned about the father of her child but she refused to divulge the required information. Had she done so, the father would

~ 186 ~

have been served a warrant and would have been forced to pay the bond.

When the mother refuses to tell the court the father's name, the woman or her parents must post the bond themselves. If no bond is posted, the uncooperative mother may be imprisoned until such time as she agrees to cooperate. Ms. Virginia Walker was remanded to the county jail this afternoon on such charges. When questioned, Ms. Walker stated that she hoped her father would be allowed to post the bond for her and that she would soon be free to go home.

Carmel stared at the paper. Was this the Virginia that the ghost was looking for? If so, then Virginia Walker probably lived in the house that now belonged to Edna and Carson Wetzel. She scanned the paper for a date and found 1889 at the top of the page. Excitedly she made two copies of the story and headed toward home. She couldn't wait to show this to the others. She'd bet anything that Tut Jackson was the father of Virginia's child. Maybe that had given him more sympathy for her situation.

However, at home she found another crisis waiting. Apparently April had done more than slash tires. Carson reported that although his tires had been replaced, his car wouldn't start. Ted Zimmerman was at the house visiting Edna and he agreed to take a look at the car for Carson. When they came back inside, both men were shaking their heads.

"Looks like the old sugar in the gas tank trick to me," Ted said. "If it is, it will require a new motor."

Carson thumped his body down into a chair and stared out the window. "After I call the police," he said, "I guess I'll call the garage and have them come and tow it in to look at it. Meanwhile, I don't have any way to get to work. I don't know what I'm going to do."

He looked so dejected that even Carmel had sympathy for him. He'd made a lot of bad choices; apparently April Mayes was one of them, but he didn't deserve this much trouble.

"I have an old truck that I don't use much," Ted said. "You're welcome to drive that if you want."

"Do you mean it?"

"Sure, after we eat, I'll drive you over to my house and you can drive it back."

Carson brightened a little after that. To change the subject and share her find, Carmel produced the newspaper account she'd found today.

"I guess they were sticklers for that sort of thing in those days," Edna said. "I heard things about it in my girlhood."

"So we think that Virginia lived here and the ghost, Tut Jackson visited her in this house. They made a child together, but when the court questioned her, Virginia refused to tell them who he was," Carson said.

"Right and this indicates that maybe her father got together the money to bond her out of jail. At least that's what she expected to happen."

"You should search the papers of the next few days. They probably reported it if she was released," Edna said.

"I didn't have time today but I'll look for that next time," Carmel agreed.

"Meanwhile, I'm going to pull the tapes from my equipment and listen to see if we have any more clues," Carson said.

Chapter 40

The next day at work, Carmel did a search on her computer during her lunch hour. She was looking for information on Bastardy Bonds. This was a term she'd never heard of before she'd located that article, and she wanted to find out a bit more about it. She found a definition under:

Poor Law, Bastardy Bonds and Maintenance Orders

When a woman was expecting an illegitimate child, Parish officials subjected her to an examination to determine who the father was. They would then attempt to have the father sign a Bastardy Bond which meant that he was responsible for supporting the child. He had to pay a sum to the mother weekly. If he refused to pay maintenance, application could be made by the Mother, Family, or the Parish to take the matter to the Justice of the Peace for a maintenance order. The child was considered "Base Born" or a "Bastard Child", and was ostracized by much of society.

Bastardy records are an important part of family records today providing evidence of parentage, which is a great help to genealogists, the article said. Carmel thought it sounded as if things were a little different in Ripley at the time Virginia Walker was scrutinized and jailed. However, as always, the woman who was with child was in a sad predicament and life was unpleasant for her no matter what happened. Carmel thought of her own situation. She was essentially in the same position since she doubted that her baby belonged to her lawful husband, Ash. Her baby would have been termed illegitimate by some.

He won't be my lawful husband for long. Too bad, he'd have been a good father too.

That reminded her that she had to go to her PO Box on the way home because the attorney had said he was mailing papers to that address. She'd decided not to get an attorney for herself. It wouldn't do any good to fight Ash. She didn't deserve any of the fruits of the marriage and she felt she should accept her fate and go quietly away. Ash deserved the chance to find someone who would be there for him, be faithful, and who would make him happy. She wasn't the one, but it made her sad to know that. She picked up the papers and sent off a reply to the attorney saying that he should proceed as planned. She was not contesting the divorce. By the time she'd finished that she didn't have time to go to the library so she went back to the house.

Meanwhile, Edna had been emboldened to question the spirit of Tut Jackson again. Going to the room, she'd read the article aloud to the seemingly empty room. All she heard at first was the whir of the recording equipment.

"Is this your Virginia? Are you the father of her baby?"

"Yes!"

Edna jumped, and then asked, "Where is the baby?"

"Virginia…" the howl erupted from somewhere near the fireplace and Edna decided to pursue this line of questioning later. Clearly, the subject of Virginia and the baby were sore points for the grieving ghost. She told Carmel and Carson about it at dinnertime, after Carmel had shared her information regarding what she'd learned about Bastardy Bonds.

"He made a horrible sound and I decided to leave him alone for a while," Edna said.

"Maybe we could think of some questions and then go in there together to ask them," Carson suggested.

"I'd like to ask him if Virginia got out of jail," Edna said.

"And I'd like to know whether he ever married her or not," Carmel added.

"I'd like to know how both of them died, but he seems to be upset by the subject," Carson contributed.

"We could go back in there and read the article again, then ask him what happened to her," Edna said.

They agreed to do this after dinner. Carmel asked what the situation was with Carson's car. He reported that the mechanic thought someone had put something, maybe sugar, in the gas tank and that it had ruined the engine.

"He's going to replace it, so I'll be without the car for another few days. I hope Ted doesn't need his truck back before then."

After eating, the three of them trouped into the "ghost's room" as they'd started calling it. Carson checked his tapes and then Edna began to read the article once again. When she'd finished, Carson asked,

"Did Virginia's father post the bond and get her out of jail?"

"Yes," the voice boomed out.

"Did you marry her," Carmel asked.

"Shot gun."

"You mean shot gun wedding?"

"Yes."

"Did her father actually have a gun?"

"A shotgun," the voice repeated.

"Did he get the money for the bond back after you and Virginia had been married," Carson wanted to know.

"Don't know."

Carson was elated to be getting all this information on his tapes. He'd found a lot of success as a ghost hunter even if he was new to the game and most of the legwork had been done by others. Now he wanted to share his findings with other people in the field. He felt he had a lot of new and important material.

"If Virginia wouldn't tell who the father of her baby was, how did her Dad know to zero in on you," Carson asked the spirit.

"He waited."

"You mean he waited for you to show up again and caught you visiting Virginia?"

"He had a gun. He held it on me and sent Virginia to get the preacher."

"Didn't you want to marry Virginia?"

"I loved Virginia. I didn't know about the baby. Don't let anything happen to the baby!!!"

Everyone jerked backward toward the door when the voice that had been speaking normally suddenly veered off into a shrieking scream.

"I think this is enough for now. I'm going to change the tapes and maybe we'll try to talk to Tut again in a day or two," Carson said.

That ended the quest for information that night. Carson went to his room to review the tapes, Carmel cleaned the kitchen and then went to her rooms, and Edna sat thinking about the ghost that was grieving and upset every time anyone mentioned the baby.

Chapter 41

"Maybe we could figure out what happened to Virginia's baby if we do some research," Carson said. "We know that Virginia died around 1889 or 1890, but did the baby die too, or was it adopted by someone?"

"Our ghost seems to have an attachment to that baby. We should ask him if it was a boy or a girl and what happened to it," Edna said.

It was the next evening and the three of them were seated around the table discussing the events of the day before. Carson had been playing the tapes from that adventure while they ate and Carmel was about to lose her appetite after that final scream. It froze her insides. They had ended their questions at that point, not wanting to upset the ghost any further. Each time they talked to him, they got some new information, but they thought it was best to go slow.

Carmel thought about her baby which was growing secretly inside her, even as she sat there talking to the others about a baby born over 100 years ago. It seemed strange somehow, but linked in a way. Funny that she hadn't realized she was pregnant but the ghost had. Had he interfered with her desire to die only because of the baby, because he had an obsession about babies, having lost his own perhaps? She hoped he'd had a little sympathy for her as well as wanting to save the baby. He had brought her to her senses at least.

Realizing that in this house people talked about ghosts as normally as they'd describe any living person who was plagued with peculiar circumstances, she wondered if they were all nuts. She no longer doubted but took the presence of Tut Jackson as fact. Even so, she was afraid when he howled out like he had last night. That sound was so eerie, like something created in Hell!

"We might be able to find out what happened to Virginia. There could be something in the paper, like an obituary," Carson was saying.

Carmel was glad that the conversation had turned to something more interesting than tobacco farming tonight, and she contributed her bit to it.

"I'll stop by the library tomorrow and search in the genealogy records. We know her name was Virginia Walker from birth, but after she was married it would be Virginia Jackson. That's the name we'd find her under," Carmel said.

"Do you mind," Carson asked. He looked pleased that she was taking part in solving the family mystery.

"Not at all, I'm good at research," Carmel said.

She was quiet the rest of the meal while Edna and Carson reminisced over the past. They were talking about something used to clean wallpaper. Carson said that it was like clay and it would be used to clean the black spots left by a coal stove off the walls and ceiling. Then the dirty mass of clay would be given to him to play with.

"You couldn't wash it out, the dirt was mixed into the clay by then but it was still soft and pliable and fun to play with," Carson said glancing toward her.

Carmel just shook her head and refused to comment. She had never heard of wall paper cleaner. Why couldn't you just wash it down like you did dry wall? She realized that in some fundamental ways she and Carson had been brought up vastly different. He'd grown up here on the river with a tobacco farming background. She'd grown up near Carmel in Highland County, the place for which she was named. Her parents lived in the country but worked in Hillsboro. She hadn't learned much about farm life, and the river culture was different as well.

The background chatter between mother and son lulled Carmel into a restful reverie as she thought about the Christmas season which was coming soon and where she'd be next year. Next year she wouldn't be alone. She'd been trying to save a little money for a place of her own and knew she'd have to save enough to carry her through the time when she'd have to be in a hospital and unable to work as well. Based on the amount she was currently making, that was a daunting task.

Now she had the problem of Christmas and what she should do about that. Since she was living in the house that belonged to Edna and Carson Wetzel, she should buy them a gift she supposed. And what about Ted Zimmerman, he'd probably be at the house for the holiday also. It was a tricky situation but she needed to do what must be done. It would be hard to buy something for Carson. Whatever she purchased it would be impersonal, she decided. She didn't want him to get the impression that she was doing anything except fulfilling her duty to her host.

I hate to part with the money but I'd better go shopping tomorrow.

I need to check my post box too.

If things were as they should be, I'd be celebrating with Ash, but that'll never happen again.

Sadness pulled at her face as the lines around her mouth turned down in despair. She wished for

Christmas to be over as soon as possible. Although she normally liked it a lot, she didn't this year. Next year, God willing, she'd celebrate her baby's first Christmas and everything would be ok.

"Have you heard anything from the ghost," Carson asked his Mother.

"No but I want to ask him about the baby. Are you game to try again," Edna said, looking at both Carson and Carmel.

"Sure," both agreed, curious.

All three of them trooped into the ghost's room again; equipment whirred as they spoke aloud to the essence of the room, hoping the spirit was there to hear them. At first everything was silent except for Edna's voice as she asked if the baby was a boy or a girl.

"Girl," the voice of Tut Jackson said, suddenly.

"What was her name?"

"Virginia."

"Both the baby and your wife were called Virginia," Edna asked him in order to clarify whether he'd understood her.

"Little Virginia; she's so cute."

"Where is Virginia? I mean what happened to your baby?"

"Vir-gin- ia!!!!!" the voice wailed into the dusty room, causing shivers to attack their spines and their hearts to race. Again they left, deciding to evaluate what information they had before trying to get more from a ghost that seemed to be having an anxiety attack.

When they were in the living room again, Carmel asked if anyone thought she should look for relatives who might have taken the baby after the mother died.

Tut wouldn't have been able to take care of her if he'd died during that time also, but the baby had a Grandfather living, and perhaps other relatives they didn't know about. Who had raised the baby and where were her descendents now?

"I think we need to find anything and everything we can," Edna said.

"I'd try to find the Mother's death record or obituary in the newspaper, and then I'd look for general information about the family," Carson said. "Who knows what might turn up?"

"Well, hopefully I'll have something to report tomorrow," Carmel said, getting up to clean the kitchen. "Don't expect miracles though."

Chapter 42

After work, Carmel drove to her PO Box where she found papers that had been sent to her by the attorney that Ash had hired. Stuffing them into her purse, she decided that she'd look at them later tonight. For now she wanted to get to the library and do some research.

The first hour was tedious and unrewarding. She couldn't find a death certificate for Virginia under either name. After that she started looking for newspaper references and finally hit the jackpot with an article that was written sometime after Virginia's death. While she sat reading it, her blood chilled as if Tut Jackson was looking over her shoulder reading it too. She could almost feel him, although as far as she knew he wouldn't be able to leave the house. What kind of limits do ghosts have anyway?

It's *my imagination. For all I know, Tut can't even read. A lot of people at that time couldn't.*

She copied the newspaper article and then searched further, finding one more reference to the subject of Tut Jackson, which she also copied. Excitedly, she headed toward her temporary home and the thrill of sharing her amazing find. Animosity against Carson had fled to the background as she focused on the mystery of the family ghost and his extraordinary history. She had a temporary family and she couldn't wait to tell the others what she'd found.

When she got to the house she found Ted Zimmerman had come to dinner tonight and that Edna had outdone herself with the meal. All this helped set the stage, Carmel thought, for later when she'd spring her news on the others. Holding it close to her, a delicious secret, Carmel waited until curiosity finally made Carson ask her if she'd found any new information during her research.

"Well, I found a couple of articles in the newspaper. Would you like for me to read them?" With all eyes on her, she read:

Tragic End to Love Affair

After Virginia Jackson's death in childbirth two days ago, tragedy has again struck the Jackson family. Some may recall that Virginia, at the time known as Ms. Virginia Walker was examined regarding the parentage of her child some months ago and was jailed when she refused to give out that information. Subsequently, a Bond was posted by her father, George Walker, and later she was married to Tut Jackson who is employed as a riverboat man on the Ohio River.

This week, tragedy first struck when Virginia died just after delivering a healthy girl child who was also named Virginia. Apparently her father, George Walker, blamed his son-in-law, Tut Jackson for her death, and is accused of having shot Mr. Jackson fatally this morning. George Walker has apparently had nothing to say for himself, other than his statement that Tut Jackson was responsible for the death of his little girl and that he'd gotten what was coming to him.

George Walker remains in our local jail, while Mr. Jackson has been taken to the Wetherby Funeral Home. Meanwhile, the baby is being cared for by Virginia's married sister Anita Williams, who lives in Cincinnati.

Carmel stopped reading and looked at the amazed faces around her. She felt like a superstar at that moment, knowing that she'd delivered an amazing and interesting story to her audience.

"I can't believe that you actually found some documentation of this supposed ghost of yours," Ted Zimmerman said, breaking the breathless quiet.

"I think the ghost is real enough," Edna said in a voice that sounded miffed. "We have a lot of taped recordings of his voice and what he's told us so far."

"Since Tut died without knowing what happened to his little girl; that explains some of his concern for where Virginia is. Maybe it's Virginia, the baby, not his wife that he's looking for. He would have known his wife was dead, but not what happened to the baby," Carmel said.

"That's right," Carson agreed. "He got upset when someone told him that Virginia was dead on one of the tapes."

"Should we go to the ghost room and read the newspaper article aloud so he'll know what happened," Edna asked the others.

"I think we should," Carmel said. "If he's been worrying about what happened to the baby all these years, it would set his mind at ease to find out."

"I wonder what happened to George Walker," Edna said. "Did he go to prison for murder?"

"I found something about that too," Carmel told her, pulling out the other clipping she'd found and starting to read it aloud.

Guilty Man Found Hanged in Cell

George Walker, who was convicted in court this morning for the murder of Tut Jackson, was found hanged in his cell this evening. There was no suicide note, but speculation is that he felt he had nothing to live for following his daughter's death and his own conviction for murder. Mr. Walker's body was taken to the same funeral home where his victim Tut Jackson had been laid out after the murder.

"I think he might like to know that justice was done. We should read this article to him too," Carson said.

After discussing the articles thoroughly over dinner, they followed their new tradition of going to the ghost's room afterward. Ted held back saying that he thought this was a foolish thing to do.

"We shouldn't meddle in things we don't understand," he told them.

"You don't have to go with us if you don't want to," Edna said disdainfully. "You can either wait in the living room or go on home."

"I'm going with you," Ted said and joined the group.

In the ghost's room, Carmel took the lead, reading the two articles aloud. When she finished there was silence and everyone looked around them uneasily. They liked it better when the ghost was talking to them. That at least gave them an idea of where he was coming from.

"Well, what do you think," Edna asked. "Your baby Virginia went to live with her aunt. That was about a hundred and eighteen years ago. By now she's dead and should be in your world, but maybe she had children of her own that you could meet."

Tut greeted that idea with silence. Everyone waited not sure if they wanted him to talk to them or not. If he'd heard all the information in the news articles, he had a lot to think about. Edna couldn't be quiet though and she spoke again.

"George Walker hanged himself in the jail cell. Aren't you glad that your murderer didn't get off Scot free?"

Quiet, and then,

"How do you know he hung himself? Maybe I helped him," the ghost said.

Chapter 43

Carson was impressed with the research that Carmel had done. He was also impressed with his own progress as a ghost hunter and was wondering who he should present the things they'd found to. Surely there were parapsychologists who'd love to know about Tut Jackson and the tapes as well as the corroborating evidence Carmel had found. He decided to look on the computer and try to find someone whom he could send his information to.

Meanwhile, he'd almost forgotten about his problem with April Mayes. He remembered though, when he found his car scratched with a sharp object and the words jerk painted in nail polish on his rear bumper. He called the police and talked to Detective Davis this time. After explaining what had happened with the fire at his house and the previous vandalism done to his car, he told him of the new damages to the car.

"The problem is we can't prove it's her that's doing this unless we get her to confess," the detective said. "We can question her but there are no guarantees that anything will come of it."

"Well, can't you at least try to stop this?"

"I'll do the best I can, Mr. Wetzel," the officer said.

Discouraged, Carson headed off to Cincinnati for a job he had there today. He'd told his mother and Carmel to call the police if they saw April anywhere around the property and that appeared to be all he could do.

The holidays were getting to him. He'd hoped earlier in the year that he and Carmel would be spending this Christmas together, preferably as husband and wife.

Now Carmel seemed farther removed from him than she'd ever been since he'd known her. Clearly she was holding a grudge because of the way he'd kidnapped her. At the time it had seemed to be the only thing to do; he didn't want to lose her. Now he wished he had tried something else. The method he'd tried had backfired; and the bitter feelings that sparked between them were worse than ever. He'd rather she had left him than to hate him.

The ghost had brought them together in a way though. Last night after Tut Jackson had hinted that he might have killed his father-in-law, who'd shot him, they had abandoned the room silent and thoughtful. Later the four of them discussed the possibility that their ghost, an entity who had almost become like an invisible friend, might be a lot more lethal than they'd thought. Was the ghost kidding, or had he somehow visited George Walker in jail and hung him? Could a ghost do that? With all the unanswered questions, the group, including Carmel, had drawn closer together for safety.

He liked the enthusiasm with which Carmel had joined into his ghost hunting project and saw that as being about their only point of agreement these days. He'd tried to leave her alone hoping that one day she'd give him a sign that she was past her anger at him for keeping her a prisoner and causing Ash to divorce her. He hadn't seen a sign though. In fact she was more distant than before, it seemed.

Carson was somewhat miffed with Carmel too because she was taking this divorce between herself and Ash so hard. If she loved him, she should be glad to move on, but she wasn't. He knew that. Still, she was here in his house, not in Ash's house, and that gave him hope. He didn't like to believe that it was his duty to give her a place to stay, as she'd said, only until she could get a place of her own. He hoped the reason she was here was that she still wanted to be near him, even if she was mad at him. Shaking his head back and forth in frustration, Carson drove through the early morning traffic toward Cincinnati and his day's work.

At the house in Ripley, Edna Wetzel was cleaning the kitchen and humming an old song when she heard a sound that made her go look out the window. At first she didn't see anything except the cold dampness of a mid December day. There was no snow on the ground but the thermometer said it was 28 degrees and she felt chilled looking at the bare trees and grey skies.

As she watched she saw a figure pop out from behind a tree and then disappear again. She couldn't tell if it was a man or a woman. Should she call the police if she didn't know who it was? Carson had left a number for her to reach Detective Davis, if she saw April Mayes hanging about, but she couldn't identify the person she'd seen. The figure had been heading down the hill and now she heard a car starting up. By the time she had run to another window where she could see the driveway; the car was gone.

Wondering what the sound she'd heard had been, Edna cautiously went outside to check. Near the front entrance she found what the intruder had left. Propped against the door was an old fashioned doll in a seated position. In its lap was a note cut from magazines. From where she stood, Edna could see two things. The doll had been mutilated with a broken neck and missing limbs.

The note said: **Send Devil Woman away.**

For a minute she couldn't tear her eyes from the scene and then Edna ran back inside the house. This had solved her problem of whether to call the Detective or not. She grabbed the phone and dialed it. Later the Detective carefully removed the doll and the note after taking photographs first. This was all evidence in his investigation he said. They might be able to link these objects to April Mayes. He handed one of the photos to Edna and said,

"Be sure that both your son and this woman, Carmel, see this photo. It sounds to me as if who ever did this is trying to threaten the woman she sees as her rival. That means that either or both of them could be in actual danger. If this is April Mayes, she's already escalated her stalking to threats. It'll only get worse."

Edna took the photo and propped it on her kitchen counter where she stared at it periodically, wondering what the others would say when she showed it to them.

Chapter 44

Edna presented the photo to the others along with the meatloaf and mashed potatoes that night. First she passed the photo around and then she explained what had happened and what Detective Davis had said. Carmel was appalled. The affair she'd had with Carson had led to nothing but tragedy in her life. Now some crazy ex-girlfriend was out to get her. Just when you think things can't get worse…!

Carson was angry.

"What are the police going to do about this," he asked.

"I don't know. You should call him yourself," Edna said. "I told you what he told me. He thinks Carmel might be in danger as well as you are, because April's jealous of the two of you."

Carson looked at Carmel but she looked away because she didn't want to discuss it. She needed to get out of this place! The reasons were piling up and she wished she had the where withal to leave today. Knowing she didn't, she just shrugged and kept eating her food.

"I think you'd better take this serious," Edna told her. "That April has a screw loose. Did you see what she did to the doll? It's her way of saying that you'll be next."

"I'll be careful," Carmel told her.

She left the table early telling them that she'd be back to clean up in a little while. At the moment she just wanted to be alone so she could think. In her apartment she sat on the couch staring at the wall and wondering how to get out of this mess. She got paper and pencil and jotted down all the things that were wrong and looked at the list as she brooded. The list said:

1. baby, not a problem but it complicates things
2. divorce
3. I need money to get my own place
4. How do I get away from both Ash and Carson before they guess about the baby
5. A ghost that kills????
6. A stalker who wants to mutilate me.

She thought the list could be longer but these were certainly enough problems to think about for the moment. She studied each listing. It was all tied together. She needed money to get away from the house so that neither of the men in her life, Ash, or Carson, would know about the baby. She needed money to take care of the child. If she left the house, April wouldn't have a reason to kill her any more and she'd be away from Tut Jackson too.

So money seems to be the key. How can I make extra money? Maybe I can search for someone who wants Holiday cleaning done. An extra two or three hundred dollars would make all the difference.

Carmel continued to think but more optimistically now. Having decided that money to leave this place was the key, she determined to do something about that. She thought about her possessions. Did she have anything she could sell or pawn? Nothing came to mind. She was earning some money but had doctor's bills, food and gas bills, and now Christmas presents to buy.

It was going to take too long to get a nest egg big enough to disappear as she'd intended. She wanted to be able to change jobs without Carson knowing it so that he wouldn't be able to trace her once she left. That was another problem. Thinking how hopeless it was, she found herself crying huge tears of self pity. As the water ran down her cheeks and dripped onto her blouse she sniffled and sobbed. Why did life have to be so difficult?

"If only I had a family heirloom or something I could pawn or sell, something very valuable that would bring a lot," she said aloud. "But I don't"

She looked at the paper again and sighed, "Well, I guess I'll have to start looking for a part time job," she told herself with resignation.

Seeing that she'd been in here over an hour and the kitchen still needed cleaned up, Carmel got up and went to do her duty. It made her feel better about using Carson's resources while plotting to leave him behind in the dust. At least she was contributing something to the household.

Behind the wall, Tut Jackson watched the drama unfolding before him with mixed feelings. What if Virginia had not told him about his baby? That would have been a tragedy! Thinking of the little baby Virginia sparked his grief again and for a while he couldn't concentrate on Carmel's pain. He knew that the other woman April was causing trouble and threatening Carmel and understood her wanting to get away from that. It sounded like she was afraid of him too, after he'd made his comment about helping George Walker commit suicide. He hadn't meant to scare her.

From what he could gather, Carmel had a husband and Carson had been her lover. She was pregnant and

~ 211 ~

didn't want either one of the men to know. She probably didn't know which man had fathered the baby. Tut didn't like that. Although he liked Carmel, he thought she'd behaved like a dance hall girl, being intimate with two men at once.

A man has a right to know about his baby.

Tut understood that she was in a bad position. He knew why she might want to go away somewhere and raise her baby alone. He had been aware that Carson was keeping her in the apartment against her will in the beginning. Tut had even considered letting her out, but since Carson wasn't physically hurting her, he'd let the situation go on just to see the drama of it. It was understandable that Carmel wouldn't want to stay around Carson any longer than she had to after he'd made her his prisoner.

The mixture of feelings inside him confused Tut in a way he hadn't been confused for decades. He felt an affinity for this woman for some reason. Maybe it was just because they'd shared a space for a couple of months, he didn't know. It felt like her baby was his baby; it was important to him somehow. Could he have transferred his feelings for baby Virginia to this unborn child which he already knew was a girl? Was he trying to act out his own drama again so he could have a different outcome?

All he knew was Carmel must not die, she must not leave, and nothing must happen to this baby. It would be like losing his family all over again.

Chapter 45

Carmel stuck to the plan she had for making extra money. Her first step was to look in the paper to see if anyone was advertising for help. She didn't find anyone who wanted a person to clean but there was an ad for a dog sitter. If she took that job she'd be responsible for the dog for two weeks after Christmas. The owner said he was going out of town during that time. When she called, she found that the house where the dog owner lived was only about a mile from Carson's house. She thought she could go to the house before and after work to feed the animal and let it out without too much hardship. The owner would pay $100.00 for her services for the two weeks. Carmel thought that would help build her nest egg and was excited at the opportunity.

She wouldn't tell anyone at the house what she was doing; she'd just leave earlier each morning and take care of the dog each evening on the way home. Meanwhile she'd keep searching for other opportunities to add to her small store of money.

That job didn't start until after Christmas which was good, because she had a lot to do before the holiday. Today she had to go shopping. She felt it was her duty to buy a gift for the people who were currently in her life but it was agonizing. It would be hard to buy for Carson because she didn't want him to read anything into the gift. It was a duty gift, not a gift for a lover.

First she checked her post box but didn't have anything more from Ash's attorney. Then she drove down toward Cincinnati looking for a store to buy the Christmas gifts. On the outskirts of town she found a department store and pulled in. Inside she was aware of the changing Christmas Carols playing, a toy activated not by a kid but by a man who looked like he was around 50, and the loud voice of a man who had his wife on cell phone and the cell phone on speaker.

Why would anyone want to have their private conversations overheard by others that way?

She finally bought an electric skillet for Edna, hat, gloves, and scarf for Ted, and a shirt and tie for Carson. As she looked at her purchases she hoped that Carson wouldn't think that clothes were too personal. She'd blanked out and couldn't think of anything else that he might need. To wrap the gifts she selected a pretty paper and some scotch tape. The entire time she was shopping she thought about Ash. What would he think if she bought him a gift?

You can't do that! The man's divorcing you! He'd think that you were trying to crawl back into his good graces!

It was just that if felt awkward to buy for people who were almost strangers to her while not doing anything for her own husband!

Back at the house, she headed to her own rooms to wrap the things she'd purchased. The house felt awfully quiet this afternoon. She hadn't seen Edna downstairs when she came in and wondered where she was. Ted might have come to pick her up; Carmel wondered if that meant that Edna would be out of the house at dinner time. She didn't choose to be left alone with Carson. He'd already tried to talk with her about their situation a time or two and she didn't want to discuss it with him. Looking at her watch, she saw that it was already five o'clock. Hopefully Edna would be home before Carson was.

Hearing a car pull up down the hill she went to the window slit and peeked out. What she saw was April Mayes getting out of her car and heading toward the house. Not wanting to talk to the police about anything, still Carmel reflected on what to do. Carson had asked her to call the police and it was uncertain what April might be up to. The last few times she'd been at the house it was to vandalize something.

There was a small click downstairs which Carmel heard through the open door to her apartment. It sounded like the click of a door closing. How could April get into the house without a key? Going to her apartment door, Carmel softly closed it and locked it from inside. Now April couldn't get to her unless she had a key to the door. However, there was no phone in her rooms; Carson hadn't wanted her to have access to the outside world when he was holding her prisoner.

She listened at the door for sounds of footsteps or some clue as to what the other woman was up to. With the door closed she couldn't hear anything. The walls and door had been purposely made thick and sound proof. It made her uneasy and gave her a feeling of being trapped. What if April set the house on fire again? Could she get out of here before the house went up in smoke and flame? But if she left the apartment and ran into April inside the house, she might have a knife or a gun. Trembling with indecision, Carmel hovered near the door, unsure what to do.

She went back to her window to see if April's car was still where she'd left it. The car was there but she could see April walking toward it. If she'd been in the house, she'd left now. What mischief had she done? After she saw April getting into her car she left her rooms and headed downstairs. Looking out the living room window she saw that April had actually driven away.

Going from room to room she looked carefully to see if anything had been added or taken away. First she checked the living room, then the dining room and kitchen. At the back of the house she looked at the mud room and then circled around to the bathroom. In the bath she saw what she'd been hoping not to find. The mirror had been shattered and written in lipstick on the glass were the words:

Sometimes you just gotta break something!

Nothing else in the room seemed to have been touched and Carmel backed out of it carefully not touching anything. She went back to the kitchen to get the number for Detective Davis and to use the phone. When she reached the police department she was told that the Detective was out at the moment but that he would call back shortly.

Did she go to all the trouble of breaking into the house just to break a mirror and to write that message? How'd she get in? Does she have a key?

Unsure how April had obtained a key if she had one, Carmel went to the front door to check for pry marks. She didn't see anything on the door and wondered if there was another way to get in. There was a door at the back of the kitchen and she checked that one next; there were pry marks near the lock on that door. The lock didn't look very substantial anyway, she thought.

"This is probably how she did it," Carmel said to herself. "Carson is going to have to secure this place before someone comes in during the night and kills us all."

Chapter 46

With her mind on how to protect herself from a stalker, Carmel called the police station again when she hadn't heard anything in half an hour. This time she talked to Detective Davis. He advised her to secure the house and wait for him to get there.

Before he arrived, Carson came home and she told him what had happened, and then she took him to see the broken mirror and the message.

"I hope this is all she did," he said, staring at the mess. "That woman's a witch!"

Carmel's stomach flipped again at the thought of April having been inside the house. She knew she had to protect herself and her baby from that crazy woman. Thinking about the dog sitting job she would do after Christmas, she vowed to look for other work to help build a nest egg faster, so she could get away from this house; a house which was haunted by a ghost and stalked by a mad woman. She left Carson to wait for the Detective but told him to let her know when he arrived so she could tell him what she'd observed.

In her rooms she sat and stared at the walls, almost paralyzed by confusion and indecision. She felt so tired and wondered if it was stress, the pregnancy, or depression. Whatever it was, she didn't feel like moving. In a few minutes she fell asleep and slept about an hour before Carson summoned her to talk to Detective Davis. She told the Detective what had happened and once he'd left, she told Carson that she had Christmas shopping to do and headed out of the house. The last thing she wanted was to be alone with Carson right now and Edna hadn't come home yet.

Out in the night she drove to a Department store and wandered in, keeping her word to do some shopping. Going aimlessly up and down the aisles she thought about how different this year was from last. Last year she'd been shopping for Ash.

Would it really hurt anything if I bought him a present?

I wouldn't have to put my name on it. I could just leave it as a surprise for him.

Now her eyes scanned the shelves with a different intensity. Each item was evaluated as a possible gift for her soon to be ex- husband. Finally she saw a sweater that was just the kind he liked. He'd look very nice in it too; his blue eyes would match the pale blue thread mixed with darker blue that made up the pattern. On impulse she bought it and a box to put it in. She didn't have a lot of money but it was Christmas and she wanted to know that Ash had at least one gift.

Confused at her own impulsive behavior, Carmel found herself driving toward the old home she'd shared with Ash. It was December 23rd, not too soon to leave a present, she thought. At the house she saw that his car wasn't in the driveway. Hastily she took her gift which was well wrapped in plastic bags and left it leaning against the front door, in between that door and the storm door. Hurrying to get back in her car she stumbled and nearly fell on the wet pavement which was now turning to ice.

I have to remember the baby. No more running on slippery surfaces for me!

In her car again, Carmel started to wonder why she'd bothered getting a gift for Ash. He'd made it clear that he wanted a divorce; he'd hired a lawyer and all. She should forget about him, and that life; she should move on to a new future. It just made her so sad to think of him sitting in the house alone with no gifts to open and no one to care about him. Now he had a gift. She wasn't sorry about that. But as she drove she wondered what he'd think when he found a gift box wrapped in plastic between his doors. Who would he think had left it for him and why?

Back at the house in Ripley, Carmel saw that Ted Zimmerman was parked in the drive .He'd probably been with Edna earlier and had stayed for dinner. Dinner; she hadn't thought about dinner. Now that she had, her stomach rumbled unhappily. Was she too late to get a meal?

Edna set her mind at ease on that issue by announcing that she'd kept a plate of food warm for her. As Carmel ate she listened to the others who had remained in the dining room this evening instead of going to the living room as usual. They were talking about Tut Jackson again. Ted seemed disinclined to discuss the ghost; but that didn't stop the others. In fact, it almost seemed they overdid it in order to keep him anxious and nervous.

Carmel wondered why Edna and Carson would harp on a subject that made someone in the group so uncomfortable. Ted had not made it a secret that he felt threatened by the adventure into the unknown and that he didn't like ghost hunting. She wasn't so sure that she liked it either although she was curious about the ghost and why he was here.

"We'll check out the tapes again after Carmel finishes her food," Carson said. "I think we should think of some questions to ask the old reprobate."

"Ask him if he has the run of the house or if he has to stay in that room only," Edna suggested.

"I'd like to know if he's dangerous," Ted said. "Can he do physical things to us? Is he really a killer?"

"He might have been teasing us when he said he could have helped George Walker commit suicide. I don't think he could travel that far from the house, but we can ask him how far he can travel, if you want," Carson told Ted.

"I can go wherever I have a psychic connection," Tut's voice boomed into the dining room, and everyone jumped. "That means that all old George had to do was to think of me and build a pathway for me to go to him."

The group looked at each other and Ted moved protectively toward Edna. They'd forgotten that the ghost might be listening to their conversation.

"Now that we're all friends so as to speak, I can travel with the four of you to wherever you go. Isn't that nice? We're all one big happy family," Tut told the shivering group around the table.

Chapter 47

"I think Ted was right, we should have left the ghost alone," Edna said after all the furor had died down and the ghost was quiet. "He might be dangerous."

"At least he wants us to think so," Carson suggested. "Maybe, he's just playing with us to see how we'll react."

Carmel had been quiet but now she spoke. "We haven't done anything to him so why would he hurt us? George Walker killed him and sent his little girl away. Even if he did kill George, he had a rational reason to do it, revenge. We haven't given him any reason to hurt us and he hasn't."

The group seemed to be comforted by this version of things and some of the static of fear left the room.

"I still think we should drop this search for ghosts and let Tut go back to sleep." I liked it better the way it was before we knew about him," Edna said.

"I don't think he's going to go back to sleep. He's on a mission to find little Virginia and the only thing that's going to satisfy him is to find her, or at least to find out what happened to her," Carmel said.

"She'd have to be dead by now," Carson said. "How could we find her?"

"We could find out what happened to her, if she married and had kids and where they are, and we might find pictures to show him how she looked when she grew up. It won't hurt us to help him find his family," Carmel said.

She couldn't explain to the others why she felt an affinity to the ghost who had brought her to her senses during a very bad time. She'd like to do something for him, in return. Anyway, she thought, that's the only way this ghost is going to move on and leave the four of us in peace. If what he said was true, he could follow her anywhere she went and the others as well.

"Since you're so good at research, you should look into that then," Carson said.

"It wouldn't hurt if I had help," Carmel said.

"I'll help you," Edna said. "I've done some genealogy research and so I know a little about it."

"Can you meet me the day after Christmas when I get off work? We'll try to find a trail on Virginia here, but I might have to take a trip to Cincinnati and look up her Aunt in order to find her. I think the Aunt's name was Anita Williams, wasn't it?"

They agreed to meet on the 26th since everything would be closed on Christmas. After that they discussed Christmas plans. As usual, Edna would cook and Carmel would clean. Edna had already shopped for the food, she said, and she showed Carmel items for decorating the table for the big feast.

Carmel wasn't sure how she'd get through the holiday but it was something she needed to face. She planned to do it with the least possible fuss. It wasn't until she'd gone off to her rooms that she realized that she had to go take care of the dog first before she could meet Edna, the day after Christmas. She made a mental note to change the time they were to meet. She didn't know how long it would take her to do what she'd contracted to do since it would be the first day of her dog sitting engagement.

In Cincinnati, Ash returned to his house, after eating out with friends, to find the package stuffed between his doors. It had no name on it anywhere. His mind flew to Carmel and hope flared that maybe she cared for him just a little in spite of all that had happened. That thought was quashed immediately, because he knew that couldn't be true. She'd made it clear that she preferred another man to him. Still he was holding his breath as he opened the package.

Inside he found the sweater which was so like something that Carmel would buy for him that he knew the package was from her. She'd told him that she liked to see men wearing sweaters. It implied strength, comfort, and stability to her. When his softly sweatered arms were around her it evoked a memory of her father when she was little, she'd said once. Her father had left when she was pretty young.

He'd liked the comfort of sweaters too and had worn them often just for her. Many of his sweaters had shades of blue in them, which she'd said matched his eyes. Holding the sweater in his arms, feeling its' texture, Ash knew that he had to see Carmel again before the divorce went through. He couldn't just leave things like this, not knowing what had gone wrong, or why his Carmel had changed so drastically.

His attorney had told him recently that Carmel wasn't contesting the divorce, had agreed to everything asked, and more, and that it would be only a matter of weeks before the divorce was final. Now Ash knew that he couldn't let it go that easily. He and Carmel had to talk first. He had to find her. Remembering that the detective hired by his attorney had narrowed down the possible locations to Aberdeen, Ripley, or Manchester, Ash decided that he must do a search himself. Maybe the detective could also be put back to work trying to trace his missing wife.

Then he thought of another thing. Carmel had a P.O. Box address which she'd given to his attorney so he could send her official papers. What if he sent a letter to her at that address? Maybe she'd agree to meet him.

Ash pulled the sweater on as he sat down to compose a letter to Carmel. The sweater gave him a more connected feeling than he'd had in months. It was time to get some answers to the questions that had been haunting him and only Carmel could give those answers to him.

"Dear Carmel", he wrote, "We need to talk."

Chapter 48

Carmel made it through the Christmas celebrations with as much ease as possible. Everyone seemed to like the gifts she'd chosen. Edna had bought a bath and body gift card for her, Ted had given her a hat, gloves, and scarf set, and Carson had bought her a necklace and earrings set. She'd been glad that Carson's gift hadn't been more personal. It would have started Ted and Edna wondering if they weren't already, and she didn't want to have to deal with that. Even so, the jewelry seemed expensive and she wished he hadn't done it. However, to refuse to accept it would attract more attention then it would to just accept it and say "Thanks".

On the 26th, she left for work early and drove to the house where she was dog sitting. The dog was a large golden retriever and she let him outside while she prepared his food as the owner had instructed her to do. Goldie, the dog finished his business outside and scratched at the door just as she finished with his food and she let him in. This afternoon, and every day, the owner had requested that she take the dog for a mile walk so he wouldn't want to tear up anything in the house. She'd have to do that after work and before she met Edna. It was going to be a busy day!

At least things were slow in the office and she was glad for that. It was going to take some getting used to, to work the dog sitting into her routine. That reminded her to look for something else since the dog sitting job was for only two weeks. During her lunch break, Carmel checked Craig's list on the computer hoping to find something local that would work for her. Nearly everything was in Cincinnati though. She'd hoped that there would be a job cleaning or taking care of an elderly person, something that she could do part time, and could work into her schedule, but she didn't see anything.

Oh, well, I'll keep trying.

The dog wasn't as easy to walk as she'd hoped. He liked to run and tried to pull her along with him. Carmel was glad that the job was only for two weeks. It would probably not be good for her baby to be jerked around so much. She wondered if a different type of collar would curb that instinct to run. Maybe she'd purchase a chocker collar and try that tomorrow; she really didn't need to be pulled on. Carmel wondered what the man who owned the dog would think about that.

After she'd walked and fed the dog, she headed to the library to meet Edna. She'd forgotten to tell her that she'd be late so Edna was probably going crazy wondering where she was.

When she got there, however, Edna was deeply engrossed in a book about the river, and the people who'd worked on it, and she didn't seem to notice how late Carmel was. Feeling she'd had a reprieve, Carmel started searching newspaper records. She reviewed the article about Virginia Walker and the Bastardy Bond as well as the one she'd found earlier telling of Tut Jackson's murder and George Walker's suicide. This time she looked more closely at the article about George's suicide. There was an interesting note at the end of the article. It said:

Officials are not clear as to how Mr. Walker obtained the rope with which he hung himself, since he was searched before entering the cell and no rope was found and the cell didn't contain a rope prior to that. That chilled Carmel's blood and she directed Edna's attention to it. Edna flinched as if stung.

"That means our ghost could be telling the truth," she said. "Tut might have taken the rope to him and then helped him use it."

"Could be," Carmel agreed.

She re-read the part about Virginia, the baby, being sent to live in Cincinnati with her Aunt. The Aunt was listed as Anita Williams, but no address was given.

I might drive to Cincinnati and check the phone books and do some research on the Williams family. There should be records of Virginia under either the Walker, Jackson, or Williams name, depending on whether they adopted her or not.

Edna was still reading the book on river lore that she'd been on for some time. Suddenly, she looked up.

"I think I've found our ghost misbehaving," she said and directed Carmel's attention to a short passage about a gambling boat fight that had resulted in two men being gravely injured in a free for all over a card game. One of them was listed as Tut Jackson.

"Could be," Carmel agreed.

The ghost had presented her with problems, and she wasn't sure where it would all end up, but this ghost hunting business was entertaining at the least. So far all he'd done in her life was to help her, so she was hopeful that his benevolence would continue. Meanwhile, she enjoyed the mystery of his life and didn't mind the research she was doing in order to find his family. She found it to be diverting. It took her mind off of her troubles.

The article that Edna had found didn't cast any light on what had happened to Virginia, but it gave them a little more understanding of the character Tut Jackson had been. He must have been common for the times, a rip roaring gambler and man of the river, Carmel thought. However, he'd made it clear to her the first time he met her that he had a compassionate heart inside him, and his search for his baby only served to illustrate that.

That was the only thing they found in their quest that day. In spite of searching for another hour, neither found anything worth their time. Back at the house, they shared their findings with Carson and with Ted who was visiting.

"It's interesting," Carson said, "But it doesn't help us track down the baby."

"No, it just gives us a little better picture of what Tut's life was like," Carmel agreed.

"I've known some men like that in my time," Ted Zimmerman piped up, surprising them all. "They live hard and die young like the song says because they use up all that's in them before their life span's done. If you ask me, that kind of life's a waste of good air."

The others looked fearfully around the room, afraid that Ted had angered their resident ghost but all they heard after a minute was a booming laugh that echoed through the house like a drum roll.

Chapter 49

Carson had been apprehensive as the holiday approached and unsure what to do about Carmel. He'd decided on the necklace and earrings in order to say to her that she was still special to him but not to alert his mother and Ted to the past relationship between them. It was an expensive set of jewelry and he'd been afraid that Carmel would make a scene about accepting it but she'd been cool. It was a tricky situation, but as housemates he thought it was appropriate for everyone to share gifts like a family would.

If only Carmel would have accepted it, she'd have had an engagement or even a wedding ring for Christmas. He knew better than to try that right now, though. The necklace and earrings had been his next best idea. Carmel was cold with him at times and at other times she acted indifferent. It seemed that all the sparks that had flown between them at first had been extinguished. Now she behaved with him as if she was his sister or something. He hated it. His feelings hadn't changed.

Sometimes he thought that her feelings were the same too. Maybe she was just trying to impress on him how outraged she was that he'd imprisoned her for those weeks. It could be that she was trying to teach him a lesson. If that was the case, she'd succeeded. He would never do something like that again. It wasn't a strategy that would work for one thing. It just made matters worse.

He'd had dreams again last night about Amanda his first girlfriend and her tragic death. The horror of that loss would never leave him. He knew that. He had latched onto April Mayes after that tragedy because she was so different from Amanda. He'd thought that the difference would help him to adjust to his loss and put it into perspective somehow. It hadn't. He'd never really loved April and when she was unfaithful it hadn't cost him much to cast her aside. Her charge that he'd neglected her was true. His emotions had been so wrapped up in his tragic lost love that he hadn't had anything to give her at that time. Now he was glad that he hadn't stayed with April. She seemed to have some very evil behaviors. He wished that he'd never dated her.

Detective Davis had told him recently that he'd taken April in for questioning but she'd denied being at Carson's house or doing anything at all to harm or harass him. When the Detective had told her that someone had seen her there the last time, she'd sloughed that off as the jealous imagination of his current girlfriend.

"She's lying," April had said, leaving it as a she said, she said, situation with no proof available that April had been at the house. She'd even accused Carmel of breaking the mirror and leaving the message in lipstick herself.

"I can't do anything with what I have right now," the Detective told Carson.

Now Carson was driving toward Cincinnati, and he thought a car was following him. It wasn't the car that April had been driving when he saw her last but she could have bought a new one or be using a friend's. The car in his mirror was making him uncomfortable. Thinking that he'd make a few unusual turns to try and lose the other vehicle or at least to see if he was being followed, Carson turned right and then left at a side street on the edge of Cincinnati. The red car behind him made the turns too.

Surely she wouldn't pick a red car to try to follow someone in; that would be certain to draw attention. But then maybe she'd believe that I'd think just that.

Still the car stayed with him. Risking that he'd be late to the job he was supposed to do this morning, Carson did a series of didos that finally lost the other vehicle. Wondering what that had all been about; he proceeded on to downtown Cincinnati, and the job he'd been hired to do.

Ash was working at home when he got a call from his attorney saying that the Detective he'd hired had spotted a car which he believed belonged to the man Carmel had been seeing, but he had lost it at the edge of Cincinnati. He'd planned to follow the man in hopes of being led to where Carmel was.

"He should stay near the place where he lost it in case the man comes back through there this afternoon then," Ash suggested.

"He didn't think that would work, because he believes the man saw him and lost him purposefully. That means he didn't stay on his regular route."

"Ok, then. Thanks for the information. Like I told you a couple of days ago, I want a chance to talk to Carmel before we let this divorce go through. Try to hold up on that if you can. I've written to the PO Box address that she gave you and I hope she'll call me or at least write to me when she gets the letter. Do you think the Detective you hired could stake out the mailbox until she comes to get her mail?"

"It's going to cost a lot to do that. We pay him by the hour and it would take hours of surveillance and then he might still miss her. I doubt that she comes every day."

"Ok, for now we'll just wait and see if she responds to my letter," Ash said.

In Ripley, Carmel had finished her dog sitting chores and was on her way to check her mailbox before going home. She hadn't been there in days and by now she hoped the attorney Ash had hired had the final papers ready so she could agree to everything and get that portion of her life behind her. She pulled up at the post office and parked behind a red cavalier. Inside the post office she fished the letter out of her postal box and without looking at it, put it into her purse and went back to her car. Driving to a fast food restaurant she went inside and ordered a cup of coffee. Then she took out the letter.

It was a shock to see that it was from Ash instead of his attorney. When she'd recovered from that she started to read it. What the message boiled down to was that Ash wanted to talk to her before the divorce was final. He wanted her to explain what had happened, he said, so that he could have peace of mind.

And if I have to talk to you, I'll lose any peace of mind I now have, Carmel thought.

Her mind in turmoil, she sat there for over an hour, thinking, before she headed back to Ripley.

Chapter 50

It was a month later and Carmel had finished her dog sitting job and set that money aside. She'd also managed to save an additional $400.00 making a total of $500.00 hidden away in her nest egg. Tut was getting worried. It wouldn't be long until Carmel would be leaving here at this rate. He didn't want her to leave. Once again the baby would be taken away. It reminded him of his own loss. He could understand why she didn't want to tell Carson about the baby and it wouldn't be long before he would guess, but Tut was desperate to prevent Carmel from going anywhere. He knew where her nest egg was hidden. He thought maybe he'd take it soon. If she didn't have that, she couldn't go anywhere.

After the letter from Ash, Carmel had agonized for days about what to do. If she talked to Ash she couldn't lie to him. She'd tell him everything. Even about the baby if he asked; or the subject came up somehow. In her mind that meant that she couldn't talk to him at all. She wanted him to think of her kindly and remember all the good. If she had to explain what had happened, he'd never see her in the same light again. He'd hate her, if he didn't already. She wasn't good for him and it was best that he move on to find someone who deserved him. She didn't.

As the days went on, it got easier to put it off and then it seemed like she shouldn't contact him after all the time that had passed. She checked her mailbox weekly but no papers arrived from his attorney. What was up with that? No more letters came from Ash either which helped her with her conscience.

She hadn't found another part time job yet but she was still looking. She'd also never gone to Cincinnati to search records in order to trace Virginia Jackson. One problem was that she worked weekdays and by the time she'd get off work and drive that far, she might not be able to do much research.

Today, however, she'd left work two hours early and was headed toward the city where she'd lived for many years. Once she'd called it home. Now she dreaded going there. The streets which she'd known well now seemed haunted and different to her.

She arrived at her destination and settled herself in for some tedious reading and sifting of information. First she checked for a marriage license for Anita Walker and a man by the last name of Williams. She found that pretty easily. Anita Walker was married to Harry Williams in 1889. That meant that she hadn't been married too long when her sister died, her father murdered her sister's husband, committed suicide, and she was left to raise the orphaned baby, Virginia.

Poor Anita; she didn't have it easy either, did she?

She lost a mother, sister and father; her entire family.

Carmel reflected on how senseless the entire thing had been. Virginia had fornicated with Tut Jackson and become pregnant. That alone was a tragedy in those days. Tut had married her with a shotgun at his head, so he'd probably resented that. Then poor Virginia had died, her father shot her husband and then died himself. Almost an entire family wiped out because of a chain of circumstances started by one forbidden love affair. She thought of her own situation and it felt similar to her. So far no one was dead but everyone had enough grief to swamp them because of one forbidden love affair. She groaned.

"Are you all right," the librarian asked her. She was restoring books to a shelf nearby.

"I'm fine. I was just thinking of something sad," Carmel said.

"Are you finding what you need?"

"I'm trying to find information on an orphan girl who was sent to live with her aunt here in Cincinnati in around 1890."

"Is she an ancestor of yours?"

"No, I'm doing research for a friend."

"You might look ahead 18 to 20 years for a marriage license. That would tell you who she married and what her married name was."

"That's a good idea. I'll check this book on marriages from 1900 to 1950. She should be in here if she got married in Cincinnati."

The woman nodded and moved to another shelf farther away. She seemed to be finished with the conversation. Carmel went over the list of names for Walker and as expected found nothing. She was sure that Virginia would have carried her father's name unless she was adopted and the name changed. Under Virginia Jackson she found a listing for someone of that name who was married in 1918 to a man named Harold Stone. She also found one that was married in 1921 to a man named John Marlowe. Well, that's great. Now I have two of them. Which one is my Virginia? She agonized over how to determine which Virginia was the right one. The librarian was back now and asked her if she'd had any luck.

Carmel told her the problem and the librarian suggested that she try to find the actual marriage certificate. It would probably tell who Virginia's parents were.

"How do I do that," Carmel asked.

"Well, you can go to the Health Department here or to the Historical Archives in Columbus. I'd go here if it was me," the woman said.

"I'm not sure if the marriage license would give her real parent or her Aunt and Uncle who raised her," Carmel mused.

"It doesn't matter if you know both names. You'll be able to identify the girl as the right one," the librarian said.

After obtaining an address for the Health Department from the helpful woman, Carmel headed back toward Ripley. Out on the open highway she noticed that a car seemed to be following her and she thought of April Mayes immediately. Instead of leaving Cincinnati, she headed down a series of alleys and took a number of turns until she was pretty sure that the car was no longer behind her.

"Soon," she told herself. "Soon you'll have enough money to rent a place and leave Ripley. "Your nest egg is growing with every pay and it won't be long. You can leave all this craziness behind you and get on with your life. No more April Mayes, no more ghost, I hope, and no more men in your life."

Chapter 51

At dinner they discussed the new information and Ted volunteered to take Edna down to the Health Department in Cincinnati to search for the marriage certificates for the two Virginia Walkers. Edna was excited to be doing the research and Carmel was glad someone else could do it while she was at work. She couldn't be taking time off, and the search needed to be done during weekdays at a time when she should be at work.

"Is there anything else I need to look for while I'm there," Edna asked.

"If you find out which is the right Virginia, assuming that one of them is the right one, you could look for children born to her and to her husband in a year or so after the marriage," Carmel told her. "If we can trace the children, some of them might still be living"

"What if they are," Ted asked, "What are you going to do, invite them here to meet their grandfather, the ghost?"

"I might," Carmel said, "It depends on what kind of people they are and if they have an open mind. If not, maybe I can get pictures of Virginia and how she looked when she was young, then again when she grew up, as well as pictures of her family. Tut would like to see how his daughter and her family turned out."

"I like your enthusiasm," Carson said, "But what will it accomplish to show the ghost his family. I mean, I know it will make him happy to see them, but how does that help us?"

"I'm trying to help him, not us. It's interesting to follow up on this story though. I'm curious to see what happened, aren't you?"

Carson admitted that he was curious.

"I contacted a man who studies these things today," he said; he wants to come here next week to listen to what we have on tape and to interview us. We might even be on TV."

"Not me!" Carmel said, "I don't want to be on TV."

"Me neither," Ted chimed in.

"I think it's pretty great to have made contact like this with a ghost. Most ghost hunters are lucky to get a scraping sound or a white light. We've got him talking to us on tape. That's fantastic! I want to share this break through with the world," Carson argued.

Outside the wind picked up to a howl, Carmel shivered remembering the ghost and his taunt about having helped George to commit suicide. Although she had a hard time thinking of Tut as a murderer, it was possible that soon after he'd been shot by George Walker, he'd acted out a desire for revenge, taking the life of the man who had shot him.

It would have been a crime of passion with a new twist.

Whoooo the wind whispered in a low roar and suddenly Carmel wanted to change the subject. All this talk about ghosts was making her nervous. As the wind whistled and shivered in the trees outside, its voice almost talking to them in a threatening way, Carmel tried to focus the conversation on something else.

"I think someone was following me today," she said.

"What kind of car," Carson asked. "I thought a red car was following me about four weeks ago. I lost it though."

"I don't know, but it was red. I lost it eventually, but it took some doing. Do you think April is following us?"

"That's what I thought. If I'd been sure about it, I'd have called the police but she's clever and doesn't give me any proof that the police can use. She didn't have that kind of car the last time I saw it though. This was a red Cavalier that followed me."

"It makes me nervous. Do you think she'll try to actually hurt one of us," Carmel asked him. "You know her, what will she do?"

"I wouldn't have said that she was dangerous before all this started, but now I think she might be. If you see her out somewhere, you should be very careful and try to avoid her if you can."

"It's not like I'm trying to seek her out," Carmel replied sarcastically.

Finding that the new topic of conversation was as unpleasant as the first topic, Carmel excused herself to clean the kitchen and then went to her rooms. The wind still seemed to have a voice tonight as it whipped against the house. She'd bet that if she could see the water in the river it would be blown into a white foam on top. The ebb and flow of wind with its various sounds was ominous, and she was afraid. When she got into her covers she covered everything, even her head.

Things looked different the next day when she headed out to her job. The sun was out and the newsman had said it would be in the 40s today. Carmel suddenly wished she could play hookey instead of going to work. Ohio weather certainly was temperamental and who knew what tomorrow would bring.

Maybe I can do something after work. I'd like to go fishing or take a walk along the river. I haven't done that for so long. Since Edna does the cooking, it won't hurt if I'm a little late as long as I'm there for dinner.

Wanting to take a holiday was unusual for Carmel these days. Often she didn't feel well. The doctor had told her that this was normal when a woman was pregnant. She was glad that she hadn't had the usual morning sickness. That would have been hard to hide from her house mates and one or both of them would have guessed that she was pregnant. So far she wasn't showing and that was a good thing. To help keep her weight down, she'd been careful of her diet, trying to buy herself a little time. Still she was coming up on three months in a day or so and it was time to leave Carson's house.

This morning she'd counted the money in her nest egg and found that she had $800.00. That wasn't much to go on her own and rent a house, but maybe she could get a sleeping room at first. She also had to start thinking about a new job. Carson knew where she worked and she didn't want him to be able to find her once she left.

Another idea she'd had was to see if she could find a place where she could exchange assistance to an elderly or disabled person for room and board. She could clean house, prepare meals and help that person with what ever was needed, which would save the cost of rent and food until she could get on her feet.

Feeling pressure from all sides, Carmel wondered how she'd gotten herself into this mess. She'd practically made herself homeless through the choices she'd made, and she didn't like the feeling.

I should be grateful that I have a roof over my head and a job. The rest of it will work out if I do the right thing.

With that firm admonition to herself, she climbed into her car and prepared to put her nose to the grindstone no matter how tempting the warm air and sunshine.

Chapter 52

Ash had taken a day off and he found himself heading toward Aberdeen where Carmel had a PO Box. The Detective had reported seeing a woman who he thought might be Carmel at the Post Office but he'd lost her. Ash still didn't know where she lived. It must be Aberdeen though since that was where she got her mail.

Wouldn't have to be Aberdeen, she might be trying to throw me off if she doesn't want me to find her. I hoped she'd respond to my letter, but I guess life can't be that simple.

Ash was nervous and restless. That's why he'd taken the first day off work in a long time, just to try to sort out some of his restlessness. It was tax time and as an accountant, his busiest season, but Ash couldn't concentrate. Maybe if he gave in to his desire to look for his run away wife, he would be able to cope better tomorrow.

The day was beautiful and he wondered how they had become lucky enough to have a day like this in the middle of the winter. It felt more like spring than winter and he could believe that things were going to get better as long as he didn't dwell on the facts. He thought he'd drive on to Manchester and look it over and then check out Ripley before returning to Aberdeen which seemed to be the most likely place for Carmel to be.

At a café where he stopped on his way, Ash sat watching a woman complaining about her coffee to the waitress. His own coffee was fine and Ash figured the woman just wanted attention.

"You served my coffee in a cold cup. Take it back and heat the cup," the woman said.

"I don't understand. The coffee is from the urn which is on the burner and quite hot," the waitress said.

"I want you to take this cup, fill it with hot water and let it set until the cup is hot, then pour the water out and put the coffee in the cup after the cup is hot," the unhappy customer said, as if that made perfect sense.

"People," Ash thought, as he watched the waitress comply with the woman's demand.

He looked at his image in the mirror in front of his booth. Someday, maybe he'd look in the glass and see that the wretched shadows had disappeared, his sorrows had become smooth, and his pale eyes were charged with bright excitement again. He remembered how Carmel's fingers had touched his hands, his face, and left him happy and serene.

But that's all in the past.

Right now I need to find her and get some answers.

After that I guess we'll go our own separate ways.

He thought of Carmel again, remembering her flawless hands, her instruments for pleasure and for music. Those slight fingers were gifted, and with them she could make music burst into smooth, sweet song, once the ivory was touched. He wondered if she even played the piano now. It would be a shame for her to stop.

Ash had believed that he and Carmel would grow old together. The dream had died a terrible death, thrashing, and denying the truth, which was that Carmel didn't want to be with him anymore. It had hurt beyond description but Ash knew he had to go on and figure out a new life for himself. He thought he could do that once he knew what had happened. It seemed to him that this crisis had dropped out of the sky without warning.

He'd shed some spiteful tears in the beginning, creating a sour fruit of furious despair inside himself. It had all seemed so unfair. His anger had been a maelstrom of fury against himself, Carmel, and the unknown man who had stolen her from him. Now he sought quiet pools of blueness to ease his pain. To make it all right, he needed to talk to Carmel one last time.

Ash was no longer amused or magically transformed by scenes of their past, scenes that wove themselves through threads of past desire. Those thoughts brought tingling to his nerves as his hopes had changed and died. They had become uncomfortable. Now he just wanted to find her, talk to her and then try to wash her memory out of his system.

Shaking his head to himself as he paid for his coffee, Ash went back to his car and continued his trip along the river. He remembered reading somewhere that Johnny Apple- seed had come down the river on his way toward Indiana. He'd carried a bag of apple seeds for planting. His idea was to help the pioneers who were traveling westward by providing a food source for them. Supposedly many apple trees that still grow in Ohio and Indiana were planted by him. Ash wondered what would start a man on a mission like that.

Maybe that's my problem. I no longer have a mission.

As he drove by the water he stared at it thinking about the men and women who'd traveled that river, had learned to read its natural indicators through the color, sound, and movement of the water. They were pioneers, gamblers, and workers on barges and riverboats. Many families had traveled down the river on the way West. Ash felt a tug of interest in the river lore, but it wasn't that strong. His mind was too perturbed. Why couldn't he feel a connection with Camel if she was somewhere nearby? In the past he would have been able to sense her presence, he thought.

After spending some time in Manchester, Ash headed back toward Cincinnati. As he drove through the streets of Ripley, he thought he saw Carmel's car. It was on a main street heading west. He fell in behind it but another car blocked him and suddenly he found himself two cars back. Trying not to lose her, he managed to get in front of one of the cars but the other one was still between him and the car he believed to be Carmel's. He couldn't get around the driver of the car between them. Meanwhile the car he thought was Carmel's turned right and by the time he got to that street, he couldn't tell which way it had gone.

Frustrated and anxious, Ash pulled to the side of the street and sat there, too disturbed to drive. He had been so close! He knew that was Carmel's car. Ripley was one of the three towns the Detective had said would be where they'd find her, and he knew he had found her… but then he'd lost her again!

Starting his car, Ash drove around and around the streets of Ripley but he couldn't find the car he'd seen. For all he knew she was from Aberdeen and had headed back there while he was driving in circles. Confused and nervous, Ash finally turned back toward Cincinnati, no better off than he'd been when he started out this morning.

Chapter 53

Carmel panicked when she saw a car behind her that looked like Ash's car. The panic caused her to bolt into full flight when she caught a glimpse of the driver and was sure it was her husband. Turning and turning and turning again, she ran north out of town hoping he wouldn't follow her. She pulled down a lane toward a farmhouse and watched to see if his car would show up; it didn't. Before she started the vehicle again she waited another ten minutes hoping the people who lived in the house wouldn't come out and question her as to why she'd parked in the middle of their lane.

Finally she pulled back onto the road and started toward Ripley. If it was Ash, he had to be looking for her. If he was looking in Ripley, he must have traced her to the town, somehow. Fear chilled her extremities as she felt an even more compelling need to get away from the house in Ripley and from Carson, to find a place of her own where it would be impossible for the men to locate her. The pressure of the growing baby, the eerie presence of the ghost, the stalking by April Mayes, and her discomfort with the man who had imprisoned her, were all problems that were now topped by her fear that Ash was about to find her.

She thought she'd die if she had to face Ash!

Carmel pulled into the driveway and was immediately aware that the police were there too. What had happened now? Fearfully, she looked around her. The officers must be in the house. She didn't see anyone. Had April been at it again? What had she done this time? Hesitant as to whether to go inside or to drive away and return later, she decided to go in because she was tired. If she could arrange it, she'd just head off to her rooms and avoid the excitement. She could find out what happened later.

It didn't work that way. The two Detectives, who'd been here before, Smith and Davis, were in the living room as was Carson, Ted and Edna. They were examining the window and discussing what had happened. Carmel sidled up to Edna and whispered,

"What's going on?"

"Someone threw a big rock through that window. It had a note wrapped around it and held with a rubber band," Edna whispered back.

"What did the note say?"

"Ask me later," Edna said, returning her attention to the others.

The Detectives had not acknowledged her presence and now they seemed to be preparing to leave. Maybe she could slip away to her room as she'd planned. Carmel turned and slowly started to exit the room.

"Ms. Simpson!" one of the men said.

"Yes?"

"You should see this," Detective Davis said.

Carmel moved reluctantly toward him. He was holding out a squashed and dirty piece of paper.

"This stalker seems to have it in for you," he said.

Taking the paper, Carmel unfolded it and read the words printed on it. It said:

Carson,
You'll never marry that woman
You'll see her DEAD in her casket first!

Carmel shuddered while Carson walked toward her to put a comforting hand on her arm, looking upset and shaken himself. He stood looking at her; she looked around the room at the others and saw that she was the center of attention, everyone wanting to know how she was taking the threat.

"It must be April again. She believes that you and I are in a relationship so she's jealous and wants to scare you away. Don't worry about her," Carson said, patting her arm.

"I disagree. I think you'd better worry," Detective Davis said. "This is how it starts with minor stalking events and then it escalates. You need to watch out for whoever's been doing this. Unfortunately we still don't have anything to go on unless we can lift some prints off this rock."

"We all know its April Mayes," Carson said angrily.

"She tops our suspect list, but we can't prove it in a court of law. She'd walk," the Detective said in defense.

"There has to be something you can do," Carson grumbled.

Carmel stood mesmerized by the web surrounding her. What a total mess! Believing it was best to think carefully before she acted, she didn't say anything. The detectives left then and she was alone with the others who were preparing for dinner.

"I don't think I'm hungry," she said.

"Oh come on, you aren't going to let April get to you, are you? Come sit down and have tea with us at least," Carson cajoled.

Not wanting to attract any more attention to her, Carmel agreed. Her mind was racing, trying to find a way out, but she kept hitting obstacles. She would go to her room later and check on her nest egg, then figure a way to get out of this situation using the money she'd saved. Right now she was going along with the group to get along and not let them know how upset she was.

Maybe she could find housing with a disabled or elderly person in exchange for services. That would be the very best thing. It wouldn't matter that she was pregnant unless the person required heavy lifting or had a disease that was contagious. But how about a job; she had to find a job somewhere else, a place where Carson wouldn't know how to find her.

I could quit my job and only work for the person who is disabled if I had room and board, but that leaves no money to pay the doctor or the hospital to deliver my baby.

"Why does life have to be so difficult?"

She realized that she'd said these words aloud when Edna said,

"It ain't no rose garden is it?"

"No," Carmel agreed, "It isn't."

After cleaning the kitchen as usual, Carmel retired to her room. The first thing she did was go to get her nest egg so the concreteness of it could motivate her to action. She ran her hand inside the small area where she'd hidden her money and didn't feel anything. Alarmed, she searched again. Her hand came out empty.

The nest egg was gone!

Chapter 54

Carson had nightmare after nightmare all night. Once he screamed loud enough that his mother came running to his room, certain that April had returned to harm her son. Once awake, Carson assured her that it was nothing, just a bad dream which he sometimes had. He didn't feel like explaining what he'd been dreaming about and told her he couldn't remember.

"If you can't remember it, how do you know you've had it before," Edna asked reasonably.

"I didn't mean it's the same dream that I sometimes have, I mean I sometimes have bad dreams. It's nothing," Carson told her.

Finally convinced that her son was ok, Edna went back to her room. Carson huddled in his blankets remembering parts of the dream. How had April known just how to scare him the most? His dreams had been about Amanda again and the scene that had occurred at her casket. However, this time the face of the woman in the casket had changed and Carmel's face was the face of the dead woman. When he'd seen her in the casket, he must have screamed because that was when his mother came into the room.

Thinking back, he couldn't remember telling April about Amanda but maybe someone else had told her. Maybe he'd had these dreams during the time they were together and had said something in his sleep that alerted her to his tragedy. Otherwise, how did she know it would upset him this much to say what she'd said about seeing Carmel in her casket? How could she have picked the words so perfectly to destroy him?

What if he'd never started his affair with Amanda? Most likely she'd be alive today, living with her husband and children, enjoying life. She wouldn't have begun drinking with him, nor would she have driven the wrong way down a highway because she was drunk out of her mind. In a way he'd destroyed her. Now, he was on the brink of destroying Carmel. He'd never be able to live with himself if anything happened to her, especially if it was because of choices he'd made.

He contemplated the state of his relationship with Carmel. April was sure they were an item; he'd caused her to think that in order to get rid of her. They would be an item if he had his way about it, but Carmel seemed to be drifting farther and farther away from him. He'd made a fatal mistake when he'd locked her in the apartment for all that time and nothing, it seemed, was going to undo it.

But she's still here. As long as she's here there's hope that we can get back together as a couple. I think Mom would like that. She likes Carmel.

Remembering how his mother had come to him in the night to comfort him as she had when he was little, Carson felt ashamed of the way he'd pushed her out of her own house so he could bring Carmel here and imprison her. Both actions had been wrong and he'd probably never be able to erase the impact they'd had on his life or the lives of others.

He wondered if he should secure his house better. It wouldn't stop another rock from coming through the window though. The doors were solid as were the window frames. Glass is always going to break when hit by a large rock unless he put safety glass in. He'd never known anyone to put that in their house. Even if he did, the glass would shatter if a rock hit it and have to be replaced. Too bad he couldn't keep a 24 hour watch on Carmel but she'd never stand for that and he had a job to consider.

You have to do everything you can to protect her. Otherwise, you'll never be able to live with yourself if something happens. Maybe you should hire a detective to follow her around during the day so she won't be attacked, and then you can make it a point to be around in the evenings to keep an eye on her.

This was the first thought he'd had that gave him any comfort and Carson was finally able to lie down and go to sleep with the feeling that there was something he could do to improve the situation.

He awoke stiff and tired at 7:00am which was an hour later than usual. It didn't matter too much though because he had some flexibility in his schedule. Dressing as fast as he could, Carson went downstairs for some coffee and an English muffin for breakfast, and then hurried off to work. As soon as he had a break he planned to look for someone to keep an eye on and protect Carmel during the times when he couldn't. He felt much better having made that decision.

Later he searched the phone book for private detective services and found a listing for a man he knew slightly, Brad Wallace. He'd done some computer work for him in the past. When he called Brad and explained that he was being stalked by an old girlfriend and that Carmel had been threatened, Brad agreed to start work the next day. It had been a slow time for him after the holidays and he was glad of the job, he said.

"I'll be at your house when she leaves in the morning and I'll stay with her until she returns to your house. You can take over from there."

"Don't let her see you. She wouldn't like it that I'm doing this," Carson said.

"I'll be discrete. How often do you want me to report?"

"How about every evening about 10:00; you can give me a call." Carson said.

After he hung up Carson wished he could tell Carmel how concerned he was and what he'd done to ensure her safety, but he knew she'd object. It would have to be his secret and Brad's until some time in the future when he hoped he could once again have a loving and trusting relationship with Carmel.

Sighing, Carson wondered if that time would ever come. He feared it never would.

Chapter 55

With everyone in the house upset for one reason or another, it was a breath of fresh air to them when Edna and Ted brought some new information to the dinner table a few days later. She and Ted had gone to Cincinnati and hit pay dirt when they found Virginia Jackson, daughter of Tut Jackson and Virginia Walker, marrying Herbert Mills. She married him in 1910. The other Virginia's that Carmel had found had been the wrong ones. Other records showed the births to this couple of Robert Mills in 1920 and of Betty Mills in 1922.

"If this is the right family, why did they wait so long to have children," Carson asked, skeptically.

"It could have been economic or something else. Virginia seems to have been a sort of feminist; maybe she didn't want children until she'd accomplished some of the things she planned to do. I saw a report that she was involved in some of the early women's rights movements. Seems like she was a regular Carrie Nation," Edna said.

"Maybe she got pregnant by accident the first time and then decided the baby needed a sibling, so she had another child," Carmel suggested.

"That could be," Ted chimed in.

Edna told them that Ted had really gotten into the research and had been a lot of help to her in her quest for information. She'd been impressed with his new found skills.

"Well, that's great, but how do we find Virginia's children," Carson said.

"That was the easiest part," Ted said proudly. "I looked in the phone book! I found Robert and called him."

"Really," Carmel said, eyes flashing with interest, "What did he say?"

"He told me his sister lived in Dayton and that his mother had died in 1950 with a brain aneurism. I debated whether to tell him about the reason we were looking for his family and then I said to myself, 'Why not'? I told him about our ghost and how we'd uncovered his family story. Instead of hanging up on me, he was full of questions."

"What kind of questions," Carmel asked.

"He wanted to know everything I could tell him about his Grandmother and Grandfather, for one thing."

"Does he want to come here and see if Tut will talk to him," Carson asked.

"Better than that, he thinks his sister would be interested too. He said that even if his Grandfather didn't talk to him, he'd like to see the house where his mother was born and where his Grandmother and her parents lived."

"This is so exciting," Carmel said, forgetting for a moment that she didn't plan to be here. "When are they coming?"

"Next week, if that's ok with everyone," Ted said proudly.

"That reminds me," Carson said, "The parapsychology researchers or ghost hunters that were going to come to see what we have and listen to the tapes, have postponed their trip. They won't be coming for two or three weeks, maybe longer."

"Is it ok for me to call Robert back and tell him to come next week," Ted asked.

"Yes, and tell him to bring any pictures he has of the family and of his mother, even of Tut and Virginia, his Grandparents, if there are any available," Carson said.

Carmel had been in a fury for days after finding her money gone. She'd made a trip to the bank and opened a savings account the next day. Thinking Carson had taken her money, either because he thought she owed it to him for room and board, or to keep her from leaving, she had been so furious with him that she hadn't said two words to him in days. She hadn't confronted him though; that would involve talking to him and she didn't want to talk to him, see him, or hear him!

She had redoubled her efforts to find a way to leave his house and had located a woman who wanted a caregiver to live in with her mother who had OCD. She'd talked to the woman, whose name was Patricia, on the phone and was set for an interview with her after work tomorrow.

Her understanding was that the mother, Alice, was a hoarder. She was completely unable to throw things away, and her house was piled to the rafters with things normally thought to be useless. The daughter's idea was to hire someone to help; then she and that woman would clean the house while her mother stayed with another daughter. The person she hired would move into the house with Alice and on a day to day basis, confront her about what to save and what to throw away as a way of controlling the illness.

Patricia understood that Carmel worked another job, but said she was willing to let her continue that while working in the home in exchange for room and board. Carmel thought that would be good, and allow her to save the money she needed for medical bills and for the baby. She hadn't told Patricia about the baby in their phone conversation and wondered if she had to.

Maybe not!

Never having dealt with a person with OCD, Carmel planned to try to find a book at the library so she could bone up on the subject. Maybe she could also find something on line during her lunch break. She wondered how hard Alice would fight to keep her from discarding things she deemed useless, and how much leeway her daughter wanted to give her as the caregiver who would decide this daily. She'd have to ask that question at the interview. She didn't want to throw something away, have Alice pitch a fit, and Patricia say that she'd overstepped her bounds.

On the way to work she thought she saw a car following her but it didn't look like the car April had originally driven nor the caviler that she'd seen behind her another day. This car was a small silver car shaped somewhat like a small mini van. She couldn't tell the make, nor could she see the driver. It stayed with her all the way to her job and then parked nearby.

Is someone watching me? Is it April in a new car, or could Ash be having someone follow me to see what I'm doing?

She wondered when this nightmare would end for her and she'd finally get back to normal.

Chapter 56

Carmel forgot about the car that had been following her when she left work and headed toward the address that Patricia had given her. She was already parked when she noticed that the car was pulling in down the street.

Well too late now. I can't leave, ditch that car, and come back later or I'll be late for my appointment.

Casting her eyes toward the vehicle and the driver who remained invisible to her at this distance, she headed toward the door and knocked firmly. Her knock was answered by a tall woman who looked to be in her 40's and who proclaimed her self to be Patricia. She lead Carmel into a room so cluttered and stacked that the windows were blocked and there was only a very small space for the two of them to sit down.

"I thought that just the two of us would meet first and then if it looks like things are going to work out, we'll set up a meeting with Mom. She knows what my plan is and isn't very happy about it. To her it's like surgery. I'm going to surgically remove all her junk, and she finds the idea painful," Patricia said, laughing.

Carmel smiled nervously as she looked around. It was hard for her to imagine a house with stuff like newspapers and magazines, old junk mail and who knows what else packed in so tight there wasn't room to live but that was the case with this house. Alice must have a real problem, she thought.

Patricia was a pleasant woman with a sardonic smile in her dark grey eyes. She managed to make Carmel feel at home during the interview, which went well.

Patricia indicated that she would hire Carmel pending her mother meeting and approving of her housemate.

"As you know, my mother doesn't like this arrangement, but she knows I'm determined. She may test you a little before she agrees but I think she'll like you well enough. If she agrees, we're looking to have you move in about three weeks from now. Is that ok?"

Carmel chaffed at the delay but agreed that would be fine. She didn't know how much each week would affect her figure, never having been pregnant before, but by watching her calories and carefully choosing the clothes she wore, she thought she could make it that long without anyone finding out about the baby.

When she went to her car, she could still see the other vehicle parked down the street. Going the opposite way, she watched as the car pulled out and followed her. Deliberately being evasive, she stopped at three stores, getting out and going inside for five minutes or so and then returning to her car. Each time the other automobile fell in behind her a few minutes later.

No doubt about it. That car's following me!

She hated it that the driver of the car had seen her go to the house to which she might be moving. One reason she was leaving Carson's house was to get away from April Mayes. Would April pursue her to another location? She couldn't see why. If she wasn't in contact with or living with Carson, why would April care where she was or what she was doing? When she returned in a few days to meet Alice she would be certain that no one was tailing her. Carmel didn't want to lead the stalker to that address twice.

It was a few days later when a man and woman walked up to Carson's house and rang Carson's doorbell. Carson was all smiles as he opened the door to Robert Mills and his sister Betty. He invited them inside where Carmel, Edna and Ted were seated with cups of tea. After offering them tea and serving it, Carson started the conversation by discussing the events that had lead up to this auspicious meeting.

"And you are telling me that all of you have heard my Grandfather, Tut Jackson, speak to you," Robert asked.

Everyone nodded their heads.

"I can play a little of the tapes we've made," Carson suggested and you can hear for yourself."

He'd already set the tapes to the most interesting conversations and now he played them for the Grandchildren of the ghost. Brother and sister sat wide eyed and quiet as the tapes played. Everyone was caught up with breathless excitement and amazement, as they listened to the questions and answers on the tape.

Carmel couldn't believe that this was really happening. What were the odds that they would have been able to make contact with a ghost who was actually willing to communicate, and that as a result they would trace his family tree for him? How unusual that the Grandchildren of that ghost would be able to come back to the house where he and their Grandmother had both died, and with luck be able to talk to their dead ancestor?

I feel like I'm living in the twilight zone or in an Alfred Hitchcock movie.

When they had finished the tapes, the conversation resumed, the siblings asking every question they could think of.

"Do you think he would talk to us," Betty asked.

"Will you be afraid if we take you to the room he seems to like and ask him," Carson asked her.

"I might be a little afraid but I wouldn't miss the chance for anything," Betty said. The six of them trouped into the room, Betty and Robert carrying family photos to share if the ghost was interested. Taking the pictures from them, Carson laid them out on a table in the center of the room.

"Hello Tut," he said. "I've brought some pictures for you. I think this is you and Virginia around the time you were married, and here is a picture of your daughter after she grew up. I also have pictures of your grandchildren and great-grandchildren here."

The room was quiet. Carmel wondered if the ghost was checking out the pictures and verifying that they were legit. The picture of him and Virginia should do it, she thought. The silence went on minute after minute. Finally, Carson said,

"The newcomers here are your own Grandchildren. This is Robert and this is Betty. They are your daughter Virginia's children, all grown up now."

"Where's Virginia?" The voice boomed out so suddenly that everyone huddled together in fear.

"I'm sorry, Tut," Carmel said, "She died sometime ago, but she had a happy life. She was a strong woman and fought for women's rights, she married and had children. Virginia had a full life. Now she's on your side of things. You won't find her here on earth. She's moved on."

She hoped that what she'd told him was true and that Virginia had been happy. Her children seemed to think she was, according to the conversation earlier. Again the silence dragged on.

"Are you really my Grandfather," Betty asked shyly.

"I spect that I am," Tut said in answer.

"I'm glad to meet you," Betty continued timidly.

"And I am glad to meet you too," Robert said. "I'd shake your hand but I don't know how to do that.

"No need," Tut thundered, "What do you do?"

Since the question seemed to be meant for Robert, he answered,

"I'm an engineer."

"Ya drive a train?"

"No, not that kind; I build and repair things for the electric company."

"I worked for the school system teaching school," Betty told her unseen ancestor. "Most women work outside the home these days."

"What about your kids?"

"They're grown now and I'm retired," Betty said.

The visit lasted for two hours with Betty and Robert getting a very rare opportunity to speak to an ancestor who was on the other side of life. At the end they said goodbye and thanked everyone enthusiastically for the opportunity they'd had.

"You should come back again," Carson told them. He mentioned the team of experts who would be coming in a week or so to listen to the information he had gathered on tape and to see if Tut would communicate with them as he had with others.

"You are invited to join us if you want," he said.

"Call me," Robert agreed, "And we'll try to come."

Chapter 57

Tut had a lot to think about after he'd met his descendents, his own Grandchildren.

For all these years he'd agonized over what had happened to his baby. He knew his wife was dead and he'd mourned for her, but he'd felt a heavy responsibility for the motherless child and had been searching for the baby Virginia ever since. Finally he knew that his little girl had grown up and had a busy and rewarding life. She'd married and had children of her own, but now she was on the other side, no longer breathing oxygen, as he himself no longer had to breathe. They were both on the same side of life and that's where he'd find her.

His Grandchildren seemed to be good people, senior citizens now, soon to pass on to the other side as well. Robert was a big man like himself, now bowed a little by life and by his old bones and gray hair, but Tut could see that he'd been a fine looking man in his time. Betty looked a lot like her Grandmother would probably have looked had she lived long enough. How strange for him to have met his Grandchildren for the first time when they were an old man and woman!

The people in this house had helped him a lot by searching for his family and setting up the meeting. It had been a privilege to meet his family, see pictures of his daughter and son in law, even to look again at his own earthly image and that of his wife, taken so long ago. Even though he was dead, it comforted him to know that life does go on. The generations come and go; there must be a plan behind it. Carmel had helped him so much by doing the initial research on his family and he owed the rest of the people in this house as well. They suddenly felt like real friends to him; he hadn't had a friend for more than a lifetime.

Guilt was consuming him as he thought about what he'd done to Carmel. The money she had so carefully saved so that she could leave had been hidden away. Tut had known where she had put it. He was dizzy with anxiety about her using it to leave the house, taking her baby with her. He didn't want her to go. Waiting until the nest egg had grown to an amount that he thought would allow her to go on her own, he had then taken the money and concealed it in another place, where she couldn't find it. Now he felt guilty after all she'd given him. How could he make it up to her?

He checked in his secret place of treasures. There it was, the bills still folded as she'd left them. He also had a favorite knife secreted here, one he'd used in his life on earth; a flask that had been his father's, a lock of Virginia's hair and a set of Irish linen that had come from the old country in 1850 with his mother, were all hidden in his special spot.

Tut took the lock of Virginia's hair and put it into his bosom and fingered the flask that had been his father's first and then his. He'd drunk many a swig of whiskey out of that flask! The set of Irish linen that his mother had treasured so much was yellow now; it saddened him, knowing how much it had meant to Mother all those years ago. On the other hand, she'd be glad to know that it had survived for so long.

He thought about his parents, his wife, and baby. All of them had gone on to where souls are supposed to go, he guessed. Tut remembered the light that had beckoned him after his death. It had called to him and he'd thought he heard voices he knew asking him to join them. However at the time he felt he needed to find his baby, to take care of her, and his mind had been rigid with that effort. He wasn't going anywhere until he knew Virginia was safe.

Now he was starting to wonder if there might be a way for him to find that light again, to go with it and to find his loved ones. Suddenly it seemed to him that everything and everyone he cared most about were on his side of things, not on earth. Even his Grandchildren, Robert and Betty were old enough that they'd be joining him soon. It was time to find the others, and be united with them again, but how could he do it? Had he missed the boat? Was the shiny white light a one time only opportunity?

Tut was thoughtful as he settled himself in his favorite spot. It came to him that there might be things he needed to do before he'd be accepted by the light. He'd have to give Carmel her money back for one thing, and maybe correct any misperceptions that he might have fostered in his discussions with the group.

He'd think on it.

Chapter 58

Carmel felt antsy and nervous as she knocked on the door to the house where Alice lived. Patricia had called her yesterday and set the appointment for Carmel to meet her Mother today. Carmel had no idea what to expect although she'd done a little research on the hoarding syndrome.

On article had said that hoarders were often indecisive, perfectionists, and people who procrastinate. They often have an avoidance personality. Carmel had taken this to mean that maybe the person couldn't decide what to throw away so they kept everything and that being a perfectionist, they might not want to make the mistake of throwing away something needed. Perhaps the person would procrastinate and do nothing because she couldn't decide what to do. Procrastination was a way to avoid doing the wrong thing.

Her research had also stated that the person's problems would be very difficult to treat unless the person really wanted to change. She wondered if Alice would try to change or if she would fight it all the way. From what she'd read, behavior therapy does show benefits. She hadn't thought of herself as a therapist but perhaps she was or would be if hired. Patricia answered the door and led her to the same spot where an additional place had been made for a third person by piling the stacks around them a little higher.

"This is my mother, Alice," she said and Alice reached across the debris to shake her hand. "My Mother knows what I'm proposing to do and she's going to try to work with us, aren't you Mom?"

"I'll try," Alice replied.

Carmel saw that Alice was a short woman of around sixty years. Her hair was a red brown in color with some wisps of grey mixed in, and her cheeks were pale as if she'd not seen any sun in years.

"I'm sure we can work it out," Carmel said. "What do you do during the day?"

"I don't work if that's what you mean," Alice said. "I watch TV, cook my meals etc. That's about it."

"How about gardening, do you like to do things outside," Carmel asked looking at the washed out complexion on the woman before her.

"I used to," Alice said. "In the last few years, I can't seem to do anything. I just hide out here. I can't have company because of the mess and I can't seem to clean it up. I feel ashamed."

Seeing that Alice was in distress and feeling sorry for her, Carmel thought it was a good time to state that it was a new day and a new beginning.

"I hope that will change. It will be spring before too long and I think maybe we should have a garden if you feel up to it. That is if you approve of me moving in here."

"So the plan is that you and Patricia will clean the house while I'm at my other Daughter's house, then I'll come back to a clean house, and we'll try to keep it that way. Is that the plan," Alice asked.

"That's the way I understand it," Carmel said, looking at Patricia, who nodded.

"Do you think you'd be able to work with Carmel and accept her judgment as to what should be thrown away," Patricia asked her mother.

"I'll try," Alice said.

"I think that once we get the house clean, you should have a tea party or something and invite some of your old friends," Carmel suggested. "It will give you more motivation to keep things clean if you know you're going to have company regularly."

"How about that Mom, would you like that," Patricia asked her mother.

"We'll see how it works. All I can say is that I'll try."

"Can we give it a couple of weeks to get the place cleaned up and then you can move in," Patricia asked. "It's hard to tell now, but there's a room back there that's pretty nice if all the trash was out of it."

"That'll be fine," Carmel agreed although she was itching from the delay.

Back in her car, on her way to Carson's place, she thought she saw a car following her again. She hadn't noticed it for a few days, but there it was behind her. It was the grey car from before. At one point it got close enough that she could read the words Honda Civic on it. She got a glimpse of the driver who seemed to be male but couldn't tell anything about him. If it was a man, then it wasn't April Mayes. Who else could it be? Maybe it was April disguised as a man.

Trying to focus on something else, Carmel thought about the monumental task ahead of her. It would be a challenge to work with Alice and her hoarding habits. The research she'd done indicated that the OCD hoarder feels trapped by the mess, feels shame but can't fix the problem. Therefore they isolate themselves away from others to keep the world from seeing their shame, to block the world out.

There is a difference between a hoarder and a clutterer the books said. Hoarding is a psychiatric condition where the person obsesses over stuff. The stuff causes distress and discomfort and limits the person's ability to live a functional and normal life, but he/she can't throw it away. In the case of a clutterer which is shared by millions of people, the person could change him/herself if desired but just doesn't seem to have the motivation to do so. This person will not usually let the junk block normal life activities such as cooking, sleeping and bathing though, as the hoarder does.

Carmel thought that Alice fit the first category because she'd indicated that she wanted to change but couldn't. The mess had limited her life to where there was no room to cook, almost no room to use the bathroom and bedroom, and most of the time, Alice admitted that she slept in the one small space in the living area where the three of them had sat. She'd stopped gardening and seeing her friends and isolated herself.

And why think you're qualified to help a sick person like Alice, she asked herself. In answer, her mind said, *I'm not a doctor but the answer to this problem lies in common sense thinking. Maybe I can teach a little of that to Alice.*

She approached the house and heaved a sigh to see that Ted and Edna appeared to be the only ones there. She was still mad at Carson over her stolen money, as well as other things, and all she wanted was to get away from him. The car that had been following her was going slowly by when she got out of her car and hit the automatic lock.

It had been following her alright!

Chapter 59

Carson had been getting some interesting reports from Brad Williams. The reports hadn't been what Carson expected to hear. Instead of finding incidents of April Mayes following Carmel, as Carson had expected, April had been noticeably absent. However, as part of his report, Brad Williams had told Carson of trips that Carmel had made to a house a few miles away as well as the normal trips to the library, grocery stores etc. Brad had given the address to him and Carson had checked it out. Seeing the house had left Carson even more confused though because it was just an ordinary house, a little run down with dirty windows and junk on the porch. He couldn't imagine why Carmel would have gone there.

Since April hadn't shown up to plague or harm Carmel, Carson decided to stop the surveillance to save money, but to keep Brad on stand by in case something else happened. Meanwhile, he continued to wonder why Carmel had gone to that house. Could she have a male friend she was visiting, someone who lived there? Was the house a place where a co-worker lived? Carson decided to find that out on his own at some future date. Right now he and Carmel were pretty much at odds with each other. He didn't want to infuriate her further by getting caught checking up on her.

The parapsychology team was coming to the house tomorrow. Carson wanted everything ready for their inspection. Therefore, he'd taken a day off to review the tapes and re-set the equipment in the ghost room so if they were lucky enough to get Tut to talk to them, it would be recorded. He'd worked all day at this and thought he was as ready as he could be.

He'd decided to talk to the others about tomorrow's visit at dinner. It would be a Saturday so he and Carmel would both be off work. He knew his Mother would want to hear what the specialists had to say and he expected that Ted would be curious too.

Saturday at 1:00pm, two men and a woman walked up the steps to Carson's front door. They were the ghost hunters and scientists of the occult that he'd talked with on the phone. The team included Mary Weeks, Martin Short, and Melvin Oberlin. They had been on TV with their exploits before but didn't bring a camera crew with them today.

Carson was glad of that. He knew that Carmel was camera shy due to her situation and he wasn't ready for national exposure himself. He had called Robert and Betty Mills but the brother and sister weren't able to attend the meeting.

With everyone seated with a hot cup of coffee or tea in the living room, the group rehashed what had happened and once again listened to the tapes Carson had made. The team of experts seemed to be wowed by his success and said so.

"We've never been able to get anyone to talk to us like this. The most we get is a sound effect of some kind or a wail," Melvin said. "This is amazing."

Carson was pleased that he'd successfully outdone the specialists but he didn't say so. He didn't want to appear to be bragging.

"Maybe we can get Tut to talk to you," he said. "At least we can try."

Everyone trooped silently to the room and waited for Carson to speak to his pet ghost as Mary had called him early in the discussion.

"Hi Tut," Carson said, "We've brought someone else to see you."

Silence filled the space. Only a collective series of human breaths could be heard.

"Are you here," Carson asked.

Nothing happened.

"I was hoping you'd have something to say to these nice people," Carson explained. "They specialize in talking to people who've crossed over, people like you, and they really want to see you or hear you. Don't you have something to say to us?"

"Goodbye!" the voice thundered from a spot near the window. Everyone flinched at the loudness of the sound.

"What's wrong, don't you want to talk to us," Carson asked once he got his voice back.

"Goodbye...I'm going away."

"Where are you going," Carson asked.

He was thinking that finally he had a real ghost and now that ghost was going to leave him in the lurch. It wasn't fair. He tingled all over with the unfairness of it.

"To find Virginia!"

"Where is she," Carson asked,

But the ghost didn't seem to want to talk any more. Carson hoped Tut would come back but after he'd tried unsuccessfully for half an hour to get the ghost to talk to him again, the group went back to the living room.

"Could we borrow these tapes to make copies," Melvin asked.

Carson hesitated. He didn't want to let the tapes go. What if Tut never talked to them again? The tapes would be the only record they had of the ghost's existence.

"No, but I'll try to make copies for you," he finally said.

After the visiting ghost hunting team had left, the others settled in the living room to discuss what had happened.

"What do you think Tut meant about going away," Ted asked the others.

"Maybe he's decided to go where dead people are supposed to go," Edna suggested. "You know, into the white light and all of that."

Carmel didn't express any opinion, and Carson also kept his to himself. He was angry with the ungrateful ghost who had used them to find his family for him and was now going to leave right when Carson stood to gain some fame for having communicated with the spirit world. To the surprise of all, Tut's voice suddenly boomed into the room.

"I didn't kill George Walker."

"But you told us you did," Carson said after he got his mental balance. "Why'd you tell us you did?"

"To get your goat," Tut replied. "Anyway, I didn't say for sure. I said I might have helped him."

"Well, I'm glad you aren't a murderer," Carmel told the unseen presence. "Thanks for telling us the truth."

Carson was so glad to have his ghost back he didn't care what the ghost was saying. Tut hadn't gone away, and Carson could still make history as the first ghost hunter to have documented discussions with a talkative ghost. Not only that, but he'd been able to find a record of the ghost's life and to trace his family tree. Pretty amazing! Carson was inordinately proud of himself.

Chapter 60

Carmel went back to her room and slumped down in her chair in front of the TV. She was exhausted. Even though she'd been off work today on her regular job, she'd gone to Alice's house and worked for six hours helping her daughter clean and toss away things. After that had come the interlude with the parapsychologists and the discussions about and sessions with Tut Jackson. Now she was very glad to get off her feet. The baby was moving now and it kicked up its heels in agreement that rest was the thing.

"Look on your dresser," Tut's voice said.

Carmel jumped, shocked again at hearing an unexpected voice in the quiet of her room.

"Don't scare me like that," she said.

"Look on your dresser."

Carmel got up and walked to the bureau where she kept her clothes. On top of it was a wad of paper money which looked like the money she'd had to come up missing.

"I'm sorry," Tut said.

"You took my money? Why would you do that?"

"Don't want you to take the baby and leave."

Carmel felt like crying. She needed this money so bad. It was like a Godsend for it to suddenly materialize again in this manner.

"You said that all we had to do was think of you and we'd pave a trail for you to come to us," she said. "If that's true, you could have come to see me and the baby. Thank you for giving the money back. I need it.

"I have to go anyway."

"Where are you going?"

"I'm going where I'm supposed to go if I can find the way," Tut explained. "I think they'll tell me how once I make right as many things as I can."

Suddenly Carmel felt all alone. She would miss this ghost. Something told her that he really was going and wouldn't be back. He would find his way to Virginia, his wife, and Virginia, his daughter. It would be a happy ending for him. In a way she was jealous. There would be no happy endings for her, no matter what happened.

The days went by and they had no further contact with the ghost. Carmel went almost every day for a few hours of cleaning and tossing at Alice's house. They were making inroads into the piles of debris. She had put the money Tut returned to her with the other money in the bank and was feeling a little more secure.

Carmel felt somewhat sorry that she'd blamed Carson for stealing her money when it had in fact been taken by Tut to keep her from leaving. Somehow it was easier to forgive a ghost than it was to forgive a living man, though. She didn't talk to Carson about it. Why should she? She'd never confronted him in the first place. He didn't even know that she had money that had come up missing. He didn't know that Carmel had believed him to be a thief.

Alice's house should be clean enough for Carmel to move into it in a few days and she had gathered most of her stuff together so that when it came time to leave she could do it in a hurry. There wasn't any need to prolong the agony. The cleaner the break, she believed, the better. Any day now someone would notice that she had thickened significantly in the waistline. She hoped it wouldn't be Carson or Edna. If she could just get away before she had to face that problem, it would be wonderful.

She wondered about Ash. After having seen him that one day, she hadn't seen him again. She'd checked her mailbox frequently but there had been no mail from his attorney either. What was causing the delay to the divorce? When she was ready to leave the area she wanted to have all loose ends tied up. No divorce hanging over her head, no one trying to get visiting privileges with her baby, no one she owed any allegiance to left behind. Everything was going way too slow.

April Mayes hadn't been pulling any tricks on them lately either. Maybe she'd seen the light and was ready to move on to another man. It seemed clear that Carson didn't want to be with April; at least that's what he'd told everyone. But without Carmel around, she guessed it would be possible for him to rekindle his old flame after all, if he wanted to.

Carmel hoped the New Year was going to be a better one than this past year. So much had happened during last year that things had to get better. Although the situation she was in had partly been of her own doing, it had been Carson's action of imprisoning her for nearly two months that had created the worse disaster. She didn't make any New Year's Resolutions. That didn't feel right. She was going to take each day as it came doing the very best with it that she could, she decided. No one could do more than that.

Her dreams had become a seeking for what she used to have and had lost. At night she relived her life with Ash, re-creating the good times before life and work and separation had twisted them apart. Their lives together had been good once. She wished her baby was Ash's child, but they'd been together so seldom during the time it had been conceived that she was fairly certain that Carson was its father.

Perhaps if the baby had been Ash's child she would have told him about it and they could have shared parenting if nothing else. As it was, she couldn't face her husband and just wanted to cut the tie and drift away. It was easier not to confront all the pain; not to see the accusation in his eyes.

Chapter 61

Ash had taken to driving to the towns along the river, where he thought Carmel might be, on weekends and sometimes during the week. He'd become convinced that she lived in either Ripley or Aberdeen but he still checked out Manchester on these trips as well. He'd told his lawyer to hold the divorce until he found her and could discuss things with her. The lawyer had agreed reluctantly, advising him against it. To hold down costs, they'd stopped using the services of the Private Detective for the moment. Ash felt that he could learn as much on his own as the Detective had after his initial narrowing down of locations.

On this Saturday, Ash was in his car driving the now familiar path from Cincinnati to Ripley, Aberdeen and Manchester. He'd looked at the map and saw the town of Rome was farther East but thought that was too far and that he had no reason to check into it.

The sun was bright and the roads were dry but the temperature was in the twenties. Ash thought that as long as he stayed in the car he would be comfortable and at the moment he had no reason to get out of the car. As he drove through Ripley he wondered where Carmel might live if she was somewhere in this town. He drove up and down the streets looking for her car. Perhaps he'd luck out and find out where she was staying by finding the car.

He didn't find the car in Ripley and drove on to Aberdeen where he did a similar search with a similar result. In Manchester he did a half hearted search, feeling that it was all a wild goose chase. He knew he should be at home getting work done for his clients but his search for his wife had started to consume him. Ash just couldn't understand Carmel's behavior. She might be unhappy enough to leave him, even have an affair with someone else, that was believable, but he couldn't believe the coldness with which she'd treated him. It wasn't like her at all. He wanted to understand what had happened. He didn't think he could ever move on until he understood it.

In Ripley again, he had a sudden urge to go to the library. Carmel always liked to read and she might be at the library on a Saturday morning. In the parking lot, he saw a car that looked exactly like hers. His heart started thumping at a pace so fast that he thought he might be having a heart attack. His nerves jumped and twitched. Could that car be hers? Could he have found her at last?

Now he was afraid to confront her, afraid of what he might hear. If she could have been so cold and unfeeling toward him in the recent past, what would make her change and become the wife he'd loved again? It was likely that she'd tell him to go away, that she never wanted to see him again and refuse to discuss anything.

As he tried to get his nerve up to go inside the library and confront her, he saw Carmel coming out of the library with a couple of books in her hands. Acting on reflex, he jumped out of his car and ran toward hers. At first she didn't see him and when she did she dropped one of the books. Both reached to pick it up, bumping heads.

Standing, rubbing his head, as he handed the book to Carmel, Ash felt the nervous fear coming back. She looked completely taken off guard and shaken too. He could see, even though she had a heavy coat on, that she'd picked up some weight. Apparently she wasn't missing him too much. She was hardly wasting away to nothing. They stood staring at each other and then at the ground, neither knowing what to say. Finally Carmel broke the silence.

"Are you bringing me the final divorce papers?"

"No, I wanted to talk to you first."

"What is there to say? You want a divorce, and you have just cause. Let's get it over with."

"I want to know why." Ash said. "It's cold out here. Will you sit in the car with me for a minute so we can talk?"

"I don't have much to say. You know that I had an affair with another man. You filed for divorce as you had every right to do. There's no need to rehash it," Carmel said. She made no move to get in his car.

"Please hear me out. Won't you sit with me for a little bit? I think you owe me that," Ash said.

Carmel rubbed her eyes, thinking about what he'd said, and then responded to his request and moved toward the car. If they had to talk about this, it would be better somewhere warm, she guessed.

"Will you please tell me why you didn't talk to me, why you turned to someone else instead," Ash said when they were inside with the heater running.

"It doesn't matter," Carmel said. "I did and that finished us."

"It matters to me."

"You were never around. When I came home from work the house was empty. We didn't have any together time on weekends even. It was like we just co-existed. You didn't listen to what I had to say, what was important to me, so why should I worry about what was important to you."

"And this other man listened to you?"

"He listened and thought that everything I said and did was special. He appreciated me."

"So, as soon as the divorce is final, you plan to marry him. Is that it?"

"No. You're the one who filed for divorce. I'll go away somewhere where I won't be an embarrassment to you."

They were silent as Ash considered what he had wanted to say for so long and now couldn't remember to ask. Carmel fidgeted and he expected her to open the door and bolt out of his life again if he couldn't come up with something.

"Why did you come and get your stuff and not stay to talk to me. You've been pretty cold in the way you've done this. I don't deserve that. I might have neglected you, but you know I loved you. You left without saying why, leaving the police to think I'd murdered you or something, and then you come and take your things and leave your keys without a word. You left no note, nothing."

"I'm sorry about that," Carmel said and he could see the tears running down her face. "I saw my things setting there and knew you were going to throw them out. I took them so you wouldn't have to bother. I didn't think you'd want to hear from me after all of this."

"I wasn't going to throw them out or give them to a thrift store or anything. I was going to store them in the basement where I wouldn't see them and have a constant reminder that you were gone."

He knew he had some tears of his own and he reached his hand to put it on Carmel's arm while turning his head to look the other way so she wouldn't see his pain. She was quiet and after he got himself under control he asked,

"Why didn't you talk to me about this before you left me?"

"Because I couldn't," Carmel said. "I didn't have a choice."

Ash couldn't see how that could be true, but he tried to go along with her. After all she was finally talking to him and that was good, even if she was trying to justify behavior that had no justification.

"Tell me about it," he said.

He was unprepared for the gush of tears and words that exploded out of Carmel. She told him everything, about how she'd wanted to break the relationship with Carson off so she could save her marriage, and how Carson had made a prisoner of her, preventing her from returning to him, only to finally let her go after all the damage was done. She even told him about the baby.

"Then come home, we'll raise the baby together," Ash said, and wondered why he'd said it. However, he found that he meant it.

"It probably isn't your baby," Carmel wailed.

"I don't care, it's not the baby's fault," Ash said. "I still love you. I'll learn to love it."

"No, I won't do that to you, I've done enough," Carmel said, getting some of her equilibrium back. "We need to go on with the divorce. I'll go away afterward and you should forget you ever knew me. Find someone who will appreciate you and be faithful to you."

She reached for the door handle and pulled it, jumping out of the car before Ash could stop her. She almost run to her car and got in. A minute later Ash watched as she pulled hastily out of the lot and headed east.

Chapter 62

Carmel was furious at herself as she ran like a fox from hounds, barreling down the street toward Alice's house. She couldn't believe that she'd actually talked to Ash, that she'd told him everything.

You just keep getting stupider and stupider! She berated herself.

Underneath it all was the knowledge that Ash still loved her and wanted her to come home, even though she wouldn't let herself look at it. It was a luxury that she didn't deserve, and she was afraid that she'd give in to the promise and temptation of it if she'd let herself. She'd had absolutely no intention of talking to Ash, let alone of telling him everything, but at the first opportunity that is just what she'd done. Why?

In answering that question, she decided that under it all she trusted Ash and didn't think he'd use the truth to hurt her. She'd been carrying the burden of her problems all alone for so long, and it had felt good to talk to someone…not just anyone, to Ash. She still loved him but how could she ever convince anyone of that? Not by her past actions, that was for sure.

Pulling up to Alice's house she got out and headed inside. Patricia had already gone to work, clearing the carpet in the living room for vacuuming and scrubbing. It had been covered for so long it had to be dust and dirt laden. They were to the point now where they only had routine cleaning such as floors, carpets, and walls, and then everything would be done. Carmel could move in by Monday night. She could hardly wait. Everything was ready. She got her tools together and started to work in the house, scrubbing and shining the woodwork. Glad that Patricia wasn't talkative, she then let her mind wander to the many things that had been happening.

Carmel hadn't told Ash that she was still living in Carson's house. Would he have believed her if she'd said that they had not been intimate since the day she'd disappeared, the day he'd locked her up in his house, making her a prisoner? Of course he wouldn't. It sounded improbable. That's a reason why she hadn't tried to press charges against Carson for kidnapping and false imprisonment. No one would have believed her, not after she'd had an affair of several months with the man.

Now she was reminded again that she was living on the charity of a man who had imprisoned her. That was an upsetting thought. Perhaps, as she'd said originally, he owed her a chance to get back on her feet, after what he'd done to her, but she'd had time and now was the time to go. She thought she'd pack and when everything was loaded in the car, leave a note for the others saying thanks and goodbye. For a brief time she, Edna, Ted, and Carson had been a family of sorts and there was some sentiment attached to that.

She thought about Tut, the ghost the group had shared. Tut had indicated that he was going to leave the house, to search on his side of things for his loved ones. Carmel hoped that would work out for him. She wondered if Carson would go on to look for another ghost now if Tut was really gone. He seemed to be quite interested in the paranormal field. Last night Carson had told everyone that when he went to copy the tapes he'd made that contained Tut's voice; he'd found them blank. Everyone in the house, including the ghost hunters and Tut's Grandchildren had heard the tapes, and could testify to what had been on them, although now there was no concrete evidence.

Carmel had felt the depth of Carson's disappointment, even felt sorry for him concerning the matter. She hoped he would find another ghost to work with. The general pool of thought seemed to be that Tut had erased any evidence of his presence before he left the house. Already the experience had started to seem like a dream sequence to Carmel. However, the history had been real, documented in newspapers, and his Grandchildren had been real people. No one could deny that.

Ash headed back to Cincinnati more distressed than he'd been before he'd talked to Carmel. Now he had a world of things to think about. Carmel was pregnant! That thought stood out. He'd always wanted a baby and had wondered why she hadn't gotten pregnant before. Now, at the worst time possible, she was. She'd told him that most likely the baby wasn't his. That was a bitter thought to absorb but he felt that he could be a good father to the baby anyway if Carmel would only let him try, would work with him.

She'd said "No."

He'd told her that he loved her, but she hadn't said that she still had feelings for him. That hurt. Maybe Carmel was right and they should go ahead with the divorce, and he should try to find someone who would be right for him; someone who would love him and stay with him.

When he got home, Ash sat down and wrote a letter to Carmel and mailed it to her post office box. Among other things he told her that he was going to let the divorce proceed, since that was what she wanted him to do. However, if at some point before it was final, she should change her mind, she was to call him and say, "I want to come home." If she did that they would stop the proceedings and try to work out their problems. He didn't have much hope of ever getting a call from her though. She seemed bent on going away to raise her baby alone.

Ash felt lonelier than he could remember having felt before in his entire life.

Chapter 63

It was a few days later and Carson wasn't having a good day. He'd been upset since finding that the tapes he'd treasured so much were now blank, and then today he'd found Carmel was gone. Her apartment had been cleaned out while he was at work and all she'd left behind was a note. The note was nothing personal, just a "Thank you for letting me stay in your house until I could get on my feet," and a "Wishing you good luck in the future," kind of note. She also left a few words for Edna and Ted and that was all.

He found it hard to absorb the shock of it. Inside him, he'd never let himself believe that she would go. He knew he'd made a big blunder when he locked her up. He'd wanted her marriage to end, so she could marry him, but forcing the issue as he'd done had been disastrous not just to her marriage to Ash, but to the relationship he and Carmel had at that time. Still, he'd lived in a day dream, reinforced by the fact that she'd stayed in his house after he'd released her. Surely she wouldn't have stayed if she didn't love him. She was just laying on the punishment to be sure he got the point, he'd thought.

Now he knew that wasn't true. She'd meant it when she'd said in the early days of her captivity that he'd killed their relationship. He'd killed or driven away everyone he'd loved, he thought. His relationships were a disaster. One woman was dead, another, April, seemed to want to kill him, and now Carmel had left him without a look back. He was feeling mighty sorry for himself. Even his ghost had abandoned him!

If only he knew where Carmel had gone, he'd go after her and try to convince her to return to him. Leaving her alone to go her own way hadn't worked, so maybe a little pressure to come back would. It seemed to him that women were inscrutable and impossible to understand. He didn't know where she was, but he supposed she still had her job. Maybe he could find her there.

Carson drove to the business where Carmel worked but her car wasn't in the lot. She must have quit the job when she quit him. Had she gone back to Cincinnati? He didn't think she'd gone back to Ash because he knew that Ash had filed for divorce. He wouldn't have let her come back, if it had been him. Where had she gone? His mind wandered from idea to idea but nothing came to him. By now she probably had saved enough money to disappear forever.

He went back home to cry on his Mother's shoulder. For the first time he let Edna know that he cared for Carmel and wanted to marry her.

"I think she's a good girl and would have made a good daughter in law," Edna said, but you can't force someone to love you."

Since Carson didn't want to tell his mother about the relationship and how he'd locked Carmel up for all that time in order to keep her from returning to her husband, he went off to his room. There he had a few strong drinks, which were intended to ease some of the pain.

In her new room, in Alice's house, Carmel was trying to adjust to changed circumstances too. She had taken a couple of days off work so she could devote all her energy to the move and to dealing with Alice. Not sure what she was going to have to deal with on a day to day basis, she'd agreed to let Alice cook, which Alice liked to do and Carmel would clean up each evening, much as it had been with Edna. She didn't think Alice could make too much of a mess in a day's time.

Alice came home, and although she seemed distressed at all she felt she'd lost, she also acted excited and happy about her new house as she called it. Carmel agreed that compared to what she'd first seen the house was new. Alice also liked the fact that she could cook again now that her stove had been uncovered and she could find her refrigerator. She couldn't wait to fix her first meal in the "new" house.

It seemed to be going almost too well those first two days and Carmel wondered what would happen when she was gone for a day. Would Alice start hoarding things or hiding them away? It was surprising how different the house looked. It was now a pleasant little house with unblocked windows that looked out on the cold sunshine of the day. With the trash off the front porch the house looked decent from the outside too.

In the spring Carmel thought she'd encourage Alice to start gardening again. She needed some hobbies to keep her occupied and to help to break the obsessions she had. It was Carmel's theory that if she could keep the woman busy and reinforce her for having a neat house, by getting her involved with friends again, Alice would find a way to overcome her problem, or at least to control it with the help of a person such as herself.

Would she even be here in the spring? Carmel had no idea. By then she hoped to have another job and to be able to leave the southern Ohio area for a place where she could raise her child alone without interference.

It surprised her that Ash hadn't demanded that she get a paternity test and that he have visitation rights to the baby if it was his. Maybe he hadn't done that because she'd caught him off guard and he didn't have time to absorb everything before she'd run off and left him. He might try to add that into the divorce agreement! She was sure the baby wasn't his. Had she believed that it was, she might have gone home with him and tried to work out the problems, if not for their sakes, for the baby's. As it was she'd feel awful having Ash work to support another man's child. It was better that she just leave the area and let Ash get his life back together.

As for Carson, she figured that since he wanted to control her and force her to marry him, he'd use the baby as an opportunity to demand access to the child, and thus to her. It could end up very embarrassing to have to prove one or the other of the men was the father, and she'd probably be forced to allow visitation to the father. It wasn't that she wanted to deny the father his rights; it was that she didn't want to have to deal with all the trouble associated with the situation. Especially with Carson, she just wanted to get away from him and forget that she'd made the terrible mistakes she'd made.

Beating herself up hourly over having told Ash about the baby, Carmel was more determined than ever not to let Carson find out. She used a part of the second day to look for another job so he couldn't find her that way, and crossed her fingers when she found a place in West Union that was hiring.

Meanwhile she was growing with the baby and no doubt her condition was going to be obvious any day.

Chapter 64

Carson was sound asleep when a scream penetrated his consciousness. Bolting up in his bed he stared around him at the darkness, his nerves a jangle with fear. Everything was silent now but he wondered if it could have been Tut making that racket. He'd been under the impression that Tut was gone, but maybe not. He sat listening to the wintry stillness of the night. Probably it was a dream after all, he decided after hearing nothing for twenty minutes. He lay down again, but his breath was coming in large gasps as he sprawled there feeling uneasy; he was certain that something was wrong.

When he couldn't go to sleep after another twenty minutes, he got up and went down to get a warm glass of milk. That worked for him sometimes and had always been his mother's answer to insomnia. Sitting at the table to drink the milk, he went over and over the sound that had awakened him. Examining it from all angles, he attempted to figure out which direction it had come from. His conclusion was that it sounded as if it had come from outside the house.

Maybe it was an animal, a fox or coyote.

He tried to accept that answer but it didn't resonate right with him. It wasn't an animal, but he didn't know what it was. Finishing his milk, he rinsed the glass at the sink and put it in the dishwasher before going back up to his bed. He straightened his covers and got them ready for sleeping and then thought maybe he should check the window. The sound that had awakened him seemed to have come from that direction.

Peering out at the darkness, he could see the river in the distance. Everything close to the house was black as ink and nothing seemed to be moving. He headed back toward his bed and sat down on it. Somehow he still wasn't satisfied that everything was ok.

Getting up again, he went to his bureau and picked up a flashlight that was lying there. He went back to the window and shined the light on the ground below. As the light moved from the shadows to the area closest to the house, and directly under his window, he saw a ladder lying on the ground. That ladder hadn't been there before! He tried to see the area directly under his window, but couldn't without opening the window, so he pushed it up and shined the flashlight downward. What he saw panicked him into hyperventilating, and froze him to the floor.

A woman, who he thought was probably April Mayes, was lying on the ground under his window; it seemed likely that she'd fallen from the ladder. There was a dark red substance around her head which he knew was blood. Grabbing his cell phone from the nightstand and his coat from a chair, Carson ran down the steps while calling 911. Outside the air was extremely cold and he wondered how long she'd been lying there. If she'd fallen at the time when he heard that scream she'd been lying unconscious for well over an hour in below freezing temperatures.

Edna had heard the commotion and come outside to stand beside him as he turned the woman's head a little and saw that it was indeed, April Mayes. She was as pale as an ice maiden and Carson paced around her agitatedly waiting for the medics to arrive.

"What do you suppose she was doing," Edna asked.

"Trying to climb up to my window I guess," Carson said through teeth that chattered with cold and fear.

When the medics arrived they confirmed Carson's fears; April was in critical condition. She'd hit her head and there had been considerable bleeding. She'd also lain exposed to the cold weather for a long time before help arrived.

"Do you think she'll make it," he asked one of the medics.

"I don't know. Her doctor will have a better idea of that. It's our job to stabilize her if we can and get her to the hospital. Do you want to ride along?"

"I'll follow you in my car," Carson said.

Edna insisted on going with him and the two of them arrived shortly after the ambulance carrying April did. The receptionist asked Carson for all the information he could supply, address, next of kin, etc. A police officer had materialized from somewhere to question him when the receptionist was through.

Carson explained the problems he'd been having to the officer, how April had been stalking him, threatening Carmel, and that he was working with the police concerning the matter. He agreed to write a statement telling them all that he knew about what had happened, how he'd heard a scream while asleep and why it took so long to figure out that April was lying injured under his window.

"You're sure you didn't see her on the ladder trying to come in your window; and maybe you gave the ladder a shove," the officer insinuated.

"No," Carson said. "I told you how it happened."

"We'll check your story," the officer assured him.

Carson and Edna sat on the hard chairs in the waiting room for what seemed like hours before a doctor came out to talk to them.

"That young lady took a hefty blow to her head," the doctor said. "It's going to be touch and go, but I think she'll make it. We've got her temperature up to normal again. She was suffering from hypothermia when she was brought in. Although she's still unconscious, I believe she'll wake up before long. She broke her right leg and dislocated her shoulder as well, but those will heal ok."

"Is there anything we can do," Carson asked.

"No, go on home. The information you gave helped us to find her mother and she'll be here any time," the doctor said.

They drove back home in silence. Carson was feeling so low that he figured he might have to crawl out of the car when they got there. Tragedy overcame every woman he touched, he was thinking. April had chosen her own course but something about him had set her off and turned her into a stalker. He hoped Carmel had escaped his toxic touch and would be happy without him. Carson had truly loved her in spite of his maladaptive method for showing it. He loved her enough that now he was finally willing to let her go.

Maybe I should take some classes on co-dependency or how to have a healthy relationship before I start dating again. I think dating married women is a part of the problem, but April was single, and that didn't work either. Why can't I get it right?

Carson climbed into his bed and pulled the covers up to blot out the morning sun which was just coming up as he had arrived back home.

Maybe he could sleep off his melancholy.

Chapter 65

Carson learned that April was going to make it the next day when he called the hospital. She was conscious now but couldn't remember what had happened. The last thing she was able to remember was that she was climbing up to Carson's window. She couldn't remember why. Her mother got on the phone and apologized to Carson for her daughter's actions.

"I've been worried about her for over a year now. She had changed and was behaving in a way I thought was unstable. I tried to get her to go for help, but she refused," her mother said.

"Well, maybe she'll get what she needs now," Carson said;

He realized that he meant it. He was still angry with April over the things she'd done but he didn't want bad things for her.

He'd been thinking about Carmel a lot, as well as his unfortunate pattern with women. She had been gone for more than a month now and it still haunted him the way things had happened. It had hurt him deeply when Carmel left with barely a word, although he'd known that might happen. If only he could talk with her a little and explain what he'd been thinking and why he'd acted the way he had. If only he could say "I'm sorry" to her, he could move on. It was too bad the way he'd devastated her life, he really was sorry about that.

Of course, she'd made the choice to have an affair, but his decision to imprison her had guaranteed the end of her marriage. If she'd gone back to Ash as she'd planned, it might have worked out for them. As it had turned out, his choice to kidnap her had guaranteed the end of his relationship with her, as well as the end of her marriage.

Remembering the house Carmel had visited while the detective was following her, Carson wondered if the people in that house would know where she had gone. Tomorrow he'd go there and talk to them. Maybe he could find her that way.

Carmel was home cleaning out the kitchen pantry which had suddenly sprouted a number of empty boxes that should have been in the trash, when someone rang the doorbell. Alice wasn't home. She'd taken to visiting a neighbor down the street most afternoons and now that the house was presentable, Alice felt good about inviting her friend to her own home as well. Since she and her friend Sally spent most of their time together, Carmel had extra time for doing the things she liked to do. Things were working out.

When she opened the door and saw Carson standing there, she almost fainted.

"Oh no," she said.

Carson seemed to be as surprised as she was. Carmel realized that her car was parked in the garage today and he wouldn't have seen it. Why was he here then?

"Hi Carmel," Carson said, and Carmel realized that he was taking in her pregnant silhouette.

"Can I come in?"

Not knowing what else to do she stood aside and let him step inside the door. She motioned him to a chair and Carson almost dissolved into it. He kept staring at her, which made her very uneasy, but she was determined to hold her own. He had no rights here, she told her anxiety ridden mind and no rights to the baby either.

"What are you doing here," she asked Carson.

"I didn't know you were here. I was going to ask whoever lived here if they knew how I could find you."

"Well, you've found me. What do you want?"

"I came to say I'm sorry for what I've done to you. I really am. I understand why you left me and it's probably for the best."

"Ok."

"You didn't tell me about the baby," he said.

"No need; I'm not asking anything from you."

"Are you planning to go back to Ash?"

"No. He deserves something better."

"But won't he want the baby?"

"Why would he want to raise someone else's baby?"

"Are you saying you think the baby is mine?"

"It probably is, but I don't want anything from you, nothing at all. Just leave us in peace."

Carson looked at her for a while as if debating something important in his mind. He shook his head a time or two and finally said,

"I guess I didn't tell you that I'd had a vasectomy, did I? I never wanted children and so I had that done to be sure I didn't have any. The baby is Ash's! It can't be mine. It would be impossible for it to be mine!"

Feeling as if she'd just been given a reprieve, Carmel looked at him closely. He seemed to be telling the truth.

"You don't want children; you had a vasectomy," she said, repeating him.

"That's right. I was never comfortable with kids and so I didn't want to put myself in the position of having to deal with them. I had the vasectomy done several years ago."

"Then you won't be fighting me for visiting rights to my baby?"

"Why should I? The baby isn't mine."

"You're sure of this?"

"Yes," Carson said. "I'm as sure as I can be of anything. It's not my baby."

Carmel sat down in a chair across from Carson and stared at him in her turn. She couldn't believe her good fortune. Not only was she not going to have a problem with Carson over the baby, but he couldn't be the father because he'd had a vasectomy. Even more amazing she noticed that Carson was no longer trying to coerce or force her to stay with him. He'd accepted that she'd left him for a good reason. Both of them could go on with their lives and try to be happy.

"Thank you for coming to tell me this. You don't know how worried and desperate I've been," she said.

"Is your divorce final," Carson asked.

"No," Carmel said, "Not yet."

"Well, I wish you the best," Carson said, getting up to leave. "I really loved you. I probably always will, but it'll be better if we move on and try to be happy apart."

"I agree," Carmel said, then acting on impulse she gave him a sisterly kiss on the cheek, showing him that she cared about his welfare too. Miraculously the bitterness she'd felt toward him for so long seemed to be gone.

When Carson had driven away and she was alone again, she sat staring out the window for almost ten minutes before she picked up the phone and dialed Ash's number.

"I want to come home," was all she said.

Finis

Saundra Crum Akers was born in Urbana, Ohio but lived in rural Southern Ohio during most of her childhood. Her family roots all date back to the early 1800's in Ohio and merge into one of four adjacent Counties, namely, Adams, Pike, Highland, and Brown. She now lives in Columbus, Ohio but visits her home territory often. Her novels are set in real towns and villages with some local history and landmarks involved in the overall plot. She believes this adds a new and unique dimension to her stories for those who live in the area, and does not diminish the storyline for those who do not. All books must be set somewhere and most seem to be in Los Angeles, New York, or the like. Rural America has its own culture; this culture is also valid and just as interesting and mysterious.

Other Book by Saundra Crum Akers

Available at www.SaundraCrumAkers.com

Made in the USA
Middletown, DE
02 July 2022

68306170R00194